Grave-Reaping Guardian

by

Everlyn C. Thompson

Grave Reaper Series

Grave-Reaping Guardian

Cover Art by *Kristian Norris*

The Wild Rose Press, Inc.
PO Box 708
Adams Basin, NY 14410-0708
Visit us at www.thewildrosepress.com

Publishing History
First Edition, 2024
Trade Paperback ISBN 978-1-5092-5283-1
Digital ISBN 978-1-5092-5284-8

Grave Reaper Series
Published in the United States of America

I closed my eyes. Immediately the ambient magic in the room leapt into my awareness. The strength of it took my breath away and left me feeling both giddy and dizzy. A steady pulse of it continued to emit from the portal, like heat from a pile of coals. The side of the room that held the massive four-post bed had an ugly dark tint to the magic. It felt ominous, and I quickly turned my attention towards something else. Unfortunately, the next thing that called to me was also the closest—the body lying at my feet.

But that didn't make any sense. The queen was dead. She shouldn't be giving off any sort of magical vibes.

I knelt without thinking, and laid both my hands on the dried skin of Safeena's arm. It was really hard not to think about what she'd been touching before she died—I knew for a fact that she hadn't washed her hands (or any other part of herself) after bumping uglies with Gus. It would be just my luck to catch the fae equivalent of chlamydia from touching her bare skin.

Magic leapt for me in a hot wave, the powerful surge knocking me backward onto my butt. The connection was so quick that it only lasted for a fraction of a second, not even long enough for me to blink, but in that brief contact something passed into me.

Oh, shit.

Dedication

This is for all the women aching to hold a child of their own. For the lucky ones that have someone to love, and for the ones still waiting. I see you.

Chapter One

The dead moose moodily stared at me, while my werewolf frolicked in the mounds of freshly fallen snow.

I rolled my eyes and ignored them both.

I was the only one who could see the dead moose (thanks to my grave-reaping magic) and nothing I could say or do would get him out of my yard any faster. The concept of time was lost on the dead, and he'd move on when he was ready, not a minute sooner.

The werewolf, on the other hand, had become a permanent resident of my tiny cabin a few months ago, so he was free to use the yard however he pleased.

I stomped the snow off my boots and carefully opened the back door while trying not to drop my armful of wood. There was no need to fumble with keys; locking my door had become unnecessary after Dog moved in. He was better than the most high-tech security system on the market and cost nearly as much since his appetite rivaled that of a sumo wrestler with a tapeworm.

After I hung my parka and mitts on a hook by the door and toed on my fuzzy pink slippers, I added some wood to the embers in the fireplace. We'd only been gone to Fairie for about three hours, so they didn't require much coaxing, and my cabin was soon filled with heat from the blaze.

The back door opened and shut once more. I turned to admire the sight as Farranen deposited a significantly larger load of firewood than I'd managed into the pine box in my living room. As the guardian of the gate, he spent a lot of his time in this realm, monitoring the fae that came and went from Fairie to Earth. In the last few weeks, there had been an exponential increase in the number of fae visiting, particularly those of the Light Court, so I was learning to treasure the few quiet moments when I had him all to myself.

Knowing it would only be a matter of time until he was needed again, I followed him into the kitchen, admiring the way his back and shoulder muscles flexed beneath his white shirt as he hung his cloak next to my coat.

"I apologize for my lengthy absence. The holding cells were full, so I had to escort the male to a secondary location." Solemn dark green eyes looked down at me.

"It wasn't a problem," I assured him with a smile. Dog and I had explored the woods surrounding the gate in Fairie while Farranen had dealt with the pompous male he had dragged back through the gate at sword point. I'd even thought to pack a small picnic, so it had been no hardship to lounge in the warmer climate of Fairie for part of the afternoon.

A quick glance out the window showed that Dog was furiously digging a hole at the back of my yard. He'd cornered a poor winter hare that had stubbornly refused to relocate to a new den. Their ridiculous territorial dispute had been going on since Dog's arrival. It would be a while before my determined shifter would concede defeat, giving Farranen and I the opportunity to enjoy a rare moment of uninterrupted alone time.

As my sworn guardian and one of the most powerful fae in the Light Court, Farranen was an imposing figure.

He was over six feet tall, with elegant good looks and the ability to wield a two-and-a-half-foot-long sword with deadly accuracy. It was still hard to believe that he was courting me—which was just an old-fashioned way of saying we were trying to figure out what a relationship between two individuals from separate realms would look like.

I licked my lips nervously, not sure how to approach the subject of *us*. Weeks ago, my guardian had declared that he would like to be "more than friends," yet he'd made no move to take our relationship past a PG rating. He'd spent every night sleeping in my bed, but he'd never once tried to cross the line from a grade-school slumber party to any number of the wickedly hot things my imagination was spitting out on a daily basis. And as a historical romance writer, I could come up with a hell of a lot of wickedly hot night-time activities for us to indulge in.

Since Dog rarely let me out of his sight, I'd been blaming Farranen's lack of interest on our scruffy chaperone. There was really only one way to be certain that it was Dog's continued presence, rather than a lack of interest on my guardian's behalf.

I wasn't the bravest of women, and my experience with seducing men was nonexistent, so there was a very good possibility that I was going to mess things up. But if he'd changed his mind about exploring the sexual chemistry that we both acknowledged was there, I wanted to find out sooner rather than later.

Braced for rejection, but hoping he'd welcome my touch, I closed the distance between us. His eyebrows climbed his smooth forehead as I traced my hands up the hard contours of his chest, and I registered the exact moment his breath caught and his heart started to race.

"My lady…" The question died on his lips but lingered in his eyes.

My magic, just as eager to join with the male standing before me, lunged for him, igniting a cascade of sparks everywhere we touched.

I had a brief moment of satisfaction as his pupils dilated, then his arms were guiding me, pulling me closer until the scant distance between us was gone. His lips curved upward right before they claimed mine.

The fabric of his shirt bunched beneath my palms, and I let out a needy sound as he deepened the kiss.

Yes.

This was what I'd been aching for.

The smell of cinnamon and fresh pine wrapped itself around me, stoking my desire for him until all I could think about was getting my hands on every part of him. My nipples scraped along his hardness as I rose onto my tippy toes, creating a delicious friction that was almost unbearable. I was just beginning to entertain the idea of dragging him to the bedroom, when the back door flew open with a *bang!* I would have jumped if Farranen hadn't been holding me so tightly.

Damn it! Living in an isolated cabin in the middle of nowhere had a lot of perks—but privacy sure wasn't one of them.

"The queen is dead!" the newcomer announced as he strode into my cabin like he owned the damn place.

Oakenlief, the dark prince of Fairie, grinned unrepentantly as his black cloak settled around his shoulders. His pale blue eyes narrowed knowingly as he took in my flushed cheeks and my companion's glower.

"Am I interrupting?" he asked innocently. Which

was laughable, since Lief was anything but innocent.

"No," I answered stubbornly, not willing to admit that I'd been caught making out in my kitchen like a teenager.

"Yes," the man next to me growled, but there was no real bite to the word.

Lief arched a dark brow and said, "Must I repeat myself? The. Queen. Is. *Dead.*"

Farranen straightened, and a rare look of surprise crossed his face. "No," he protested, but it was half-hearted; he would have known if Lief had been lying. "When?" he demanded. "Who?"

"I only found the body this afternoon; it appears to have happened some time ago. Most likely right around the time that Augustus announced his sovereignty over the Light Court."

A hoard of agitated wasps took up residence in my belly. I'd known that the queen's body would eventually be discovered, but I'd hoped for more time to come up with a plausible explanation. Because, yes, I had been the one to kill her.

"The Gray Knight killed her?" Farranen asked in disbelief, referring to Gus by his formal title.

Lief shrugged one of his wide shoulders. "In all honesty, I came to see if you had been the one to do it. Augustus was my next likely suspect."

"Why would he tell everyone he was mated to the queen, rather than admitting he felled her?" Farranen mused.

I looked up at Lief and realized he'd been staring at me while talking to my guardian. I quickly looked away from his multi-faceted eyes that always seemed to see more than I wanted them to.

5

"Theo."

His voice demanded that I look at him, but I stubbornly kept my gaze on the worn linoleum floor. I had the world's worst poker face, and my guilt was written all over it.

About two weeks ago, a female in the queen's army kidnapped me and took me to Fairie. After I was forced to watch the queen and Gus engage in a very sweaty display of physical intimacy, Gus used glamour to trick the queen into thinking they'd become mated. Once he left to spread the word that he was the new king of the Light Court, I tried to tell the queen that she'd been duped. She didn't take the news very well and tried to kill me. I probably should have seen that coming.

Fortunately, Gus had left a handgun behind in her private chambers. Since the fae couldn't handle it—due to the iron in it—the queen wasn't expecting me to be able to use it either. I hadn't actually wanted to kill her, but the gun ended up going off accidentally, shooting her in the head.

Lief must have picked up on the tale of supernatural homicide that was going through my head, because he stepped forward until the toes of his black boots were less than an inch from my fuzzy pink slippers. "Theo?" His voice was decidedly less suspicious and far kinder as he tipped my chin up with a single finger so I was forced to look at him. "Tell me."

I swallowed hard, unable to look away from his commanding presence. He towered over me, with his black hair falling around his shoulders and blending into the black clothing he wore. His hard jaw and strong features softened into those of a compassionate ruler, and I realized if I had to confide my crime to someone, I wanted it to be him. I didn't know what the punishment for regicide was, but Lief was fond of me, so hopefully he'd be lenient.

"I…" The words of confession for my heinous act died on my lips.

"You know who did this." Lief sounded bewildered. "Who are you protecting, Theo?"

Me, I thought guiltily.

"Theodora?" Farranen asked. I looked over to where he was watching me. Confusion had brightened the green of his eyes to something that reminded me of fresh grass in the spring. I'd nearly forgotten he was in the room with us. He was the last person I wanted to find out that I was a murderer. He already knew that the ankou magic I'd been infected with last fall was defective and that I'd failed the transition from human to changeling. I wasn't sure how many more of my flaws he would tolerate before he decided I wasn't worth courting anymore. Although, judging by the kiss we'd just shared, I was hoping he might be willing to overlook the manslaughter charges.

I took a deep breath and pushed past the two males who had me cornered in my small kitchen.

It wasn't like me to feel so insecure. I wasn't sure if it was because I was unaccustomed to trusting other people, or because I'd finally found someone I was afraid of losing. Either way, I didn't care for the guilt and unease that were crawling across my conscience.

I could hear Farranen and Lief speaking in hushed voices in the kitchen. It was probably safe to assume they were talking about me.

I dropped onto the ugly striped couch in my living room and buried my face in my hands. I'd felt different ever since I'd accidentally taken Safeena's life. I couldn't actually point to one specific thing that was different, but something inside me felt *off*.

I held out my hands and turned them so I could see the creamy white skin that went from my fingertips to my elbows. The scars that had once been a part of me were gone. Maybe that's what was niggling at the back of my mind—the fact that every one of my scars and imperfections had been wiped away a few weeks ago. I didn't recognize myself when I looked in the mirror anymore. Yes, the straight brown hair and hazel eyes were the same, but the woman staring back at me was a virtual stranger. She looked…lost.

Maybe the feeling that I'd lost myself came from my guilty conscience. Whatever condemnation my actions had earned me might be more palatable than continuing to suffer in silence.

My guardian approached cautiously and knelt in front of me. "Theodora? The dark prince and I will help however we can, with whatever it is that ails you."

I looked into his eyes and saw the sincerity of his words.

My limbs began to tremble, and I felt shaky like I hadn't eaten enough, even though I had. I looked from Farranen to where Lief was leaning against the dining room table. "Can we go for a walk?" I asked. If the men were surprised, they didn't show it.

"It's thirty degrees below zero out there," Lief pointed out.

"I need to go to Fairie," I told them.

****

Now that it was winter, the dead animals that wandered through the woods were easier to spot. By my way of thinking, anything that didn't leave tracks in the snow was dead. They were drawn by my ankou magic, and I hadn't yet figured out a way to stop them from visiting.

So, when a little fox blinked up at me from his perch on a snow-covered tree stump, I didn't bother acknowledging his presence. The men I was with couldn't see him, and it would have been cruel to taunt Dog with another furry woodland creature that he couldn't see or chase.

I'd been visiting Fairie every day for the last few weeks, sometimes two or three times a day.

Gus's supposed ascension to the throne, combined with Lief's rebellion, which had come to a standstill since the queen was MIA, had led to an increase in the number of fae passing through the gate. Farranen had been extra vigilant about monitoring who was coming and going, and I often tagged along with the excuse of wanting to spend time in the warmer temperatures. While Tamarac was still blanketed in mid-January snow, Fairie had slipped from late autumn back into summer. My guardian thought it had something to do with Fairie's unstable magic.

In truth, I was going because my magic became weak and erratic when I was in the Earth realm. I sometimes wondered if it was related to the vampire magic in my body, but since there was only one other known case of someone possessing both fae and vampire magic, it was hard to say for sure.

As soon as Dog and I stepped through the magical doorway in the hawthorn tree that allowed people to travel between Earth to Fairie, I sank to my knees and ran my fingers through the lush grass. Like an addict, my magic fumbled until it merged with the ambient magic that saturated every part of Fairie. Instantly, the jitters faded, and my head felt clearer.

I quickly shed my winter jacket and toque.

Thick velvety green leaves filled the branches above me, blocking out the clear blue sky. The scent of fresh fruit drifted over from the woods that surrounded the clearing.

I felt, rather than heard, Farranen and Lief join us. Their worry prickled at me, like fire ants marching along my nerves. My own anxiety ratcheted back up in response. I hated that I'd been keeping something important from them.

After I'd been attacked by Lebolus and infected with his fae magic, I'd been dragged into more life-threatening situations than I cared for. I was sick and tired of reacting to whatever drama life threw my way, so this time, I decided to act first.

If Lief had already found the queen's body, I knew my involvement wouldn't stay a secret much longer. Fairie might not have crime scene investigators, but anyone with half a brain would be able to figure out that the list of people who could handle a gun was shockingly short. I'd have to face the consequences sooner or later; at least this way I'd get to do it on my terms.

Taking a deep breath, I let myself enjoy the feeling of my magic joined with the magic of Fairie for a few more seconds. It welcomed me, like a warm blanket on a cold night. Then, before I could chicken out, I opened my mouth and let go of the words that I'd been holding onto for the last few weeks. "Gus didn't kill the queen."

Lief knelt next to me on the grass and was the first to speak. "How do you know?"

I risked a glace at his face, and his unguarded expression was better than the distrust I was expecting. "I was there."

"You were where?" my guardian asked, in a soft tone that he usually reserved for delivering bad news.

"In the queen's private chambers." My voice shrank to a whisper, but I forced myself to continue the awful tale. "After you left to find Lief, Celesta showed up. She dragged me to Fairie." I left out the part about Gus and Safeena's mutual enjoyment of each other. "Gus announced that he'd given the queen a mating mark, but I could see it was just glamour."

They already knew I was able to see through glamour that was being used to conceal or cover something up, so I didn't have to elaborate on why it hadn't fooled me.

"The queen should have been able to see through even the strongest of glamour," Lief said.

"Her mental state has been deteriorating for some time. It's possible that Augustus was able to trick her into seeing a mark, especially if that's what she most desired to see." Farranen's voice was full of contemplation, and I knew there would be a tiny wrinkle in his forehead if I was brave enough to look. I wasn't.

"After he and Celesta left, the queen wanted to know what it looked like, and she would have known if I tried to lie, so I told her it was just glamour." I let out a humorless laugh. "She didn't believe me."

Nobody bothered to question why Safeena hadn't seen Gus's announcement for the lie that it was. The fae were notorious for their ability to twist their words, and the way the gray knight had phrased the discovery hadn't technically been a lie.

Your Highness, can it be? I see a mating mark! Of course he'd seen a mating mark—because he'd been the one to glamour it onto her skin.

"If Augustus didn't kill her, then who did?" Farranen asked as his eyebrows slanted downward. I wanted to hug him for not immediately seeing the most obvious answer.

"She did." Lief sounded absolutely shocked, and for that, I wanted to hug him too.

I nodded and made no move to wipe away the tears that were crawling down my face. "It was an accident." I sniffed. "I didn't mean to."

A strangled sob escaped me when Farranen dropped to his knees and pulled me into his arms. Soft words of comfort surrounded me, and I clung to his shirt like it was about to sprout legs and run away.

"You should have told me," he said finally, but not unkindly. "I knew something was amiss; you haven't been yourself since we left Fairie."

His assessment wasn't wrong; I'd been stumbling through the days like a trauma victim with dementia. I hadn't thought that he'd noticed.

"It didn't seem real." My tummy was still tied up in knots from not knowing what my punishment would be. But I wasn't stupid. There would be some far-reaching consequences for my actions. And as much as I didn't want to face them, it would be better to get it over with now, before my guilt could continuing eating me alive.

Chapter Two

It was shocking how few words it took to succinctly relay such a life-altering tale.

My guardian sat close enough that his magic was a steady buzz in my peripheral, and I appreciated that nobody interrupted my stuttering confession.

After I'd laid out the bare facts, some of the pressure filling my chest eased, and I could take a deep breath again. Any possibility of me making it as a criminal mastermind was shot to hell; if keeping secrets literally made me sick to my stomach, then I'd better stick with writing romance novels.

"Oh, I almost forgot—there was a body." My eyes burned with fresh tears as I thought about the naked merdain fae I'd discovered on the floor next to the queen's bed, discarded like garbage. "It was Harvey."

I'd first met Harvalin of the Light Court when my ankou magic had gotten out of control and I'd accidentally pulled his ghost through the veil into our world. He'd saved my life on more than one occasion, and he was one of the few friends I had. I still wasn't sure if he'd recognized his own body when he'd felt me fighting for my life in the queen's private chambers and showed up to help. He'd been strangely absent in the last few weeks, and I hadn't thought much of it, since my life was oddly danger-free these days, but now a little thread of doubt filled my head. Did his absence have something to do with my fluctuating magic? Damn, I'd been so caught up in my guilt that I'd been neglecting my favorite ghost.

"Yes, I found Harvalin's body. Arrangements have been made to return him to his next of kin." Lief stood with his back to the hawthorn tree while his fingers absently ran across the hilt of the dagger strapped to his waist. His crystalline eyes were unfocused as he watched the sunless sky.

"I think the queen and Gus killed him in some sort of BDSM thing gone wrong," I told them hesitantly.

"He would not be the first to fall victim to her extraneous proclivities," Farranen murmured.

I wanted to kill her all over again. I hadn't known Harvey in life, only in death, but he was a thoughtful and intelligent male, if somewhat awkward and nervous. I doubted that whatever circumstances had led to his death had been consensual. Maybe it had something to do with his status as a soldier in the queen's army; I wouldn't put it past the bitch to use her position of power to coerce those under her to get what she wanted.

I tore my thoughts away from my murdered friend, and back to the two males, who seemed lost in their own thoughts. Since neither of them had given me any indication as to how I'd be reprimanded for my crime, it was as good a time as any to voice the question that had been haunting me since my misdeed.

"So, who's been ruling the Light Court for the last few weeks?" I tried to sound casual as I ran my fingers back and forth in the grass, but it came out a touch apprehensive.

I'd heard the phrase *whoever takes the head, takes the crown* a few times and had assumed the interpretation was pretty straightforward. Since I'd been the one to blow the queen's brains out, I sure as hell hoped there was an unspoken clause about whoever took the head having to be fae. Because I had some serious commitment issues in regard to inheriting the crown of an entire court in a realm that I wasn't even a resident of.

"I don't recall there ever being a case such as this, where someone from outside the court was able to overthrow the current ruler," Lief answered thoughtfully. "It's been theorized that the realm itself will choose the successor."

I let out the breath I'd been holding. "Fairie will pick the next king or queen?" That was a nifty idea. It's too bad my realm wasn't smart enough to do the same. "So how do we know who was chosen?"

Lief offered a casual shrug. "The realm may still be deciding. Or perhaps the individual hasn't yet realized the power that's been bestowed upon them."

"Thus, the increased turmoil in Fairie," Farranen added.

I nodded, relieved beyond belief that I hadn't been saddled with another supernatural label. I mean, Queen Theo? Have you ever heard anything more stupid? I smothered a laugh against the back of my hand and ignored the odd looks from the males.

Dog let out a little whine and inched closer until his head was resting in my lap.

"How were you able to get into the queen's private chambers? I thought only the queen could make the portal open?" I asked Lief. The fact that it had opened for me had been bugging me.

"The rulers of both courts can access any of the portals, regardless of who created them or who they are keyed to." Lief straightened and glanced down at me, losing some of the vacantness in his gaze. I'm pretty sure he'd just caught on to the fact that I'd managed to enact the age-old murder mystery that involved a dead body in a windowless, doorless room. "How were *you* able to exit through the portal?"

"Um, I just asked it nicely?"

"You *asked* the *portal?*" Lief's dark brows rose even higher on his forehead like they were trying to escape into his hairline.

"Did you make a blood offering?" Farranen asked, leaning in closer to where I sat and making me feel crowded, even though we were in a big empty clearing.

"No. And *eww.*" I'd seen some of the fae cut themselves and then use the blood to open the magical doorways, but I hadn't thought to try it myself at the time.

The men exchanged a heated look that made me wonder for the millionth time if they could read each other's minds. When Lief finally turned his gaze on me, I fought the urge to fidget.

"We should consult the lideeram fae; they've managed Fairie's written library since we began recording our histories." He nodded once like the matter was settled, and his shoulders relaxed a bit. My body relaxed in response; the dark prince's uncertainty had been adding to my own anxiety.

Farranen rose to his feet, and I followed, albeit a lot less gracefully. I reached for my coat and toque, prepared to leave now that I'd soaked up a fair bit of Fairie's magic, but before I could pull them on, Lief and Farranen turned toward the woods in an eerily synchronized move, complete with them both reaching for their swords.

With a low growl, Dog moved to put himself in front of me.

The brief whisper of fabric against leaves was the only audible signal I had before a dark figure stepped off the path and into the clearing.

"My lord," the figure panted, and I immediately recognized the scratchy rasp of her voice.

"Mary!" I darted around Dog and wrapped myself around her skeletally thin body. She was close to eighteen inches taller than my five foot and four inches, so the best I could do was to wrap my arms awkwardly around her waist—or what I assumed was her waist, since her long black robe completely hid her figure. After a brief hesitation, she gave me a little single-handed pat on the back.

I detangled myself and smiled up at the black hole beneath her hood where her face should have been. The last time I'd seen her, we'd both been lying in puddles of blood on the dirt floor of the queen's dungeons, sporting injuries that were potentially fatal. I was delighted to see that she'd survived.

"Theo, it's pleasant to see you again," Mary said in a surprised tone.

I wanted to hang my head in shame. I wasn't proud of the fact that I'd initially treated the female with prejudice and fear because she was an ankou fae. I'd unfairly assumed that she was no different from Lebolus, even thought she'd been acting as my guide while I was in Fairie to rescue Farranen. My suspicious nature had gotten the better of me, and I owed her an apology.

"I'm sorry I was such a bitch to you." I stared directly at the inky darkness that was her face, willing her to see the sincerity in my eyes. "And I'm really glad that you're all right."

She tilted her head to the side like she was having trouble understanding me. I was just starting to think that maybe the word "bitch" wasn't part of the fae vocabulary, when she told me, "What my brother did was unforgivable. Your apology is unnecessary."

I thought about hugging her again, but I decided against it since I really wasn't much of a hugger. The one I'd already given her was more than enough to push the boundaries of my comfort levels. Still, I was ridiculously glad that she wasn't holding a grudge against my inexcusable behavior.

Mary turned toward Lief and bent in a shallow bow. "My lord, there's been a development."

The way she said development gave me a shiver. Whatever it was, I doubted it was good.

"What happened?" he asked.

"The Army of Light has engaged the weeden fae; there were many fatalities. The survivors are being overseen by your supporters." Mary delivered the news in an impassionate tone, but I could tell by her sudden stillness that she wasn't unaffected by the dire announcement.

Lief let out a collection of profanities, some of which must have been fae because they made no sense to my ears. "*Why?* Why would they go after the weeden?" he demanded of no one in particular.

Farranen, who'd moved next to me when I hadn't been paying attention, bent down and murmured next to my ear, "The weeden reside in the southwestern edges of the Fallow Woods. They are highly skilled in woodworking and are indirect cousins to the pixies."

"I believe it was upon the light king's instruction, my lord," Mary answered. "We also suspect that the orders extend to those of the Light Court rumored to support the uprising."

Farranen sucked in a breath; for my stoic guardian, it was the equivalent of anyone else shouting, "Holy hairy monkey balls!" and looking dumbstruck.

"Wait—Gus is using the Army of Light to kill anyone involved with the rebellion?" I asked in shock. That was crazy. Since the fae couldn't reproduce by having babies or making changelings anymore, their population was on the verge of extinction. With less than three thousand fae left, they couldn't afford to lose any more.

My thoughts took another turn that had my stomach dropping like I was on an amusement park ride. Farranen was one of Lief's most well-known supporters—which meant he had a giant target on his back. And it wouldn't be hard for the Army of Light to track him down since he had to remain close to his gate.

I looked up and realized the conversation had continued without me while I'd been humoring my inner panic.

"Take Theo home and close the gate. They know where she lives, and I don't want them to get any bright ideas about going through her to get to me," Lief was saying.

Farranen's eyes narrowed, and he put his hand on my back as if to guide me toward the gate. I dug in my heels and turned back toward the group of fae intent on dragging me out of Fairie.

"You can't close the gate!" I told them, a tad desperately.

"Augustus has been to your residence," Farranen said, and I bristled at his barely concealed condescension.

Dog growled at the mention of Gus, or maybe he wanted to remind the men that I wouldn't be alone and unguarded at my cabin.

"I know that! But if you shut the gate, I won't be able to reach Fairie's magic."

Green eyes softened with understanding, and Farranen assured me, "I will return as soon as I am able; and as always, my own personal magic will be yours to draw from."

I shook my head. "You don't get it. Ever since I, um…When I…you know—" I still couldn't bring myself to give voice to what I'd done to the queen. "I *need* to be here. My magic starts to *die* if I don't come." I fumbled for words to explain how dependant I'd become on my daily visits to the fae realm. I was too ashamed to mention my very real fear that if I couldn't get back to Fairie, and I attempted to pull magic from another fae, I'd end up taking too much and accidentally kill him or her.

Lief moved silently, like a living shadow, until he was directly in front of me. There was no judgment in his eyes, and when he held out his hand, I took it without hesitation. Since my metaphorical battery was fully charged from already being in Fairie, I wasn't worried about stealing from him.

His magic was a warm familiar caress that I welcomed. It tasted like fresh winter snow and brought a smile to my lips. His eyes widened briefly, before settling back into their usual knowing look. I wanted to ask what he'd found surprising, since the brief exchange hadn't felt unusual to me, but he spoke first.

"Your magic…It's started to form a permanent connection with the magic of our realm." The dark prince spoke slowly, with the barest hint of a smile curling his lips upward. "This is most…unexpected."

I looked over to Farranen, hoping for some clarification, since I wasn't exactly grasping what Lief was hinting at. His lips parted in a smile—

A thunderous *BOOM!* filled the air, and I

instinctively covered my ears against the onslaught. The ground beneath me shuddered, and I staggered until someone grabbed me around the waist and lifted me off my feet. Before I could call out to Dog to make sure he was okay, we were hurtling toward the woods at the edge of the clearing.

Broken pieces of wood bounced off my back and shoulders, like I was standing downwind of a woodchipper in use, and then the terrifying sensation of falling filled me. I let out a shriek that was cut off when I landed on my back and all the air was forced from my lungs.

Lief's angry cry sounded like a far-off echo with the ringing in my ears, and I couldn't make out the words he was shouting.

I blinked a few times and realized I was pinned between Farranen's hard body and the equally hard ground. His shoulders were hunched protectively around me, blocking the rest of the world from my sight. I pushed against him with a shaking hand, and he made a small sound of protest as he shifted some of his weight off me.

The bright blue of the sky filled my vision, only this time it was tarnished with a thick plume of black smoke. My eyes traced the column back down to the ground, finally coming to rest on the hawthorn tree—or what was left of it.

Chapter Three

The tree that held the gate between worlds had been easily three or four stories tall, with multiple trunks and an elaborate canopy that boasted brightly colored summer leaves. Now it was a smoldering tower of charred wood. Some of the smaller trunks had broken off and lay in the grass like fallen soldiers, while black tendrils of smoke continued to escape higher into the sky.

I sucked in a breath to ask the obvious question of what the hell had just happened, but I choked on the acidic smell of uncured wood burning.

"Theo!"

I caught a glimpse of Lief's face, his eyes wide and his lips drawn into a tight line, as he rolled Farranen off me.

My guardian let out a muffled groan, and from somewhere behind him came Dog's familiar whine.

"Theo!"

I looked up as Lief knelt over me.

My feeble attempt to push him away was ignored as he ran his hands over my body, hopefully checking for injuries and not just trying to cop a feel, until I could choke out, "I'm okay. Where's Dog?"

The dark prince helped me to sit up, and I got a better view of the extent of the damage surrounding us. Less than half of the original hawthorn tree remained standing. "What happened?" I gasped.

He shook his head. "I don't know." A small trickle

of blood ran down the side of his face from his hairline to jaw. Apparently satisfied that I wasn't in need of any first aid, he focused his attention on Farranen.

I stared open-mouthed at the remains of the tree, unable to process what I was seeing. Had it been struck by lightning? There wasn't a cloud in the sky. Did Fairie even have lightning?

A wet nose shoved its way under my jaw, eliciting a gasp from me and drawing my attention away from the burnt tree. I didn't reprimand Dog for the breach of my personal space; I just wrapped my arms around his scruffy neck and took comfort in the fact that he was unharmed.

Lief pulled Farranen to his feet, and together they surveyed the destruction. The clearing was littered with bits and pieces of the hawthorn tree, like a massive tornado had torn it apart but left every other tree in the area untouched.

I jumped when another figure appeared next to me, only to realize it was Mary. When she extended her hand to me, I took it, fighting the urge to cringe as her triple-jointed fingers grasped mine before pulling me to my feet. Her grip was gentle, but I knew firsthand that ankou fae had retractable razors in their fingertips.

"This was no accident," Mary grated, gesturing to the smoking tree.

My gaze automatically shot to her face to see if she was joking, but the swirling black mist made it impossible to read her expression.

"You think someone set the tree on fire?" I asked incredulously.

"No, someone tried to blow it up," Lief stated flatly, as he and Farranen joined us. My guardian weaved on his feet, and the dark prince's shoulder was the only thing holding him up. I wedged myself under his other arm, and the fact that he didn't protest scared me more than if he'd been screaming in pain. Knowing one of his fae gifts (aka superpowers) was the ability to heal himself, I tentatively pushed some of my magic into him. It flowed smoothly, merging with his, which was shockingly depleted.

"Why?" I asked. Why would anyone want to blow up the beautiful old tree? Without it, the fae wouldn't be able to travel between realms—

Oh my God—the gate!

I turned and looked at the soot marks; they spread outward from a central point, with the blackest being right where the doorway between the realms had been. *How the hell was I supposed to get home?* My arm tightened around Farranen, like I was suddenly the one in danger of falling over. Could the gate be fixed? How long would it take? I glanced back at the semicircle of fae watching the flames at the top of the tree; the males' flat eyes and tight jaws let me know they'd already moved past the shock and denial I was currently struggling with, and on to grim acceptance. Which only served to catapult me straight to pissed off.

"Someone did this on *purpose?*" I demanded of no one in particular. "Where are they?" I took an angry step forward, to see if maybe the arsonist was hiding on the other side of the tree.

"There's nobody here, Theo," Lief told me. The fact that he had his sword still strapped to his back rather than in hand, did more to convince me than his words. "Whatever happened, occurred in the Earth realm."

I blinked at Lief's steely tone. Good. I shouldn't be the only one irate. If someone had purposely damaged the gate, he should be furious too.

"Get Theo out of here," he told Farranen in his I'm-a-bossy-ruler voice.

"If this was an attempt on our lives, they'll try again. My temporary residence won't be sufficient against an attack of this magnitude." My guardian stood up a little straighter, seeming to shake off some of the lingering weakness from being thrown across the clearing.

I looked back and forth at the tense posture on both males and realized they were expecting another metaphorical shoe to drop.

"Take her to the Dark Castle. I'll send word to any of my court who may be targeted and have them join you." Lief turned to Mary. "Can you reach any of the Light Court who have given me their allegiance?"

"Of course, my lord." With a surprisingly graceful bow, Mary departed.

"I'll join you as soon as I'm able," Lief told us and moved to take the path that led away from the Dark Castle.

Farranen was content to accept Lief's dismissal and nodded. But I wasn't one of his subjects and had no problem questioning the high and mighty dark prince when I thought he was running head-first into a dangerous situation. "Where are you going?" I demanded.

"To the Earth realm," he answered curtly. Yeah, he definitely didn't like having his royal self questioned.

"What? How?" I gestured at the smoking remains of the hawthorn tree.

"There are other gates, the closest being fifty miles west of here. That will be their next stop to either cross back into Fairie or destroy that gate as well. They won't be expecting any resistance." A brief slash of smile promised that he was looking forward to providing the implied resistance.

I wanted to tell him not to go, but I kept my mouth shut. If this were my realm to lead and protect, there was no way I'd sit back and let someone else deal with the threat. "Be careful," I told him softly, letting every bit of my worry and sincerity show on my face.

Something passed in the depths of his blue eyes, gone before I could name it. He looked to my guardian, and they silently exchanged a lengthy look. Tension crackled through the air, brushing up against my magic like an itchy wool sweater.

Suddenly Lief reached forward and pulled Farranen into an embrace, inadvertently including me since I was still playing the part of a leaning post. Slightly uncomfortable with the group hug, I thought about saying something sarcastic, but if one of us really was being targeted by someone with access to explosives, I could live with the overly enthusiastic good-bye.

Lief whispered a word or two that I couldn't understand and then pressed his lips to my forehead in a chaste kiss. I blinked in surprise, and when I looked up, it was to the sight of his black cloak fluttering in the breeze as he walked away.

****

I felt like a new me.

Not that there was anything wrong with the old me.

Well, actually, I could think of a few things I'd like to improve, but that wasn't particularly relevant at the moment. What I meant was that the combination of spending the afternoon in Fairie, followed by the subsequent return trip, was doing wonders for my attitude. The tightness in my chest had faded from imminent-zombie-apocalypse levels, down to oh-dear-I-burned-the-Christmas-turkey levels. Until then, I hadn't realized how extreme my anxiety had become.

My magic bubbled happily beneath my skin, and I was forced to constantly brush away tendrils of Fairie's magic that continued to reach for me. I'd always been aware of the magic that permeated everything in the realm, but now it was…more. More intense. More tactile. More alive. Just…*more.*

And speaking of *more*, my traitorous brain kept jumping to all the physical ways I'd like to enjoy *more* of the man next to me. Physical ways that left us both gasping and sweaty. Which should have made me feel guilty since he was moving at a pace that any mall-walking granny could beat.

If someone hadn't been gunning for the males I cared about, I would have been positively giddy.

The few fae we encountered on the road to the Dark Castle either greeted Farranen with respect and Dog and I with curiosity or ignored us all completely. The realities of civil war had apparently come crashing down on those who, until then, had been doing their best to remain ignorant.

The sky had faded to darkness before we arrived at the castle, and I stared at the growing shadows suspiciously. Whoever had bombed the gate was stuck in the Earth realm and couldn't be lying in wait for us, but that didn't mean that they'd been working alone. Any number of their co-conspirators could be wandering around Fairie looking for us.

My scattered thoughts were interrupted when the Dark Castle came into view.

It was identical to the Light Castle, only predictably darker in color. Outer walls of large hand-cut slabs of stone rose over half a dozen stories in the air, bookended at the four corners with square towers that were even taller. Flying buttresses with intricate carvings gracefully supported the monstrous structure. Sharply arched windows topped with stained glass, combined with the somber colors and a multi-peaked roof, gave the building a gothic feel. I was still slightly disappointed that Lief didn't have any gargoyle statues. That would have been epic. Although, this was Fairie, so maybe there were real gargoyles roaming around with better things to do than hang out at the Dark Castle.

The massive doors to the castle opened silently as if we were expected, and after Farranen exchanged a few brief words with the fae guards, he led us down a long corridor with thick wooden doors inset at even distances. The whole place felt somber, like everyone that lived within its walls were collectively holding their breath and waiting for something to happen. I wasn't sure if it was because they'd already caught wind of what happened to the gate, or maybe it was just from being in the midst of a civil war. Either way, it made me realize that I wasn't the only one affected by the explosion. These were the people that Lief and Farranen were working so hard to improve the realm for.

Dog pressed his body against my thigh as we walked, and I absently scratched behind his ears to let him know I appreciated having him with me.

Farranen had stopped leaning on me for support before we'd reached the castle, and the set of his shoulders and brisk pace had returned to normal. And yeah, I only know because I was ogling his back as we walked. Guilty as charged.

For the hundredth time, I was grateful for his speedy healing. And a little jealous, since I had a few bumps and bruises of my own that were making themselves known. Girls my size just weren't cut out for getting tossed around.

And speaking of getting thrown around—if my guardian truly was feeling better, I wouldn't mind tossing him on the nearest horizontal surface and climbing on top—

Stop it! I sternly chastised myself. There were more important things to worry about than getting physical with the hottest male in the realm. I just couldn't remember what they were right now.

We stopped at a wooden door that was identical to all the other doors in the hall. "Where are we?" I asked in a hushed voice, hesitant to disturb the bleak atmosphere.

"This is where I stay when I have business at the Dark Castle." He uttered a single foreign word and then reached out and turned the silver knob. I shared a curious look with Dog before we followed my guardian through the door.

The simple room was spacious and well appointed. A large bed graced the far wall, its bedding a neutral beige and cream. The floors were more of the same dark stone as the rest of the castle, with their starkness broken up by a white rug. Books were stacked in neat orderly piles on the table like tiny little models of perfectly engineered high-rise buildings. A large wardrobe nestled in the corner of the room, while a box of firewood sat next to the large fireplace.

Farranen crossed the room and knelt in front of the empty hearth.

My eyes were immediately drawn to his long graceful fingers as they set about the task of lighting a fire. I could think of at least a dozen ways those beautiful digits could be put to better use.

"Don't," I told him hoarsely.

He shot me a look over his shoulder with his eyebrows drawn. "Don't what?" he asked in confusion.

"Don't bother with a fire," I answered, barely recognizing my own voice.

Something like shock crossed his face, only to be replaced with a contemplative suspicion, followed quickly by confusion. He got to his feet and approached me slowly. Wariness echoed in each hesitant step he took. "It's cold, and we may be here for a while," he said.

"I can think of a better way for us to keep warm," I told him honestly, without a single trace of the uncertainty I was expecting to hear. Weeks of sleeping in the same bed as him but seeing zero indication that he was interested in sex was making me crazy. And desperate.

Until the mind-blowing kiss that we'd shared in my kitchen, he'd kept his hands to himself since he'd declared his intentions to court me. If he had changed his mind and was no longer interested, then I wanted to know now.

"Theodora?" The fragile hope in his face helped to chase away some of my doubts, but it was the hungry way that his eyes traveled down to my lips before returning to my eyes that told me the attraction wasn't one-sided. It was a look that I'd never get tired of seeing.

I took the last step to close the distance between us and rose on my tippy toes as my hands reached up to caress the back of his neck. The smell of cinnamon and fresh pine went straight to my head, making me dizzy. The strong hands that slid around my waist were firm as he gently pulled me into the heat of his body.

A low whine cut thought the fog of pheromones that surrounded me.

Without breaking eye contact, Farranen told Dog,

30

"You should have no trouble finding the dining room. Word of your arrival will have already reached the staff; they'll treat you as they would any guest of the dark prince."

Another uncertain whine filled the air, and I shared an exasperated smile with the male in front of me before turning to look at Dog. "Go find something to eat. I'll be fine."

His sad yellow eyes were filled with indecision. He was clearly torn between not wanting to leave me alone in a hostile realm, and the prospect of trying to satisfy his never-ending appetite.

I detangled myself from Farranen's arms and knelt next to my worried shifter. "Do you really think anyone can get to me when I'm with him?" I gestured to where my guardian was patiently waiting. Which was pretty impressive since I was practically vibrating with the need to toss Dog's furry butt out the door and lock it behind him.

Dog silently evaluated the tall fae, and some of the fear melted from his expression. He gave a chuff that I took to mean that we'd better behave ourselves while he was gone.

I stood and opened the door but wisely made no promises about what sort of shenanigans Farranen and I might engage in during his absence. After all, this was Fairie, and I wasn't sure exactly how the whole the-fae-can't-lie thing worked. And I was already compiling a mental list of shenanigans that I was looking forward to.

Dog stepped out into the hall and lifted his nose to sniff the air. He must have caught the scent of something tasty, because his tail gave a brief wag before he trotted off in the direction we'd originally come from.

I shut the door before turning to look at my guardian.

"How long do you think he'll be gone?" Farranen asked in a casual voice that didn't match the heat in his eyes.

"How much food is there in the Dark Castle?" I replied mildly.

"Enough to feed a flock of greckle demons for a month." His lips curved up, and I couldn't wait to taste them again.

I took a few steps toward him, completely out of my comfort zone. Until now, seduction had been a concept that I practiced on paper, not in real life.

With shaking hands, I tugged my sweatshirt over my head and tossed it over the back of a comfortable looking armchair where I'd deposited my coat earlier.

"My lady…" Farranen locked eyes with me and slowly unclasped his cloak.

My heartrate tripled when I heard it land on the floor at his feet, but I refused to look away from the passion in his eyes. It was my lifeline, the only thing I had to hold onto in the sea of uncertainty and desire that I was floating in.

He closed the last few steps between us. Our combined breathing was too loud in the emptiness of the large room, and I was proud of myself for not trying to break it up by making a sarcastic comment.

His hands slid back around my waist and pulled me against the hardness of his body. My head tilted back of its own volition, and I sighed when he pressed his lips to mine in a kiss that started gentle but quickly became demanding. A low moan escaped my throat as he slowly backed me up until I was trapped between a cold stone wall and the heat of his chest. It was a glorious place to be.

My hands wandered over his shoulders and back as

his tongue continued to delve and explore. Feeling the hard strips of scars that ran beneath his shirt was intimate in a way that increased the tingling in my lady parts. There was a strength and beauty in the ridges that brought out my possessive urges. If anyone tried to hurt this man again, they were going to have to go through me first.

A prickling of fae magic surged against mine a few seconds before the door across the room banged open, shattering any sense of privacy that I'd been enjoying.

Chapter Four

I jumped and probably would have fallen if I hadn't been locked in Farranen's embrace.

Damn it! Why was the world so determined to keep me from some much-needed time spent in the arms of my hot guardian?

Lief stormed through the doorway with his black cloak and hair swirling around him like he'd just stepped out of a wind tunnel. His sword was still strapped to his back, and his hands were clenched into fists at his side. Whatever had the dark prince on edge must be a pretty big deal; the only time I'd seen him so worked up was right after I'd died, and then again when I'd almost fallen off a cliff.

Farranen, picking up on the fact that Lief was two seconds from stroking out, thankfully skipped the awkward topic of us getting caught fooling around red-handed. "What happened?" he asked as the veil of his stoic guardian mask slid firmly back in place.

"A scout intercepted me before I could reach the secondary gate," Lief announced as he came to a stop at the foot of the bed. "The dead lands are expanding, and the southern half of the Fallow Woods are gone."

I'd seen the dead lands firsthand when I'd come to Fairie to rescue Farranen. The name wasn't very creative, but it fit the ominous black shadow that was slowly swallowing the land. It was like Dog's stomach and devoured everything in its path. Even the immortal fae.

"Half the woods are *gone?*" I asked, shock making my words sound hollow. First the gate, and now the woods? If I looked outside, would I see the sky falling in? Something was seriously wrong with Fairie.

Lief gave a curt nod. "Gavriel was the one to discover the trouble, so I haven't seen it personally, but he's reporting that half of the Fallow Woods are gone. The Ragnier Woods that border them are still intact, but at the rate it's moving—"

"What about the pixies?" I demanded breathlessly. The pixies lived in the grassy hills next to the Fallow Woods. They'd played a major part in helping me rescue Farranen last month, and I was rather fond of the bloodthirsty little fae.

Lief gave me a brief smile and said, "I have no doubt that Karista and her flock have fled somewhere safe."

I thought about the feisty leader of the pixies, with her bright pink hair and tinkling voice, and realized he was right. Despite being only twelve inches tall and built like a voluptuous doll, she was perfectly capable of keeping the pixies safe. Not to mention the fact that I'd seen her rip golf-ball-sized chunks out of another fae with her razor-sharp teeth. She was tiny but all kinds of scary.

"That's hundreds of hectares gone"—the skin on my guardian's forehead creased as he thought out loud—"in a matter of weeks?"

"Days," Lief stated somberly. "I was down that way a week ago, and nothing seemed amiss."

"How?" Farranen voiced the question we'd all been thinking.

Lief's jaw clenched as he exhaled. "I don't know, but I suspect it has something to do with the imbalance of power between the courts." The weariness in his voice spoke to the centuries that he'd lived through, despite appearing to be in his mid-thirties.

Guilt filled me, unwelcome and suffocating; this was my fault. If I hadn't deprived Fairie of one of its rulers, then the balance of power wouldn't be out of wack.

"What can we do?" I asked.

The men exchanged a knowing look, and Lief nodded like he was giving my guardian permission to spill the beans.

"We need to find the key," Farranen declared.

"What key?" I asked, my eyes bouncing between the two males.

"The leader of each court inherits a key that holds half of the power of the realm when they ascend to the throne." Lief tugged a chain from beneath his shirt to reveal a small black key. "This one is magically bound to me and can't be controlled by another."

I stepped closer, so I could admire the delicate design as it hung from Lief's neck. It was one of those old-fashioned keys with a long narrow neck and multiple flat teeth that would fit in the corresponding lock. The head was shaped like a three-leaf clover with a small purple jewel embedded in the center. It was deceptively simple and elegant for something that radiated with power.

I reached out, wanting to know exactly what the magic would feel like, but stopped short of actually touching it. Who knew how my messed-up magic would react? I decided it wasn't worth finding out and lowered my hand.

Lief slid the key back under his shirt, and the press of the strange magic disappeared from my awareness as soon as it touched the smooth skin of his neck. Which explained how I'd never noticed it before.

"How come I've never seen it before?" I mused aloud.

Last fall after I'd been attacked by Merrick (for the second time), Lief and I had showered together. We'd been fully dressed, but afterward he'd glamoured our wet clothing into fluffy bath towels, giving me a good view of everything he had from the waist up. I would have noticed if he'd been wearing the key. And I'd had multiple chances to ogle his bare chest when I'd posed as his consort, but still no memory of the key surfaced. If he'd been hiding it with glamour, I would have noticed the tell-tale shimmer.

"The keys must remain in Fairie," Lief told me, and I knew by the way he was looking at me that he was thinking of all the times I'd seen him half naked. "But I don't always keep it on my person in this realm either. It must be close by so I can use its power to sustain the Dark Court, but there's no point in making it easy to find if someone should think to steal it to weaken my power base."

"But the queen wasn't wearing one when—" I ignored the way my voice shook and continued lamely with "—ah, the last time I saw her." After seeing Safeena in the buff, I knew for a fact that she hadn't been wearing any sort of magical key. Or anything for that matter. "And what does finding the key have to do with the dead lands growing?" And why wasn't there a manual for all the random fae knowledge I was lacking? It was impractical (and embarrassing) to keep using Lief and Farranen as my tutors.

"The magic stored in the key is different from my personal magic. I use it to sustain the realm and all the inhabitants of my court. As of lately, it's become quite taxed."

"Which indicates that nobody is in possession of the key to the Light Court," Farranen interjected. "Thus, giving the dead lands the ability to grow at an accelerated rate."

I thought back to my time in the queen's chambers. Had I seen a small key anywhere? I hadn't exactly been looking for one, but I think I would have noticed the magic radiating off it, if it hadn't been directly touching Safeena's skin.

"So how do we find it?" I asked of no one in particular. "Does it have some sort of magical GPS tracker?"

"Unfortunately, it's not that easy," Lief said with a hint of his usual smile. "We'll have to do it the old-fashioned way."

Things would be so much easier if I'd just left the regicide to someone who knew what they were doing.

****

Dog waddled down the hall like a pregnant hippo, and I could tell by his distended belly that he had enjoyed a fair amount of the local cuisine.

Nobody spoke as the dark prince led us through the silent halls of the Dark Castle with a determined stride. Once we were outside, Lief knelt next to Dog and looked into his wary eyes. "Dog of the Earth realm, as the ruler of the Dark Court, I would like to formally request your assistance with a matter of great importance."

"You want Dog's help?" I asked in surprise. What could Dog do for the fae realm that the dark prince couldn't?

"Your shifter senses would be a great help in discovering who besieged the hawthorn tree," Lief told him before looking up to where I stood. "Theo will be in good hands, and I would welcome an ally at my back that I can trust."

The muscles in my shoulders tightened at the thought of Lief bringing Dog into a dangerous situation. Until now, I'd assumed the four of us would head off on an epic journey full of adventure and camaraderie to locate the missing key—like the four musketeers—thus putting us in a position to watch each other's backs. I could understand Lief's desire to split up, since someone needed to find out who was responsible for destroying the gate, but I wasn't loving the idea of being separated from my faithful shifter.

Farranen wrapped an arm around my waist, and his thumb massaged little circles into my hip. It was probably his way of telling me that Dog was a big boy and could speak for himself. The part of my brain that ran on emotions, rather than logic, wanted to wrap my arms around my furry friend and keep him by my side. But he was capable of making his own decisions, and it was probably safer for him to go with Lief anyway since trouble had an uncanny knack for finding me. I'd seen the dark prince use a sword; Dog would be as safe as a shifter could be in Fairie if he stayed with Lief.

As if sensing my thoughts, Dog gave me a toothy grin and bobbed his head. Something about the dark prince's proposal must have appealed to the part of his nature that loved to hunt and chase things.

It was surprising that he was so quick to agree. He usually got separation anxiety when I left the cabin to get a load of firewood. Still, it was good to see that my little shifter was growing up.

I bent at the waist so I could look into his big soulful doggy eyes. "Take care of Lief, okay?" I whispered, horrified that I was choking up.

He gave a low whine and shoved his shaggy head into my hands until I was forced to wrap my arms around him or fall over. I took one last deep breath, savoring the knowledge that he was safe with me, and then I let him go.

"Merry meet, Dog," Farranen murmured.

Before I could protest, Lief tugged me into an embrace that lacked the usual flirtatious vibes he enjoyed teasing me with. "I give you my solemn oath that I will bring him back to you," he whispered against the top of my head. A small snap of magic settled over us, forging his words into an unbreakable bond that eased some of the worry in my heart.

"Thank you," I told him sincerely.

"I know that no harm will befall the guardian with you to watch over him." He pulled back far enough so I could see myself reflected in his eyes.

Was Farranen still a guardian, now that the gate was gone? I wondered.

"We'll send word as soon as we locate the key," Farranen told him.

Lief released me and stepped back onto the path that would take him toward the closest working gate. With a jaunty wave, he turned on his heel and walked away with Dog trotting along behind him.

Farranen's arm came around my shoulders, and I let myself be pulled against his body. It was comforting, just like he'd probably intended for it to be, and I reminded myself that this was just a temporary separation from two of the males that I'd come to care about.

"So where are we headed?" I asked, trying to steer my melancholy thoughts away from Dog and Lief.

Taking my hand in his, Farranen told me, "To the

Light Castle."

"Is that safe?" I asked as we started walking. I did a quick mental recap of the times I'd been to the queen's castle, and every visit could be categorized as "life-threating and terrifying." I really wasn't looking forward to another visit.

"The gray knight and the Army of Light were last seen in the wild lands. The castle should be relatively empty."

"And that's where the key will be hidden?" This was beginning to sound like an impossible task. Finding something as tiny as a key in a massive magical castle was like searching for a proverbial needle in a haystack. If it was even in the castle. And what if the queen had used glamour to hide it? I'd be able to see the key if it was hidden behind a layer of glamour, but if it was glamoured *into* something else, I'd have no idea. Hopefully my guardian had some nifty fae tricks up his sleeve to give us a fighting chance.

But what if Gus had taken it? I already knew he was a master of deception and murder; it wasn't a far stretch to think he might be a klepto too. My eyeballs had been firmly pointed at anything but Gus's nudity when he'd been getting dressed after his tryst with Safeena. It wouldn't have been hard for him to slip something small into his pants pocket.

"The queen would have kept it close. Since that is where she died, it is likely still there."

I latched onto the confidence in his voice, hoping it would bolster my own. "And nobody else could have gotten through the portal since then?"

"Only the dark prince." He came to an abrupt stop, and I was forced to stop with him or let go of his hand.

I stopped.

"And you," he murmured thoughtfully. "*You* were able to open the portal." His eyes narrowed in a way that made me feel like I was a frog about to be dissected. "But only the leaders of the courts can create the portals and determine who they open for—only those who possess the power of a key."

Oh shit.

"I don't have the key!" My voice was a little too high-pitched and came across as defensive. "I mean, I'd know if I had a key, right?" It's not like I'd accidentally stepped on it and it had been stuck to the bottom of my boot for the last two weeks. And hadn't Lief said that the key couldn't leave Fairie?

Farranen shrugged a single shoulder, and the gesture made him look more human than fae. "I'm unsure what to think when it comes to you, Theodora. It would be unwise to assume the same rules apply to you as they do everyone else."

Ouch. His logic was sound, but it sucked to hear him say the words out loud.

****

The thirty-minute walk from Lief's castle to the Light Castle was relatively silent. I'm not sure if that was because Farranen was lost in contemplation of where the missing key could be, or if we were trying to get there unnoticed. Most likely he was thinking; sneaking anywhere with me was rather pointless. I made more noise than a grand piano falling down a flight of stairs.

When the castle came into view, I gasped and Farranen stopped dead in his tracks.

It was still a soaring architectural masterpiece, but instead of the pale gray I'd been expecting, it was stark white, like someone had leached all the color out of the rough stones.

"What happened?" I asked in shock. How had the entire castle changed color in only two weeks? Even the bright stained glass that topped the tall narrow windows had faded to dull shades of gray.

"More proof that no one wields the key to the Light Court."

I didn't like his grim tone, almost like he was resigned to the fact that his realm was dying.

"Will things get better once there's a new king or queen?" I asked quietly.

"In theory." His eyes were bright as he stared at the castle, making his skin and blond hair paler by comparison.

"Well, let's get in there and find the damn key so Fairie can pick a new ruler for the Light Court and we can all go back to our lives until the next bit of supernatural drama sneaks up and bites us on the butt," I told him earnestly. Because I really couldn't wait for life to go back to normal—or whatever passed as normal in my world.

And if a new ruler was appointed, there would be the bonus of calling out Gus on his farce. Not to mention, I'd finally get a chance to tear the clothes off my gorgeous fae and act on some of the naughty fantasies that frequently occupied my imagination. Of course, then we'd still have to deal with him not having a gate to guard anymore...But for now, we could only focus on one problem at a time.

Farranen looked down at me, and once again I was left a little speechless at the affection that I saw in his serious face. "An excellent plan."

Chapter Five

Breaking into a castle was easier than you'd think.

We didn't march up to the front doors and use a battering ram to bash them in. Nor did we don clever disguises, knock politely, and sweet-talk our way in. No, it was much less exciting—we snuck in the back door.

Considering that this was where soldiers had spent hundreds of years training to serve in the Army of Light, I wasn't real impressed by the lack of security. Perhaps if the queen had spent a little more time preparing for the possibility of war and less time on sadistic bedroom sport, there would have been a guard at the back door.

I was just thankful there was no bloodshed involved with breaking and entering.

I almost asked how Farranen had known where to find the seldom-used door, but judging by the confidence in his steps as he led me down one narrow hall after another, he'd obviously done this before. If this was the route he'd used to rendezvous with a female living in the castle on the down-low, I didn't want to know about it.

The hall was lined by torches every ten feet that lit by themselves as we passed by. Even the flames looked white, like something had sucked all the color from them. A quick peek over my shoulder revealed that they extinguished once we were a certain distance away. I wasn't sure if Farranen was controlling them, or if the castle had some sort of motion-sensor system.

We passed a number of rooms that held old furniture

covered in sheets. After I poked my head into another room, Farranen took my hand and pulled me back into the hall.

"These rooms are used for storage; it is unlikely the key will be here."

"How can you know for sure? It's dark and spooky down here—perfect for hiding something," I stubbornly pointed out.

"You're more likely to find a clutter of vernaim than the key."

"What's a clutter of vernaim?" My imagination was already compiling a list of cool options.

"A cluster of insects, much like the spiders of Earth, but larger. *Much* larger."

I didn't stop to snoop behind any more closed doors.

After climbing two different sets of stone stairs, the narrow hallways finally gave way to wider ones that had the occasional window to let in ambient light from outside.

The mouth-watering aroma from multiple foods lingered in the empty kitchens. If the cooks in Fairie were as talented as my nose was inclined to believe, it was no wonder Dog had gorged himself at the Dark Castle. Farranen led us around another corner, and the smells faded.

Every once in a while, I held my hand out to run my fingertips along the walls as we walked. The building wasn't just constructed from giant slabs of rock; magic was as much a part of the castle as the stone and mortar. Little tendrils of it reached out to me, clinging to my fingers like sticky blades of invisible grass. I hadn't been able to feel them during my previous visits, and I wondered why I could now.

My steps slowed when I realized we were getting

closer to the queen's private chambers. There were no physical landmarks to hint at our location. I could just feel the energy of the room from up ahead. The buzzing intensified as we got closer, and my own magic prickled under my skin in protest.

Farranen glanced back at me with his eyebrows drawn. "What is it?"

I jumped at the sound of his voice. "Nothing. I'm just on edge from sneaking around like a cat-burglar." The fact that the castle appeared to be empty should have been reassuring, but instead it upped the creepiness factor tenfold. I offered him an apologetic smile and took a deep breath to calm my nerves.

Pulling his sword from his back in a practiced movement, Farranen slid around the corner into a hall that appeared no different from the last one, aside from the panel of frosted glass that marked the entrance to the queen's chambers—which was kind of weird, since the portal wasn't usually visible unless it was in use.

I was going to ask why he felt the need to be armed in the empty hallway, but I realized this would be a really good spot for someone hidden to ambush us. I gave the corridor an analytical once-over and came up empty-handed. Unless someone had glamoured themselves to look like one of the paintings on the wall, we were alone. "There's nobody here," I told my guardian in a whisper. If anyone was trying to hide behind a layer of glamour, I would have been able to spot them.

He lowered his sword but didn't return it to the scabbard on his back. His eyes were thoughtful as he stared at the motionless section of glass, as if he was confronting a particularly complex algebra equation that might jump off the page and attack him.

I knew from my previous visits that the portal

shouldn't have been visible until someone said the magic word and made a blood offering. The fact that it was already the size of a door was weird. Had I left it like this when I'd escaped through it? I'd been so focused on getting away, that I hadn't looked back to check.

Lief had been here since I had; maybe he'd left it open.

Farranen must have reached the same conclusion, because he reached out and rapped his knuckles on the glass. The hollow knock echoed back down the hallway behind us. Okay, so maybe it wasn't exactly open. This was the point where we should have been able to walk through it, but it was as solid as a brick wall.

"Why is it like that?" I asked, my curiosity winning out over my desire to avoid being heard and possibly discovered.

"I'm uncertain. It's like the portal has been left in some sort of stasis." He frowned. "The whole castle feels like it's in stasis." Sudden understanding filled his eyes. "It *is* waiting—for a new ruler."

I wasn't sure what the frozen portal had to do with it, but I'd already picked up on the anticipative vibes that flowed like an undercurrent in Fairie's magic. Like a blushing bride waiting breathlessly at the alter, she was ready for whatever was coming. "So, let's help her find one," I softly suggested.

I'm not sure when Fairie went from being an "it" to a "her," but sometime in the last few weeks, during my many visits to the realm, I'd come to feel something other than fear and aversion for the realm. Now that I knew she was stuck in some sort of limbo with no one to rule the Light Court, I wanted to help her.

I moved toward the magical doorway, but Farranen grabbed my arm. "We don't know what's in there. It might be a trap."

I gave him a look that implied I was no longer the craziest one in this relationship. "Who would set a trap for us? In *there* of all places?" This was the last place I'd willingly be if the fate of the realm wasn't dependent on finding the stupid key. There was nothing nostalgic about revisiting the scene of a murder I committed.

"Why would someone blow up the gate?" he countered. "Until we know exactly what and who we're up against, it would be wise to err on the side of caution."

Well, I couldn't argue with that logic. Especially since my overly suspicious brain agreed. I took a step back and said, "Harvey? Vanessa? Can you hear me?"

Immediately the two ghosts appeared next to us. When I'd been learning to control my magic, I'd accidentally pulled them through the veil between worlds into this one. They were both able to travel with me between Earth and Fairie until their energy became depleted. Then they were forced to return to wherever it was ghosts went to recharge.

"What the hell, Theo?" Vanessa demanded, propping her hand on her cocked hip, while flipping her long brown hair over her shoulder with the other hand.

"Hey, guys. Did I catch you at a bad time?" I asked with genuine curiosity. If I was ever done running for my life, I was going to sit these two down and make them spill all the gory details about the afterlife. *Research for an upcoming novel,* I told myself. Riiiiight.

"Seriously? We're back *here* again?" Her disgust was understandable. After Gus had killed me, Lief had brought my body here, and Vanessa had tagged along. Since I was the only one that could see her, she hadn't had many other options. Combined with the fact that she'd had a front-row seat when I'd murdered Safeena, I was sympathetic to her desire to be anywhere else than the Light Castle.

I decided to skip over the complicated tale of how we'd ended up back at the scene of the crime, and told her, "It's kind of a long story. Would you guys mind checking in there"—I gestured toward the portal—"to see if anyone's waiting to ambush us?"

Harvey nodded once, causing a curtain of indigo hair to fall in his eyes, before stepping through the wall that separated us from the room in question. As a former soldier in the Army of Light, he was really good at taking orders without questioning them. A small niggle of guilt tickled my chest; I wasn't his boss. Though I was grateful that he'd switched his allegiance from the queen to me, I tried not to take him for granted.

Harvey's head popped back through the wall, and his lips split into a small grin. "There's nobody here. No traps either, magical or otherwise."

Even as a ghost, Harvey had the typical pale metallic blue skin of all merdain fae. He'd once showed me the gills that ran diagonally across his pecs, used for breathing underwater. He still wore a light gray shirt with gold buttons that was neatly tucked into tight black pants and tall boots. I had no idea why, but ghosts were only allowed one wardrobe choice in the afterlife. With my luck, I'd probably end up in a really hideous muumuu if I was ever brought back.

"The room is clear," I told Farranen since he couldn't see or hear my ghosts. It was a pain in the butt to always be the translator, but it was only fair because I'd been the one to create the flawed ghosts in the first place.

Normal ghosts could be seen by anyone with fae magic and disappeared back behind the veil after a few hours. My ghosts had been hanging around for almost a month and didn't seem to be inclined to leave anytime soon. So, yeah. I made broken ghosts. I didn't think it was a big deal, but not everyone saw it my way.

"Ugh. If I step in any brain bits, I'm going to be pissed." Scrunching her pert little nose, Vanessa disappeared through the wall.

I tapped on the glass with my fingertips and felt the sluggish buzz of magic that the portal was made of. It reached for me, like the trembling hand of a loved one that was on the verge of dying.

What had I done last time? I'd been terrified and desperate at the time. Probably in shock.

I bowed my head until it rested on the cool surface and took a deep breath. The scent of fresh pine and spicy cinnamon teased my nose, and my breathing slowed. I wasn't running for my life this time, but it was just as important that I get in and find the key.

"Please, just open," I whispered as I finally remembered the words I'd uttered the night that I'd been trapped and feeling hopeless.

The portal dissolved into a swirling eddy of silver light, and I tumbled through it until Harvey caught me by the shoulders on the other side.

"Thanks." I gave him a self-deprecating smile.

"You're welcome," he responded amiably, and I was grateful he didn't comment on my clumsiness.

Everything in the room was exactly as I'd left it. Books and small bottles of lotion and powder were strewn across the floor. The wardrobe was askew with one of the doors hanging open. Shimmering gowns in an array of colors had fallen on the floor like someone had sprinkled expensive jewels over a puddle of melted rainbows. No flames graced the pile of ash in the hearth.

And the bed...I forced my eyes to take in the mauve sheets, complete with dried blood splatter and other bodily fluids that made my stomach flip. Lief had said that Harvey's body had been returned to his next of kin, so at least he wouldn't have to see his mutilated remains if he decided to peek around to the other side of the bed.

The scent of the spilled perfumes and lotions hung in the stale air, but there was none of the decomposition smells that would normally be associated with a dead body.

Farranen stepped cautiously through the doorway and joined me where I stood next to the queen's body.

After taking in everything else in the room, including the small droplets of blood and brains that had sprayed in an arc across the wall and ceiling, I risked a glance down.

Yep. She was still dead.

The baby-soft skin of her head had shrunk, tightening around her face like a mask made of jerky that possessed the consistency of thick plastic wrap. Long blond hair tipped with sage green still clung to her scalp, except for the top part that had been blown away. Her graceful limbs were askew and just as naked as the rest of her. Nothing hung around her neck.

I'd been braced for an overwhelming surge of guilt to hit me, but all I felt was pity and relief that she couldn't hurt anyone anymore. I didn't want to think about what my lack of remorse said about the woman that I'd become.

"Where would she have hidden the key?" I asked, mostly to take my mind off the direction my thoughts had taken. If Farranen already knew where the key was, we wouldn't just be standing here twiddling our thumbs.

"Here in her private chambers, would be the most

likely solution." He moved toward her dresser and began opening drawers. I wanted to tell him that there was nothing in there but a mountain of uncomfortable lingerie, but if the key had been glamoured, it might be hiding among the thongs and G-strings. But if it was, would Farranen be able to recognize it for what it was? I had no idea how the fae's glamour worked. Once an object was changed into something else, was there a way to tell? Perhaps a magical signature or lingering trace from the fae who glamoured it? I decided my brain wasn't up for an in-depth discussion on something that I probably wouldn't understand anyway.

I crossed to the bookcase to shuffle through the books. Most of them looked older than I was. "Will the key still feel the same if it's glamoured?" I asked.

"Feel the same?"

Something heavy hit the floor, and I looked back to discover that my guardian had moved on from the dresser to the wardrobe and was tossing shoes out by the handful. Which seemed kind of impossible, seeing as he'd already pulled out enough clothing and shoes to clothe an entire ballroom of dancers. After all the weird things I'd seen in Fairie, I didn't even blink an eye when the law of physics were not just broken, but blatantly smashed to pieces.

"Yeah. Will the magic coming off it be all staticky feeling, like Lief's key?" I didn't have a better description for the electric hum of power that had radiated from the key for the brief time it hadn't been in contact with his skin.

The rustle of evening gowns being pulled from the wardrobe stopped. "You could feel the magic of the dark prince's key?"

Fingers of unease tiptoed down my spine at his

carefully neutral tone. I turned and met his gaze.

"Yes. Couldn't you?" I was proud of how I was able to match his faked indifference, when all I really wanted to do was slap a hand to my forehead and shout, "Damn it!" Anything that surprised Farranen and involved magic, usually didn't bode well for me.

"The keys and their powers are undetectable to all but the rulers who control them. Most fae wouldn't even be able to recognize them since they have never seen them."

Sigh. Of course, they were indistinguishable. I mean, it made sense that the leaders of Fairie wouldn't want a giant bull's-eye on the most powerful items in the realm. But still—I'd been hoping for something that wouldn't fall into the category of just-one-more-reason-that-Theo's-an-oddball. Although maybe my awareness of the key's power was a good thing. Maybe I could use it to zero in on the key's hidey-hole.

I shrugged, because I didn't know what to say. I had no idea how to explain why I'd been able to perceive Lief's key on a magical level.

I closed my eyes. Immediately the ambient magic in the room leapt into my awareness. The strength of it took my breath away and left me feeling both giddy and dizzy. A steady pulse of it continued to emit from the portal, like heat from a pile of coals. The side of the room that held the massive four-post bed had an ugly dark tint to the magic. It felt ominous, and I quickly turned my attention toward something else. Unfortunately, the next thing that called to me was also the closest—the body lying at my feet.

But that didn't make any sense. The queen was dead. She shouldn't be giving off any sort of magical vibes.

I knelt without thinking and laid both my hands on

the dried skin of Safeena's arm. It was really hard not to think about what she'd been touching before she died— I knew for a fact that she hadn't washed her hands (or any other part of herself) after bumping uglies with Gus. It would be just my luck to catch the fae equivalent of chlamydia from touching her bare skin.

Magic leapt for me in a hot wave, the powerful surge knocking me backward onto my butt. The connection was so quick that it only lasted for a fraction of a second, not even long enough for me to blink, but in that brief contact, something passed into me.

Oh, shit.

Chapter Six

I let out a startled gasp. Whatever it was, it pushed against my magic, seeking and shoving as it fought for space inside me.

Get out! I thought in panic. Or maybe I said it out loud. Either was possible.

I was dimly aware of Farranen as he rushed across the room toward me, and I held up a hand to ward him off. I didn't want him to touch me; for all I knew, I really had just caught something contagious and might pass it on to him.

"What happened? Theodora, talk to me!"

His alarm only served to increase my own. I could taste my heartbeat in my mouth and tried to slow my breathing.

Whatever foreign magic had invaded me was slowly settling in, nestling into the spaces that my own magic wasn't occupying. *Oh, no you don't!* I told it. *Get the hell out.* I didn't want any foreign magic hitchhiking inside me. There was barely enough room for the weird mishmash of fae and vampire magic inside me.

After a few moments while I held myself perfectly still, the foreign magic stopped moving and gave off an oddly contented vibe. If I didn't know better, I'd say it even sighed.

"Theo?" Farranen's smooth forehead was pinched into a valley of fine lines that matched the worry in his voice.

"I'm fine," I said, surprised to find it was true. The unfamiliar magic was disturbing, but it wasn't actually hurting me. If my own magic wasn't bothered by it, then I shouldn't have been so quick to panic either.

"What happened?" He looked to the body that I'd briefly touched and then back to me. "When you screamed and fell back, I assumed...Well, I had no idea what to assume."

His uncertainty wasn't something I was used to, and my heart clenched. A reasonable answer would go a long way to chase away the lingering fear in his eyes, but I honestly had no idea how to explain what had just happened.

"Her magic just kind of jumped inside me." I stopped because that didn't sound right. "No, wait— magic jumped inside me, but it wasn't hers." I knew firsthand what Safeena's magic felt like, since I'd stolen some of it when she'd been trying to kill me. Plus, I was certain her magic was long gone; the part of me that shared an affinity for death had recognized the exact moment when her life and magic fled her immortal body.

"What magic?" Apparently, my vague answer had only increased his perturbation.

I shrugged since I couldn't answer that either. "It's definitely fae." Which should have been pretty evident, since we were in Fairie after all. I had yet to encounter any vampire or shifter magic in this realm.

With a small frown, Farranen stood and offered me his hand. I debated the likeliness of accidentally shocking him with the excess of magic in my body, but it had been a while since I'd lost control and let off any magical flares. It should be safe to touch him. Hopefully.

As soon as I put my hand in his, the familiar graze of his magic slid into me. It was brisker than the usual sensual caress I was used to; he was on a mission to examine every inch of my magic, and I didn't protest as he poked and prodded. I felt the exact moment when he bumped up against the new slumbering magic and then continued on as if he hadn't found it.

"Whatever it was, it's gone now," he told me with a relieved smile.

"No." I frowned. "It's still here, right next to mine." I tapped my chest for emphasis, even though I couldn't actually point to a specific location on my body where the foreign hum of power was curled up.

Now we were both frowning like little old ladies who'd just lost a crib tournament.

Our difference of opinion was interrupted when Harvey dashed through the wall and came to a stumbling halt next to us with Vanessa a few steps behind him. Her pale pink sundress with dainty white daisies was askew, and one of her bra straps had slipped off her pale shoulder from her mad sprint.

"Twenty light soldiers just arrived," Vanessa informed me breathlessly.

"They're planning to search the entire castle." Harvey didn't sound quite as apprehensive as Vanessa, but his throat bobbed nervously.

"Three guesses who they're looking for…" Vanessa gave me a hard look.

I had to admit she was justified—she didn't know about the missing key, so I couldn't blame her for assuming I was at the center of whatever shitstorm was about to rain down on us. Even if they weren't looking for me, I knew what would happen if they found me.

"Ghosts?" Farranen cut in, reminding me that he couldn't hear or see them.

"Yes. Vanessa and Harvey," I told him,

unnecessarily since I only knew two ghosts. "Twenty soldiers are here to search the castle."

Farranen looked back to the doorway that was still a swirling mass of silver. "We need to go, before they corner us in here."

As much as I loathed the idea of being trapped with a dead body in the queen's torture chamber of kink and horrors, I really hated the idea of leaving without the key. I mean, the castle was *huge*, and it would take hours, or possibly days, for twenty men to search the entire place. Maybe we should stay and search just a little longer—

"Theo! Move your ass!" Vanessa shoved me toward the portal, snapping me out of my dangerous thoughts. Yeah, we should go. Farranen was a formidable warrior, but against twenty of the men he used to serve with? It wasn't exactly great odds.

****

Vanessa and Harvey were able to get us out of the Light Castle and into the woods without running into any soldiers. I asked them to scout ahead and make sure nobody was waiting to ambush us as we made our way back to the main road. It might have seemed like overkill, but I wasn't going to take any unnecessary chances, especially since my ghosts seemed happy to help. Well, Harvey looked happy; Vanessa just seemed less bitchy, which I interpreted as happy.

Once the road ahead was deemed clear, I asked my ghosts to return to the Light Castle. Whether the soldiers found the elusive key or came up empty-handed, I wanted to know the second they left.

"Where are we going?" I asked as we tramped past bushes with summery blossoms.

Okay, I tramped. Farranen prowled silently, like a sleek panther on the hunt.

"North." He reached back and offered me a hand as the ground rose sharply before us.

"What's to the north?" Nobody had ever taken the time to show me a map of the fae realm, but I was pretty sure I'd never been any farther north than the Light Castle.

"Most of the ankou have settled there. They prefer the solitude of the Phantom Cliffs."

A snort of laughter escaped me. Seriously, I shouldn't have been surprised that the grave reapers of the realm had chosen to live in a place with a name like that. Or maybe it was named that *because* they lived there.

"Why are we going to see the ankou?" I asked.

"They'll be able to send a message to the dark prince. He needs to know we were unsuccessful in locating the key and won't be able to try again until the Army of Light retreats." He stopped to shield his eyes from the brightness of the sky and survey the land around us before veering slightly to the right as we continued through the trees.

"How can they reach him? We don't even know where he is." It was possible that he wasn't even in Fairie anymore. If he'd reached another gate, he could have crossed though to the Earth realm to hunt down whoever had destroyed Farranen's gate. From what I could tell, ghosts were stuck in whatever realm their creator was in. Or maybe that rule only applied to my broken ghosts.

"The dark prince has a court of devoted followers, who will be eager to help locate him." He paused with a somber smile. "In truth, he has inspired more loyalty from his subjects than the queen ever earned through fear and intimidation. I cannot change what court I was born into, but I shouldn't have waited so long to pledge my allegiance to him."

What a stupid system. The fae should be free to reside in whichever court they wanted to. In my realm, people were free to switch nationalities. Some even had dual citizenship. Fairie needed to implement some sort of an application process for switching courts. Maybe I'd suggest it to Lief when we finally caught up to him.

****

The Phantom Cliffs were every bit as spooky as the name implied.

After a few hours of walking, we'd arrived at the top of a massive chasm that had been cut into the ground by time and weather. Shaped like an irregular circle, the hole was at least half a dozen stories deep and as big across as four full-sized hockey rinks. Tall windows and doorways were cut into the vertical face at irregular intervals, most connected by a series of staircases. The smooth black walls appeared to absorb the ambient light from the sunless sky to create the illusion of a bottomless pit of shadows. Or maybe it really was bottomless. I kept a healthy distance from the edge, lest I trip and fall in. Tumbling into the hole and spending the rest of my life falling until I died of old age wasn't something I wanted to chance.

I followed Farranen as he skirted the edge of the giant hole, shivering as my magic prickled beneath my skin. As soon as we'd gotten close to the unique landmark, I'd known why it was called the Phantom Cliffs.

There were ghosts here. *Lots* of ghosts.

My magic itched to be set free so it could yank every single one of them through the veil and into this realm. I wrapped my arms around my middle, determined to remain in control of my roiling magic, instead of being controlled by it. Thankfully, the lump of dormant magic that wasn't mine didn't seem to be affected by, or even aware of, the nimbus of death that surrounded us.

A rough staircase was cut into the side of the black rock, and I cautiously peered over the lip of the embankment into the darkness below. I pretended not to notice when Farranen put his arm around me; his concern that I might topple over the edge was well founded.

"We're going down into the giant pit of death, aren't we." My words came out flat since I wasn't really asking. Of *course* we were going down into the giant shadowy abyss that the grave reapers of the realm called home. It's not like I'd expected them to live in a castle made of gingerbread and gumdrops, but the macabre chasm of death seemed a bit over the top, even for the ankou.

My guardian's answering smile was apologetic, and I sighed in resignation. If this was the best way to get a message to Lief, then I'd do it. But I sure as hell wasn't looking forward to it.

When I moved to take a step onto the first deadly looking stair, Farranen caught me by the wrist and spun me back around.

"What—"

He silenced me with a kiss; the simple act shut down not only my speech, but my thoughts as well.

His lips were warm and firm, tugging a breathless gasp of pleasure from my chest.

My fingers curled into the fabric of his shirt, and I melted into the heat of his body. God, I could spend the rest of my life kissing this man and die a happy woman.

Every stroke of his tongue sent shivers down my spine, causing my magic to pulse in a lazy wave against his. When he pulled away with a pained laugh, I gave him a frustrated growl in return.

"Sometime very soon, you and I are going to find a modicum of privacy, and then I'm going to take my time learning exactly what pleasures you," he whispered against my temple.

My hormones stood up and did a little happy dance at his declaration, and I nodded dazedly. My body was literally thrumming with the need to explore every hard inch of him. And not just his body—I wanted to merge my magic with his until we could no longer tell whose was whose. Yes, we'd shared magic before, but I instinctively knew that once we were finally able to act on the sensual chemistry that was growing between us, things would be even more intense.

"That sounds…" My voice dried up, and I had to clear my throat before I could continue with "…nice."

His masculine chuckle made my belly clench. "I assure you, my skills at love-making exceed *nice.*"

I'll bet they did. I'd even bet good money that his skills were mind-blowingly spectacular. Why the hell had I said "nice"? I was such an idiot.

"Merry meet, guardian." A gravelly voice rolled out of the darkness of the pit, startling a gasp from me. "Welcome, Theo. I anticipated that you would arrive soon."

I turned, just as Mary finished ascending the stairs and joined us on the grassy forest floor. If not for her voice, I wouldn't have been able to tell her apart from any other ankou fae. Although, Mary and Lebolus were the only ankou I'd ever met, so maybe not all of them were tall skinny hunchbacks with a preference for long black hooded cloaks? Life would be so much easier if there was a *101 Local Fae You're Likely To Run Into* app I could download to my phone.

"Merry meet, Mary." Farranen delivered the

alliterative greeting with a straight face that I tried to mimic.

"Hey, Mary." I offered a little wave.

"We need to get a message to the dark prince." My guardian sure wasn't one to waste time on small talk.

"Of course. Follow me." Mary also got right to the point. Maybe it was a fae thing?

She turned and descended the roughly cut stairs with a grace that made me envious. It probably had something to do with the way her knees bent at an unnatural angle and the long length of her limbs. Following in her wake, I was forced to take two steps on each stair since they were taller and longer than normal stairs.

Farranen followed behind me, close enough that he'd be able to reach out and steady me if I stumbled. I should have been embarrassed, but I was just grateful. There was nothing to hold onto, and no barrier or rail between me and the sheer drop into the darkness of the hole to my left. I kept my right hand firmly on the smooth black wall. The steps were only two feet wide, so there was very little room for error if I lost my footing.

The press of darkness increased as we descended farther into the hole. After we passed six separate landings with arched doorways, Mary led us through the next one. An equally dark hallway waited for us, wide enough that we were able to walk two abreast. Farranen laced his fingers through mine, and I gratefully accepted his guidance.

If the ankou had a penchant for the darkness, why had Lebolus been wandering around Earth on a bright sunny morning? Then again, his psychogenic atrophy had probably been messing with his ability to think logically.

I'd already lost track of all the twists and turns we'd

taken when we entered a new room. It was vast and mostly empty, judging from the echo of Mary's words when she told us, "We can summon in here."

I wasn't exactly claustrophobic, but knowing that I was in an underground cavern with billions of tons of rock between me and the sky was a bit unnerving. A small trickle of sweat slid down my back between my shoulder blades. Why was it so dang warm this far underground? And what the hell did she mean by "summon?"

Once we came to a halt, I tugged my sweatshirt over my head and dropped the navy fabric on the floor next to me where I should be able to find it again when it was time to leave. The bold white words THERE'S ALWAYS TIME FOR CAKE! were the only part visible in the near darkness.

"The ankou prefer to use the same location when they pull from beyond the veil. The residual magic from previous summonings lingers, making it easier for each subsequent user." Farranen spoke in a hushed voice, like the ghosts might overhear us.

Now that he mentioned it, I could feel the lingering magic that saturated the area. It had a distinctive ankou feel to it, reminding me of stargazing in the fall. The same breathless awe that came from lying on a hill, surrounded by the earthy scent of decomposing leaves, while Mother Nature worked her own unique magic in the sky above was evident in the underground chamber.

"The veil is especially thin here," Mary informed me, matching Farranen's quiet tone. Maybe the ghosts really could hear us. If I hadn't known that Harvey and Vanessa were tired from helping me earlier, I would have called them to see what they thought of the spooky space.

"Why are we summoning a ghost?" Wasn't the plan

to send a message to Lief?

"Ghosts make excellent messengers, as they are visible to all fae," my guardian patiently explained, politely not mentioning that my ghosts were only visible to me.

I nodded, because that seemed like a practical solution for a realm that had no cell phones, computers, or postal system.

Something moved, catching my attention from across the large room. I opened my eyes even wider, trying to see who, or what, the darkness was hiding. Maybe I'd been imagining things—no, wait…There it was again! I took a step closer to where the air was shimmering.

"There's something over there." I directed my words to Farranen, even though I knew anyone in the chamber would be able to hear me.

The familiar slide of Farranen's sword being unsheathed was a welcome sound, but it was the glow emanating off it that truly filled me with relief. I pointed across the cave with one hand, while shielding my eyes from the sudden brightness with my other hand.

His boots scraped against the stone floor as he slowly spun in a circle. "I don't see anything," he finally said, breaking the heavy silence that had been slowly building.

"She sees the spirits beyond the veil," Mary grated.

"Beyond the veil?" I blinked a few times as my eyes adjusted to the dim light radiating from the sword.

"Yes, your magic must be strong for you to unintentionally see those on the other side." It almost sounded like pride in her words. I couldn't be entirely sure, her raspy voice made it hard to tell.

The thing on the other side of the room moved again.

Now that I knew what I was seeing, it was hard not to notice the distinctly human shape it had. My magic simmered beneath my skin, reminding me what it could do if I would just set it free.

Farranen lifted the sword over his head, and when I realized he was going to put it away, I stopped him with a little squeak of "Don't!"

He froze with a foreign look of confusion wrinkling his forehead.

"Sorry!" I hadn't meant to sound so demanding. "I just meant, can you please keep the sword out so it's not so dark in here?" It was a miracle I hadn't walked face first into a wall yet.

"The darkness bothers you?" He dropped his arm so the sword was at hip level again, casting weird shadows on his face that would have been perfect for telling scary stories around a campfire.

"Well, yeah. I don't want to accidentally fall down any stairs because I can't see." Or get eaten by whatever other fae might live down here with the ankou. Or fall off a cliff since I still wasn't sure if we were on the bottom level of the pit or not. Generally, Fairie seemed to be lacking any type of guardrails, so it was up to me to watch where I was going if I didn't want to end up dead. And that would be a whole lot easier if I could see.

"Sometimes I forget that you're human." None of the irritation that I expected to hear colored his words, just a small underlying tone of endearment, and perhaps some embarrassment. "Please accept my apology."

"Don't worry about it," I told him. It had never occurred to me that he and Mary had been able to see in the dim lighting, so I couldn't be mad that he'd overlooked my pathetic human eyesight.

He gestured toward the ceiling, and a handful of

sparks shot from his cupped palm. The small kernels of light quickly grew to the size of softballs and floated up to hover about ten feet above our heads. They were similar to the floating orbs that Lief used when we'd shared a tent in his war camp. They were essentially air glamoured to look like floating lights. My wonky ability to see through glamour made them waver if I looked straight at them.

I was dimly aware of Mary settling herself on the hard floor behind me as I continued to glance uneasily at the shadowy recesses of the room. A few more shimmers of movement stood out against the gloomy black stone, and I turned to get a better look. More spirits peeking through the veil at me. My brain wasn't nearly as fascinated as my magic was by their spectral appearance.

My guardian sucked in a breath, and I quickly turned to see what had startled him.

Chapter Seven

"What—" Whatever question I was about to ask was cut off when he grabbed me by the shoulders and spun me away from him.

"*Theo…*"

Still caught in his firm grip, I twisted around until I could see his shocked face over my shoulder. He didn't meet my eyes as he continued to stare at my back like an entire family of cockroaches had decided to make a nice home for themselves on my pale blue tank top. A shudder rippled across my body, and I squirmed in his grasp. Why didn't he just smack them off already?

Mary joined him, and her raspy intake of breath was harsh in the silent room.

"What's going on? You guys are freaking me out." I knew I was safe with the two fae at my back, but *damn*, their silence was terrifying.

Mary asked, "Is that a—"

"I don't know," Farranen murmured thoughtfully.

My imagination was starting to come unglued, right along with the rest of me. Gah! What the hell were they looking at? Was there a giant cancerous mole thriving on my back? Had I grown a tail? Was the world's largest mosquito slowly sucking me dry? The not knowing was killing me!

I still had my head craned around, so I caught the flash of Mary's claws as they reflected the floating lights when they swiftly rose and then slashed downward across my back. I choked out a scream that ended as abruptly as it started when I realized she wasn't trying to eviscerate me from behind.

Cool air caressed my bare skin as Farranen pulled the two halves of my shredded shirt and sports bra apart. I clutched at the front of the ruined fabric, shocked speechless that they'd destroyed the only shirt I had with me.

"What the hell?" I demanded, squirming away from his gentle touch.

"Theo…You're *marked*." He delivered the prognosis with an odd mixture of bewilderment and hesitant awe.

I stared at him blankly until a scowl took over my face. God, I hated that word. *Marked.* Nothing good ever came from someone using that word.

Through some mystical process that I didn't completely understand, the fae were able to brand their true mate with a mating mark. Which sounded kind of romantic, until you realized that it was just a pretty way of saying "nonconsensual marriage without the possibility of divorce." From what I understood, it was permanent.

"What do you mean I'm *marked?*" I wasn't intentionally trying to sound like a crazy bitch, it just kind of happened that way.

"You have a mark on your back." He reached out with tender hands and turned me so he could see my back again. "It's beautiful…The detail…It's the largest I've ever seen." His long slender fingers traced over the skin between my shoulder blades, and I shivered. "It wasn't there when you dressed this morning."

I shot him a disgruntled look over my shoulder. He'd still been asleep when I'd gotten dressed this morning. The big dummy must have been faking it.

"But we didn't…" I glanced to where Mary hovered a few feet away. A mating mark was supposed to appear once two people had consummated their relationship in a physical way, but Farranen and I hadn't gotten that far yet. I wasn't sure how to ask what that meant, without advertising our lack of a sex life to Mary.

Farranen must have sensed my discomfort and saved me from having to elaborate. "I don't know what the mark means, but we'll figure it out."

The familiar hum of his magic flowed across my back and then around to my front. When it reached my breasts, it teased my nipples into hard points, and I bit back an embarrassing moan. Too soon it faded, and I found myself in a freshly glamoured black tank top and new bra. When I raised an eyebrow at the color change, Farranen offered an elegant shrug.

"We should keep your mark hidden until we can discern why it appeared."

Well, that made sense; most fae had amazing eyesight and could see through paler fabrics. And as for keeping the mark hidden? I was all for that. While the fae regarded mating marks with unbridled reverence, I still wasn't convinced that's what we were dealing with. The fact that I'd been celibate for over six years threw a huge wrench into his theory. I was going to reserve judgment until I got a look at the thing on my back—which needed to happen asap. Until I found out what the mystery mark looked like, my imagination was going to be working overtime. I had all my fingers crossed that it wasn't something outrageously mortifying like a chimpanzee with a boner, or a machete-wielding body builder wearing a banana hammock.

But for right now, all I could do was focus on one

task at a time—the most important being summoning a ghost so we could get a message to Lief.

I took a seat on the floor where Mary had been sitting earlier. It was time to rustle up a ghost.

"So, how exactly does this work?" I asked nervously.

Farranen gave me a reassuring smile from where he leaned against the hard wall next to the doorway. Despite his casual stance, I knew he was ready to leap into action at the slightest sign of trouble.

"I will summon a ghost to deliver your message, and you will pay attention so you can learn how it is done."

There was no censure in Mary's words, and it occurred to me that she might not know that I'd already brought two ghosts through the veil. Vanessa had been the one to warn us when we'd walked into the trap in the queen's dungeons, but Mary hadn't been able to see her…Yeah, if she didn't already know about my flawed ghosts, there was no point in bringing it up.

I took the hand that Mary offered me, not at all bothered by her triple-jointed fingers and razor-sharp claws.

Her magic slid down my hand to wrap around my arm, before continuing up and over the rest of my body. I'd have thought that since we both had ankou magic, hers would have been similar to mine, but they were as different as night and day.

"*Whoa…*" I ground out.

It wasn't exactly unpleasant; I was just a bit surprised when it didn't immediately flow into me like Farranen and Lief's did. It kind of hovered over top of my magic, like oil floating on water. It tasted like freshly turned dirt and a dusty attic full of newspapers on a hot day. I wondered how she'd describe my magic?

"First, I'll weaken the veil," she intoned in a calm voice that set my own nerves at ease.

There was nothing for my eyes to see, but I felt her magic grow and stretch until it filled the cavern.

"We must be careful not to damage the veil. If the spirits were free to enter this world unchecked, there would be some that would seek to dwell here permanently."

"That doesn't sound so bad," I commented, thinking that Vanessa and Harvey were basically stuck on this side of the veil until I found a way to return them.

"Ghosts can be helpful but rely on our magic to sustain them for the short duration they're here. A spirit without any ankou magic supporting it will appear as it does beyond the veil—as a mere glimmer of its former self, with no way to be heard or seen by those still living."

Yeah, I could see why that would be a problem. I was pretty uncomfortable with the idea of getting a visit from a deceased loved one without knowing they were there. I visibly shuddered at the thought of my ex-husband hanging around while I showered every morning. Then again, most people weren't able to see the spirts beyond the veil, so only those with ankou magic would know they had unwanted company.

"It is believed that if the spirits were able to travel into our world, they would seek out those with ankou magic, just as they congregate beyond the veil at the Phantom Cliffs. It would be possible for the strongest spirits to drain enough magic from an unsuspecting ankou to become a ghost—but with no obligation to obey the fae they stole it from."

The hypothetical picture Mary was painting was grim. Escaped spirits stealing magic from me? No, thanks.

"Got it—don't rip the veil." I sure as hell didn't want to be the one responsible for unleashing a ghost apocalypse on both realms.

"Some spirits are willing to cross over and serve us, and they will make themselves known."

As if they could hear Mary's words of wisdom, a few shimmers around the room increased until they resembled a bright kaleidoscope of light refracting off something shiny.

The other female gestured toward the expanse of room around us. "Now you choose one to pull through."

That's easier said than done, I thought to myself. The last time I'd pulled a spirit through, he'd been the one to initiate things. I'd just gone along for the ride and was grateful to have an outlet for all the magic that had built up in my body.

I scanned the room, noting that most of the glimmering spirits were the same size and shape as a fully grown human, but the one that called loudest to my magic was only about three and a half feet tall. It had moved closer to us than any of the others, and when it held out a hand in my direction, I knew it was asking to be pulled through into Fairie.

"That one," I told Mary, never taking my eyes off the small spirit.

She held out her free hand, and I nearly lost sight of the shimmering mass as it leapt forward. As soon as it contacted Mary's fingers, the magic in the room collapsed into a single point, directly in the center of the spirit. I blinked. The shimmering spirit was gone, and in its place was a small boy, probably about six or seven years old, with tall pointy ears. The features of his face were set into solemn lines, and he slowly withdrew his hand from Mary's. It was hard to tell if his expensive looking clothes were navy or dark green in the dim lighting, and the glowing orbs reflected off the row of silver buttons on his shirt.

"I am Mary of the Dark Court. I have brought you through the veil; do you agree to willingly serve me until I return you to whence you came?" The anticipation of magic buzzed through the air with Mary's words, and I held my breath to see what the little ghost would say.

"Yes, Mary of the Dark Court, I will serve you." The sharp snap of a promise being made accompanied the boy's words. Would Mary have sent him back if he didn't agree to do her bidding?

So, this was what a professionally made ghost was supposed to look like…He didn't really appear any different from Harvey or Vanessa. If he had any ghostly characteristics, I wasn't seeing them. He looked just as solid as the cavern we were standing in.

"Can you see him?" I asked Farranen.

"Yes. A young male from the Light Court. An excellent choice for a messenger. The darteen are nearly twice as fast on their feet as any other type of fae."

I looked back at the ghost, who'd been following our conversation.

"What's your name?" I asked, trying to sound friendly rather than like a creepy human woman who didn't spend much time around children.

He blinked his wide blue eyes at me once before answering, "Svencer of the Light Court."

I gave him a genuine smile. "Hi, Svencer, it's nice to meet you. I'm Theo, and that's Farranen." I gestured to where my guardian lingered next to the doorway.

Svencer's thin blond eyebrows rose. "A guardian of the gate," he breathed with all the reverence usually saved for sports heroes. It didn't surprise me that Farranen had rock star status in the fae realm, but how had the little guy known that Farranen was a guardian? Judging by his young age, he must have been dead a while since there hadn't been any fae babies born in over five centuries.

"Svencer, you will search out the dark prince of the Dark Court and deliver a message to him." Mary looked to where Farranen was standing, and the little ghost turned as well.

My guardian unfolded himself from the wall to stand at his full height as he addressed our new messenger. "The dark prince was last seen headed for the westernmost gate. You will tell him that we were unable to retrieve the item we sought, and that his vision of the lady in white has come to fruition under mysterious circumstances. Any counsel he can offer, in regard to either matter, would be appreciated."

Well, that was a really sneaky way of telling Lief that the key was still missing, and that I'd gotten a weird mark on my back.

Svencer quickly repeated the message word for word and stood attentively like he was waiting for orders. Were all ghosts so well behaved? Just another glaring difference between a professionally raised ghost and my bizarre versions.

"Once you've located the dark prince and delivered the message, you will return to me." Mary's raspy voice left no room for negotiation, and the ghost bowed solemnly to her. After a small pause, he offered a bow to Farranen, and then one to me. I wasn't sure I warranted a bow, but he'd probably sensed my magic and assumed I was fae.

Before I could offer up so much as a good-bye, the

ghost took off running. Farranen hadn't been kidding when he said that the darteen fae were fast. Svencer rocketed out of the dark cave like the local comic book store was going out of business, and his weekly allowance was about to burn a hole in his pocket.

"Will he be able to find Lief?" I asked in surprise. I mean, there were three thousand fae living here, and I wasn't sure exactly how big their realm was, but it sounded like he'd be hunting for a needle in a stack of needles.

"The fae love to gossip. Word will spread if there are any sightings of the dark prince so far from his castle." Farranen retrieved my sweatshirt from the floor and offered his hand to help me stand.

"What if he takes the back roads and nobody sees him?" When I'd died, Lief had carried my body from the queen's dungeons to the Light Castle without being seen by anyone. Well, except for the pixies—okay, so maybe Fairie did have eyes everywhere.

"With the tumultuous state of the realm, there will be many seeking his aid and reassurance. He is not a ruler who will let his people's cries go unheard."

A warm fuzzy feeling burned in my belly at Farranen's words. Lief was exactly what the people of this realm needed, yet he only had sovereignty over those in the dark court. Why couldn't Fairie see that he'd be an asset to both courts and hand him the damn crown to the Light Court already? And what the hell was she waiting for, anyway? She was literally being consumed by the dead lands!

Gah, I was back to referring to Fairie as "she."

Chapter Eight

After a fun afternoon of nearly being blown up, followed by an educational session of communing with the dead, I was ready to fall into bed and sleep for a week. Unfortunately, my guardian had other plans.

We had no idea how long it would take Svencer to contact Lief, and Farranen wasn't inclined to sit around the Phantom Cliffs indefinitely, so we set out on foot toward the low hills that were visible in the distance.

Trees grew in large clusters, none of them familiar to me, but their bright green leaves reminded me of the woods surrounding my cabin in the summer. Actually, the rolling landscape had the same rural component that made my property feel serene instead of lonely. I smiled, enjoying the solitude. Even my wonky magic was able to recognize that there weren't any fae nearby. The relaxed set of Farranen's shoulders also convinced me that danger wasn't hiding around the next corner, ready to jump out and sink its teeth into us.

"It's beautiful here," I murmured, hesitant to disturb the silence but grateful to have something to say that didn't involve death or destruction.

"Yes, I spent a lot of time here before I became a guardian." His voice was wistful, making me wish I'd gotten to meet him before he'd become the super-serious protector of the gate. It was hard to picture him in the early stages of adolescence, full of innocence and ambition. Did he smile more back then?

"Where are we going?" I asked, dragging my thoughts from the hypothetical man he used to be and back to the formidable warrior he was now.

"There's a glade, not far from here. We can rest there and wait for your ghosts to bring word that the Light Castle is empty once more."

That sounded like a great idea. Thanks to Mary's thoughtfulness, we had a pack full of food and soft bedrolls to make our campout under the stars even more luxurious. And really, the possibility of a night alone with my strong guardian was something I'd been craving longer than I'd like to admit.

Unfortunately, the practical side of my brain had coughed up an idea that was slowly evolving into a plan for tonight. And, no, it didn't involve hot, sweaty, aerobic sex. I'd come up with a strategy for locating the key that didn't involve us searching all eighty thousand square feet of the castle. The only problem would be getting Farranen to go along with it. Wanting to avoid the argument that my proposal was likely to cause, I kept my thoughts to myself for the time being.

A small stream wound its way past us, flowing in the opposite direction to where we were headed. When we stopped to drink from it, it was deliciously cold and crisp. Far better than anything that came from a tap or out of a vending machine back on Earth.

My feet protested as we continued on. How long had we been walking? I squinted at the bright sky above me. "What time is it?" I asked suspiciously.

"I suspect it is near dawn."

Son of a gun. I'd forgotten that the diurnal cycle of Fairie was controlled by its rulers—and with one of them dead, the regular pattern of night and day was awry. No wonder I was so tired, I'd been awake for almost twenty-four hours.

I was nearly asleep on my feet when Farranen led me into a small valley that was cut into the landscape where several hills intersected. The stream widened into a tranquil pool that was bordered by smooth round boulders, before continuing past us on its journey to meet up with a larger river at a lower elevation. Tall trees with droopy branches hung out over the water, creating an archway of green leaves and pink and purple flowers. Before my first visit to Fairie, *this* was what I'd imagined a magical realm would look like.

"If you want to unroll the beds, I'll start a fire," Farranen suggested.

I tore my eyes away from the charming landscape of the of glen and unpacked the thick sleeping beds. And yes, I spread them out so that one would be under us, and the other would be on top, rather than us each sleeping in a single roll. Yeah, you could say I'm an opportunist.

"Why do we need a fire?" I asked, to distract myself from the intimate sleeping arrangements.

"It will be dark soon, and the temperature will drop."

A quick glance at the sky confirmed that it was indeed darkening. I could even see a few faint stars twinkling into existence. I was grateful the fire was for warmth; I wouldn't sleep nearly as well if I knew he'd built it to keep hungry wildlife at bay. Having already been stalked and attacked by a tibber, I wasn't eager to see what other predators lived in Fairie.

After a meal of bread, cheese, and some sort of fruit that looked like pink and yellow kiwis, Farranen added some more branches to the fire. The blue sky had slowly faded until all that was left was a deep purple backdrop with streaks of amber in the distance. Thousands of stars stood out in stark relief against the darkness, giving off enough light that I could see the entire glade, but everything beyond was lost in shadows.

My eyes felt like they had sand in them from the combination of a full belly and not enough shut-eye. But I wasn't ready to sleep yet.

Farranen sank gracefully onto the makeshift bed next to me, and I let out a startled little yelp. Maybe I was more tired than I thought.

"I was thinkin—"

My guardian leaned in and pressed his lips to mine, effectively shutting down what I'd been about to say. I opened my mouth to utter some form of protest, but his tongue swept against mine in a caress that left me breathless. I clutched the back of his neck, tangling my fingers through his long ponytail as the lightheaded feeling grew.

His hands found my waist, and he slowly urged me back until I was lying on the bedroll. I sucked in a greedy breath of air when his lips left mine to feather kisses across my jaw. His touch was achingly gentle as he continued down to the column of my neck, and I let out an involuntary whimper.

The dark masculine chuckle he gave me in return sent a twist of desire spiraling through my belly and lower.

"We should…" God, it was hard to think with the way his hands were exploring the skin under my tank top. What the hell had I been saying? Right, the stupid key…

His lips continued their assault, lingering on my collarbone, as I struggled to think past the haze of lust that had clouded my brain. Something incoherent escaped my lips when one of his hard thighs nudged mine apart and settled against the ache that was growing between my legs.

"I have longed to explore every inch of you," he whispered against my neck, sending a ripple of shivers over the sensitive skin. And for the first time in my life, I was grateful for every single one of my many inches that were available for exploration. Heck, I'd draw him a freakin' map if he wanted me to.

"Wait…" I needed to tell him that I'd figured out how to locate the key. Saving Fairie was more important than sex…Right? And while I was pretty sure I would self-combust if he wasn't in me in the next three seconds, the tiny part of my brain that wasn't ruled by hormones whispered, *The fate of the realm is more important than getting lucky, you slutty cow! Stop groping him and find the damn key!*

His leg shifted, increasing the friction to nearly unbearable levels.

God, I wanted to lose myself in the pleasure he was offering…But the lingering threat to Fairie was more important than my selfish desires. With a frustrated groan, I forced my fingers to stop clutching at his broad shoulders and push them away. Of course, from my helpless position all I succeeded in doing was putting a few inches between us. Still, it was enough that I could see his face as he hovered above me.

His green eyes, dark with desire, silently asked for permission to continue with the seduction that I'd interrupted.

Damn it. My stupid moral compass had never been such an inconvenience as it was right now. I silently promised myself that once we had the key safely tucked away, I was going to drag him onto the nearest surface and make love to him until we were both satisfied.

"I'm going to summon the queen's ghost," I told

him, destroying my libido's last hope of this ending with an earth-shattering orgasm.

His perfect lips formed a surprised little *O* before compressing into a hard line that warned me that playtime was over.

"*No.*" The single word would have been enough to make an entire army of hardened soldiers fall into line cowering. But it didn't really do much to intimidate a sarcastic hermit.

"She's the only one who knows where it is—"

"Absolutely not." Anger still lurked in his gaze, but his face had reverted back into the impassive frozen mask that let me know he'd already donned his emotional armor.

"It'll only take half a minute to ask her where the key is hidden, then I'll send her back. Easy peasy." Assuming I could figure out how to banish her back through the veil once she revealed the key's location. But, really, how hard could it be?

"Theodora, *no.*" His jaw clenched in an adorable way that let me know he was seriously ticked off.

"It's the quickest way!" I shoved at his shoulders. Having this conversation on my back with him looming over me like a giant sexy god of war was making it hard to focus on what we were arguing about.

"She will kill you!" His thunderous expression didn't match the gentle way he cupped my face in his palms. "If she arrives corporeal, as Harvey and Vanessa are, she will wrap her pretty little hands around your neck and *kill you.* And there would be nothing I could do to stop her."

Oh. He had a point. I'd forgotten that my record for creating ghosts wasn't exactly pristine. But I'd seen how Mary had done it in the cavern, and I was extremely confident that I could replicate the process. Well, fairly confident. Mostly.

His voice dropped to an anguished whisper that spoke louder than any amount of shouting would have. "Would you have me stand by helplessly and watch as someone tries to kill the woman I love?"

My breath caught in my chest. He *loved* me? No—he'd only known me for a few months (most of which he was locked in the queen's dungeons) so he couldn't possibly love me. Could he?

A painful lump took up residence beneath my breastbone, as hard and unyielding as a piece of glass. At one time, my ex-husband, Will, had loved me, but in the end it hadn't mattered. Eventually, he'd left. Love was temporary and not something I wanted.

"Yes, Theodora Edwards of the Earth realm, I am very much in love with you." A discordant snap of magic accompanied his words, turning them into a promise. The fae couldn't lie, and he'd said that he loved me. As hard as I tried, I just couldn't find a hidden loophole that would make his statement make sense.

A soft sigh escaped my lips, while a single tear spilled from my eye. It streaked a path downward until it was lost beneath Farranen's slender fingers as they stroked the hair at my temple.

It was too much. Too soon. He wasn't supposed to love me. I wasn't ready to give him that power over me. I'd worked hard to make sure I'd never again be in a position where someone who cared for me could hurt me.

"We need the key. I'm doing this with or without you," I told him in a thick voice, purposely not commenting on the bombshell he'd just dropped.

Understanding softened his features, and I had to look away. I wasn't sure if the look was because I was being predictably tenacious regarding the issue of creating a ghost, or because I'd avoided the topic of his feelings for me.

"Theo…" Sadness and resignation lingered in the air as his words trailed off.

I still couldn't look at his face. I shoved at him again, and this time he rolled away from me without protest.

After a moment of yanking my tank top back into place, I tugged my sweatshirt overtop of it. I had no idea how good a ghost's eyesight was, and I didn't want to risk the queen spotting the mark on my back. And something about wearing a thick layer of warm fabric made me feel safer, so some of the lingering vulnerability faded.

I stood, feeling stronger as soon as I was supported by my own two feet.

"The veil will be harder to breach here," Farranen advised, and I was grateful that he accepted the change in subject. I'd rather scoop my own eyeballs out of my head with a dull spoon than consider the possibility of letting him love me.

"I know," I replied, trying to sound confident about something I'd already proven not to be very good at.

At least he wasn't trying to talk me out of doing this anymore.

"Vanessa? Harvey? Can you hear me?" I scanned the clearing and smiled when I found my ghosts waiting next to the trunk of a large tree.

Following my gaze, Farranen stood and crossed to a thick tree about half a dozen feet away from where the ghosts were lounging, giving him a clear view of the entire glade. Even though his face remained impassive, I got the sense that beneath his bored expression he was brooding.

I cleared my throat and turned back to my waiting ghosts. "Hey, I was just wondering, have you guys ever touched each other?" My gaze darted back and forth between them.

Vanessa let out a throaty laugh and said, "Theo, you dirty little vixen!" Her eyebrows rose suggestively.

Harvey's throat bobbed nervously, but he made no comment about Vanessa's slutty remarks.

I rolled my eyes. "I meant, you guys are tangible to me, but can you physically touch each other?"

Vanessa punched Harvey in the arm, harder than I would have expected possible, and he staggered back half a step before regaining his footing. Very cool. And a good reminder not to piss off the pretty brunette, because she had an arm like she pitched for the Blue Jays.

"So, if I created another ghost just like you guys, you could restrain them if they potentially tried to kill me, right?" My hopes rose even further when Harvey nodded with a calm determination that spoke to his time spent as a soldier in the Army of Light's ranks.

Vanessa gave a whoop of excitement. "We're going to kick some ghostly ass!" She might look like a sweet girl in her pink sundress and sandals, but when I'd met her, she'd been working as a waitress at Tamarac's local dive bar, the Boot Scoot. I had no doubt that the small-town Saskatchewan beauty knew how to handle herself.

"See?" I glanced to where Farranen stood. And, yeah, he didn't look any happier about what I was about to do. "Harvey and Vanessa will step in if things get out of hand."

"Are they armed?" Now he was just looking for excuses that this wouldn't work.

"No." The ghostly reconstruction process didn't

apply to weapons. Thankfully, my ghosts had manifested with clothing—naked ghosts would have been all kinds of awkward. "But Harvey has been a soldier for hundreds of years! Are you seriously doubting his ability to take on one itty bitty little queen?"

"You're summoning the *queen?*" Shock and horror washed over Harvey's pale blue features, turning them an ashy gray. "Theo—*no!*"

I frowned. It was true; the queen had been one scary bitch when she was alive, but she was dead now. Without a castle full of lackeys to do her evil bidding, and no magic to turn me into a lump of coal, she didn't seem like much of a threat.

Still, it was unlike Harvey to act like such a scaredy cat. "What's wrong?" I asked him. Maybe he knew something I didn't? I mean, the guy was a ghost, which pretty much made him an expert on the subject. "We need to find the key, and she knows where it is. Unless we want to search the *entire* castle—"

"You *killed* her, Theo! Do you really think the queen will kindly answer your questions?"

I would have taken offense at Harvey's condescending words if I hadn't heard the apprehension in his voice. He was genuinely worried for me, and my heart squeezed a little at the thought. I was still getting used to having people in my life that cared about me. Instead of saying something snarky, I gave him a small smile.

"Fairie needs us to find the key." I looked around the clearing at the two ghosts and my guardian. "Without it, the dead lands will keep growing until there's nothing left of her."

"Her?" Farranen arched a perfectly shaped eyebrow.

"Fairie," I clarified. "If there's a possibility that I

can use my magic to help her, then I have to at least try."

Some of the tension dropped from his posture, and he stalked toward me. I held his gaze until there was nothing but a few scant inches between us. His hands were gentle as he gripped my shoulders.

"What is your magic telling you?" he softly demanded.

I'd been expecting an argument from him, so the simple question caught me off guard, and I didn't immediately have an answer. Closing my eyes, I focused on the magic that resided inside me. The vampire and grave-reaping magic twined together throughout my body, merging until their edges were no longer as defined as they'd once been. Now they were a beautiful pulsing thing that twisted casually around the lump of alien magic that I'd acquired yesterday.

So, what was my magic telling me? I wasn't sure…I looked closer, examining the edges of where my magic ended and the magic of Fairie began. Tiny tendrils of the realm's magic continued to reach for me, the edges of the tingling strands blurring where they touched me. They put off a forlorn vibe, and it felt like…like they were asking for me to help them.

"My magic is pretty content, but Fairie's magic needs help." As soon as the words left my mouth, I felt the rightness of them.

Farranen smiled, but instead of joy, it was full of resignation and tenderness. "I suspected your connection with Fairie would become permanent."

I remembered Lief saying something like that right before the gate had been blown to smithereens. At the time, I'd assumed it was a good thing. Now I wasn't so sure.

"What does that mean?" I attempted to keep my

cynicism to a reasonable level.

"You're bound to the realm now. It's why your magic flounders at home and thrives in Fairie."

Well, damn.

I'd known something was off, but I hadn't thought it was because I'd accidentally developed an addiction to being in Fairie. Maybe there was some sort of rehab for situations like this.

My guardian continued, unaware that I was mentally freaking out. "It could explain why I was unable to revive you from the coma until you'd spent a sufficient amount of time in Fairie. And possibly why your wrist was healed. It's hard to say for sure; I'm unaware of anyone that's not fae having a bond."

I still wasn't cool with the fact that Fairie had taken all my scars, but at least I now had a possible explanation for why it had happened.

"If this is truly what the realm needs, then we should try," Farranen quietly acknowledged.

I wanted to do a little happy dance because I'd finally won an argument against the intimidating male, but all I could do was nod.

Holy shit.

I was about to summon the queen of the fae.

Chapter Nine

The smart thing to do would have been to get a few hours sleep before trying to summon the queen. But you know me, I rarely do the smart thing.

I folded my legs, miming the cross-legged position Mary had used earlier.

All I had to do was reach through the veil, find the queen, and drag her back into this world. No big deal, right?

Vanessa and Harvey hovered behind me, ready to intervene if Safeena went homicidal. Knowing that I had two capable ghosts watching my back went a long way to calming some of my nerves.

After a few deep breaths, I tried pushing my magic outward, much like Mary had done in the cavern. *Weakening the veil*, she'd called it.

It resisted at first, clinging to my body like I was trying to exorcise it for good. I continued poking and prodding at it until sweat beaded on my lower back, but I was finally able to nudge it out into the clearing. The move was by no means as smoothly executed as Mary's had been, nor did it encompass a very big area, but I'd done it.

I let out a shaky breath and gave everyone an equally shaky smile before turning my attention back to the dark clearing.

There were spirits here. Slight shimmers of movement danced around the edges of my peripheral, but it was too dark to see exactly how many. Not nearly as many as I'd hoped for though. Maybe I should have waited until I was back at the Phantom Cliffs, where the spirits tended to congregate. What were the chances that the queen was among the handful of spirits watching me now?

With thousands, or even millions, of dead fae spirits lingering beyond the veil, how was I going to find the one I needed?

Vanessa and Harvey had found me. It wasn't like I'd gone searching for them specifically.

"How do I find her?" I asked aloud, hoping someone could provide some magical insight.

Farranen answered from a dozen feet away. "Call to her. Use her true name and picture her likeness in your mind. The newest spirits are usually not far beyond the veil."

I nodded, grateful that he was helping me despite his reservations about my plan.

"Safeena of the Light Court, queen of the Light Court, come to me." If I'd had more time, I would have written something more suitable for summoning a ghost in the eerily beautiful setting. Something spooky, yet articulate. Something that rhymed like a kid's Halloween poem. Maybe next time.

A drop of sweat ran down my neck, reminding me that I couldn't keep this up forever. The longer I had to force my magic to hover outside my body, the weaker I felt.

I repeated the call twice more before something vibrated against the edge of my magic. I stared at the spot it came from, about ten feet in front of where I was seated. The barest glimmer of movement let me know there was a spirit nearby, but I had no way of knowing if it was the queen or just another random dead fae looking for a way through the veil.

There's only one way to find out.

Exhausted by the effort of using so much magic and not getting any sleep, my hand trembled when I extended it toward the spirit.

I was the only one who could see the figure beyond the veil, but my companions must have sensed what was about to happen. I could hear them collectively holding their breath.

In a smooth graceful movement that reminded me of the way Safeena used to glide rather than walk, the spirit drifted closer and touched my proffered hand.

All the magic that had been hanging in the air outside my body collapsed, concentrating into a single point directly in the center of the spirit—who was no longer a spirit.

The former queen of the Light Court, now a ghost, yanked her hand back with a look of confusion on her pale face. Wide violet eyes, above a perfectly pert nose, reflected my own shocked appearance.

"What—" She glanced around, taking in the two ghosts and my tense guardian, before returning her gaze to me.

I quickly stood, not wanting her to have a single advantage. We were the exact same height, and I stuffed as much bravado and confidence into all five feet and four inches of myself that I could. Despite my grungy sweatshirt, dirt-stained yoga pants, and disheveled hair, I wasn't going to let the bitch look down on me.

Before I could demand that she tell us where the key was, her beautiful face twisted into a furious scowl and she launched herself at me. Her nails, as sharp and pointy as broken glass, aimed for my unprotected face. I let out a shriek of panic that was lost beneath her howl of rage as she rushed me.

My boots tangled in the layers of bedding on the ground, and I fell backward onto my butt. A small *oomph!* choked out of my lungs, and I threw my hands in front of my face to keep from getting mauled.

When nothing happened, I cautiously opened my eyes.

I was surrounded by huge mounds of crimson fabric from the gown Safeena was wearing, while the queen herself sat on my lap, straddling me. Actually, she sat *in* my lap. Everywhere she touched me, she just sort of disappeared into my body. And, yes, it was every bit as strange as it sounded.

With a disgusted grimace, I scuttled backward until there was some space between us. I hadn't been able to feel the queen when she'd been in me, but there was no way I could talk to her when we were literally sharing the same space. I liked to think I was able to deal with some pretty freaky things, but this was a whole new level of weird.

My eyes sought out Farranen, and I was relieved to find him staring in disbelief at the queen. When he looked up and met my gaze, approval brightened his features, and my heart gave a happy little thump in return. I'd done it right!

The sounds of a scuffle broke out, cutting through the haze of prideful achievement I'd been basking in.

"She can't hurt her—"

I turned and found Harvey blocking Vanessa from reaching the queen. Her angry grunts punctuated the sharp kicks she was giving his shins. I opened my mouth to find out what the hell they were doing, but a well-placed knee to Harvey's groin made him drop like a sack of bricks.

He cupped his balls like they were made of broken eggshells and lay there gasping for a few seconds before disappearing completely. I hoped he was going back to his ghostly realm so he could recharge instead of being gone for good. I didn't know enough about ghosts to comprehend if a case of smashed balls would end his existence permanently. Right now, he was probably wishing it would.

"Damn it, Vanessa!" I shouted.

Oblivious to me, she marched over to where the queen was still kneeling on my bedroll, and pulled her arm back in a classic foretelling that someone was about to get punched in the face.

"*Don't*—" I was too late to stop her from launching her fist directly at the queen's pretty little nose—and then falling on her own face when her fist continued through the queen's head without any resistance.

"What the *fuck*?" she shrieked, still on her knees on top of the queen—or in the queen. I'm not sure what the correct characterization was to describe two separate ghosts taking up the same space. Actually, the words bizarre, perplexing, impossible, and hilarious would have all worked to describe what I was seeing.

Safeena, who'd been looking slightly less murderous and decidedly more aghast, rose to her feet in a wave of crimson satin and blonde-and-sage-colored hair. Her violet gaze landed on Vanessa, and her eyes narrowed before moving on to Farranen.

If he felt anything other than wariness, it didn't show on his impassive face.

"Theo! What the *hell*?" The irate brunette rounded on me, and I backed up a step. Unlike the nutso queen, Vanessa could literally kick my butt if she wanted to.

"Why can't I touch her?"

Oh man, how to explain that one? It would probably be easier to distract her.

"Why did you try to hit her?" I demanded. "We need her to answer our questions." Which would have been infinitely harder if all her teeth were knocked out.

"She deserved more than a knuckle sandwich for trying to kill you!"

Aww, she was trying to avenge my honor? That was kind of sweet. And unnecessary since I'd already repaid the queen's failed murder attempt with a bullet to her head.

Farranen patiently caught my eye with a raised eyebrow that I took to mean I'm-only-hearing-half-of-the-conversation-so-please-let-me-know-what's-going-on.

I gave a forlorn little sigh. It looked like it would be up to me to play translator. God, I was tired. I hadn't used nearly as much magic as the first two times I'd made a ghost, but summoning the queen had definitely taken its toll on me. As if he could sense my exhaustion, my guardian dug through one of the packs and handed me a canteen of water that I gratefully accepted.

"Vanessa tried to punch Safeena in the face." A quick glance confirmed that the two women were still trading hostile glares. "On the bright side, I made a legitimate ghost! Oh, and Harvey left with his nuts in a sling." I hoped he was okay. He'd looked a little blue around the gills—ha! I made a merdain joke!

The mystery of how the queen was able to see my two ghosts was something that I'd have to deal with at a later date as I just wasn't up for a round of metaphysical ponderings this early in the morning.

I let out a little giggle at the absurdity of our odd

group, and it came out sounding hopeless and a bit deranged. Good lord, I needed to get some sleep.

If I'd truly done the ghost thing properly, then the magic that I'd pumped into Safeena wouldn't last forever. I needed her to tell me where to find the key, and that would be a lot easier without Vanessa antagonizing her.

"Vanessa, I think it would best if you went to check on Harvey and maybe do your recharge thing..." My suggestion was met with an affronted glower strong enough to peel the paint off metal.

"Fine! If you want to hang around with the murderous psycho bitch, then be my guest!" The fuming ghost winked out of existence, leaving me feeling guilty. I'd clearly hurt her feelings. Living like a hermit had squashed the need to take other people's emotional well-being into account, but now that there were ghosts in my life, I'd have to remember that their opinions counted too.

Later, I'd have to apologize to Vanessa; right now, I had a dead queen to deal with.

Some small naïve part of me had been hoping that death had mellowed Safeena out.

I should have known I wasn't that lucky.

She was just as much of a bitch as I remembered. The only difference, aside from her being dead, was that the glassy shine of insanity was gone from her eyes. The cold, calculating shrewdness that stared back at me was no less terrifying than the craziness I was used to seeing.

She wore her new role as a ghost with the same haughty confidence as when she'd ruled over the Light Court. Her lips contorted into a scornful grimace as she inspected me with a thoroughness that made me hyper-aware of my many flaws.

"A weak human," she scoffed. "For her, you betrayed our court?" Her eyes continued to bore into me like bright purple lasers, but her words were for my guardian.

He tensed, and I quickly cut in with "This *weak human* just brought you back through the veil. But go ahead, keep underestimating me. It's totally working in your favor."

She took a step forward, like she wanted to hit me or claw my eyes out, but I stood my ground. We both knew she couldn't touch me.

While I would have gladly stood there all day hurling sarcastic insults at her, I needed to find out where she'd hidden the key.

Farranen, clearly the smarter half of our duo, calmly demanded, "Where did you hide the key to the Light Court?"

Some of the viciousness left her expression, and a single tiny wrinkle marred her forehead. "It will make itself known to whoever wears the crown." If she'd been any less of a lady, I'm pretty sure she would have followed it up with a *duh*.

Starlight reflected off Farranen's pale hair as he slowly shook his head. "The realm has been in disarray since your death, but no one has been crowned."

Her perfect porcelain skin paled a few shades, and there was a quiver in her voice when she spoke. "How long…"

"Two weeks," Farranen supplied, with more kindness than I would have used.

"Two *weeks?* But who—" She made a sound like the words she wanted to say were caught in her throat.

Harvey and Vanessa hadn't been able to recall their own deaths, and it appeared the queen couldn't either.

"I did," I told her, keeping all traces of guilt and horror from leaking into my voice.

Her eyes widened, and she looked at me like my hair was on fire and she'd be happy to extinguish the flames with a baseball bat. "*You*?" Her disbelief was insulting, and I bared my teeth at her. "The crown cannot be worn by a human!"

Wow. The entire realm of Fairie was about to collapse, and she was worried about me polluting it with my humanity. What a racist.

"Does it look like I stole the precious crown!" I demanded. "We just want to find the damn key so we can give it to someone who will take care of the Light Court! I wouldn't be here at all if Fairie would stop taking her sweet-ass time to pick a new ruler!"

I was breathing raggedly from my little outburst, so when Farranen came over and put his arms around me, I didn't protest. My fists slowly unclenched as I stood there surrounded by the reassuring scent of fresh pine and cinnamon. My frustration at facing one more roadblock was understandable, but throwing a tantrum over it? That was inexcusable. And embarrassing.

"Why is it dark?"

The queen's soft musing tore me from my thoughts, and I looked over to where she stood with her face tilted toward the constellations that blanketed the black sky.

"The strain of supporting both courts has taken its toll on the dark prince," Farranen told her, while keeping his arms firmly around me. I wondered how the queen knew what time it was. I didn't see a watch on her dainty wrist.

A haunted look flitted across her expression, which was better than the bigoted indignation she'd been aiming in my direction.

"It's not just the diurnal cycle that suffers. The dead lands are growing; they consume dozens of hectares every day."

"And Oakenlief does nothing?" she demanded. Great, she was back to blaming others for the problems she'd caused. Typical.

"Lief does *everything*," I growled. Even before I'd killed her, he'd been managing more than his fair share of the duties required to keep Fairie going.

Farranen massaged his thumbs over my skin in a soothing gesture, probably to remind me that I sounded like a petulant toddler. I sucked in a deep breath and tried to will my heartrate back to normal while Safeena studied me like I was a massively deformed bug.

"Why do you care what happens to Fairie?" Her voice was deceptively soft, and I wouldn't have recognized the predatory curiosity for what it was if it hadn't been shining in her eyes.

I shrugged and saw no reason to bother lying. "My magic cares. And since it's become a part of me, I care." I thought about the permanent connection I'd formed with the realm, as well as the relationships I'd formed with some of the fae that lived here. Farranen and Lief were more than enough reason for me to care what happened to Fairie. "Even when my short pathetic human life is over and I'm dead, I'll still care." I gave her a contemptuous look. "A better question would be, why don't *you* care?"

Her mouth fell open, and she gaped at me. It only took a few seconds for dark fury to replace the shock on her face, but I knew what she was going to say before she even said it.

"Don't." I gave her a beseeching look. "Don't pretend you care. If you really did, you'd just tell us where the key is, instead of playing stupid mind games and acting like everyone has wronged you."

"I have ruled over the Light Court for over eight hundred years—"

"Yeah, I've seen how well that worked out for all your subjects. Infertility. Psychogenic atrophy. Both courts trying to kill each other instead of working together to make the realm stronger. The only thing that grows here are the dead lands. Sounds like you did a bang-up job while you were in charge." The bitter words slipped out before I could sugarcoat them. Then again, there was no point in trying to lie to a fae.

I closed my eyes and rested my forehead against Farranen's chest. I owed him an apology. He'd told me summoning the queen wasn't a good idea. I should have listened. I'd wasted time and energy trying to find the key the easy way. But nothing ever came easy for me. I sighed. I'd have to apologize to Vanessa too.

"Who will you give the key to?"

I looked up at Safeena's bleak inquiry.

"Who have you deemed worthy to possess my key?" she softly demanded.

"I don't know," I told her honestly. I really hadn't given it any thought since I didn't know many fae from the Light Court. "I think it will be safe with Lief."

Her head tilted to the side, like I was speaking a foreign language. "You would hand over the power to my court, to the dark prince?"

"Yes. At the very least, he'll keep it safe until Fairie makes up her mind." I knew without a shadow of a doubt that Lief would do what was best for the entire realm, not just his court. Safeena probably thought he'd withhold it from whoever ended up in charge of the Light Court or something equally sinister, since that's what she would have done in his position. But Lief was a far better ruler than she'd ever been, as well as a far better person. Still, it seemed tacky to point out that little truth, so I kept my mouth shut.

"Very well," she huffed. "I can't say with certainty since my last memories were stolen by death, but it should be here." One slim hand reached up to tap the skin directly above her impressive cleavage.

Chapter Ten

Farranen and I both leaned closer, staring at the queen's chest like the holy grail itself was tattooed there.

When it became apparent that the key wasn't going to sprout out of her bosom, I said, "I don't see anything."

"Not *here*," she snapped, drawing my eyes back down to her cleavage when she gestured for the second time. "It is here, within the corporeal body I left behind."

Oh. I understood—it was back at the Light Castle inside her dead body. And, *eww*. I wasn't looking forward to retrieving it.

Could it really be that easy? A sudden wave of relief left me feeling light-headed.

"How were you able to store it within yourself?" Speculation filled Farranen's voice, and my own suspicion rose, along with some revulsion. I doubted I wanted the details on how it had gotten inside her body. There were only so many nooks and crannies it could be tucked into.

Damn it. Of *course,* this wasn't going to be easy.

"The lideeram libraries date back millennia. When one of their scholars stumbled upon a scroll telling how our long-forgotten rulers were able to merge themselves with the key, he brought me the knowledge."

And she hadn't thought to share the info with Lief. Shocking.

"The key was fused to your body?" The bewilderment in Farranen's tone was almost comical. I'd been forced to adopt an I-never-thought-that-was-possible-but-I'll-just-roll-with-it-so-my-brain-doesn't-implode attitude since discovering the fae existed, but my poor guardian wasn't used to having his beliefs challenged on a daily basis.

"Not fused; just stored inside my physical self." The queen's blasé attitude made me think that she must have been living with the key inside herself for quite a while. "Accessible whenever I needed it, hidden from those that would steal it."

Dang. We'd been so close. I'd literally been standing over her body and the key and had no idea.

I looked at the rumpled bedroll longingly. If I didn't get some sleep soon, I was going to be one grumpy bear.

"We have the answers we sought. You can banish her back beyond the veil if you'd like," Farranen whispered against my hair.

I didn't want to tell him that I didn't know how, so I let myself enjoy one last moment of being in his arms before I stepped back and sized up the queen. The jewels on her red gown caught the starlight and reflected it onto the ground in a million different directions with her every movement amplifying the effect.

After a few tense moments of trying to gather my magic, I lifted my hands toward the queen. If I pushed the magic into her ghostly body, it might make her stronger, or possibly even corporeal like my other ghosts. The safest bet was to aim it at the veil and hope I could weaken it enough for Safeena to slip back through.

Choosing a spot just behind her, I crossed my fingers and released my magic. It moved sluggishly at first but gathered momentum faster than it had last time. As soon as it reached the exact location I'd been focused on, I felt the resistance of the veil. I nudged it a few times with my magic until it shifted.

Safeena let out a startled shriek as she was sucked backward through the veil in a tangle of crimson satin and pale skin, like she'd been plucked up by an invisible hand.

I let out a matching shriek, stunned by the force of her departure. If I didn't know better, I would have said she'd been eaten by a baby black hole.

Farranen offered me a hand, and I realized I'd fallen to my knees at some point. It looked like I'd need to practice if I wanted to be able to banish ghosts without falling on my face.

"Thanks," I told him with a smile as he pulled me to my feet.

When he didn't immediately let go and pulled me into the warmth of his body, I went willingly.

****

I woke to the smell of fresh snow.

Blinking sleepily, I looked around expecting to see Lief, but all I found was an endless expanse of actual snow. The entire glade was covered in a thin layer of the fluffy white stuff.

"What the…" I sat up and was relieved to see that my bedding was surrounded by a circle of dry grass. The bright green leaves of the tree above me were weighed down with so much snow that the limbs actually touched the ground in some places, creating a cozy wall between me and the rest of the world. "…wow," I finished lamely.

A masculine chuckle let me know I wasn't the only one awake.

I quickly scooted back down under the covers where it was warmer, turning onto my side until I was nose to nose with my handsome guardian. Those sharp cheekbones and chiseled jaw must be indicative to the fae; I'd never seen a human with such a perfectly sculpted face. Before I knew what was happening, my fingers reached out to trace the contours that I'd been memorizing. My magic followed in an eager wave, joining the power that lived just beneath his skin.

He was so beautiful; it literally took my breath away.

No—it wasn't just his physical good looks that made it hard to breathe; it was the look in his eyes. The way they filled with tenderness and awe whenever he looked at me. Like they were looking at me right now.

"Farranen?" My mouth was dry, and his name came out with a tremor.

"My lady?"

"I think I just found us a modicum of privacy."

His lips twitched, and I shivered as his eyes darkened. I didn't look away when he pulled my hands away from their exploration of his face so he could kiss each fingertip with infinite care before capturing them against his chest. The smooth planes and hard ridges of scars were equally warm against my skin.

"I want to be naked." My candid words hovered in the air for a moment, and I tensed, remembering the first time we'd come close to having sex. He'd told me to leave my clothes on, and now my head filled with doubts. What if my body turned him off? I certainly wasn't a runway model.

He didn't respond to my request. He just leaned in and pressed his lips to mine in a lazy movement that clashed with the eagerness in his eyes. When I started to make the appeal a second time, he swallowed my words and slid his hands under my shirt. At some point during the night, I must have gotten hot and tossed off my sweatshirt because I wasn't wearing it anymore.

In a move that was too smooth for it to be the first time he'd done it, he tugged my shirt over my head, only breaking the kiss long enough for me to inhale before his mouth settled against mine again.

"Still not naked…" I murmured against his lips.

"So bossy…" The fascination in his voice let me know he had no problem with me making demands, so I made another.

"I want this—" I reached down and palmed his manhood through his pants, eliciting a strangled hiss from him. "—inside me."

The rejection I'd felt when he'd denied me the most intimate part of himself so many months ago still brought an ache to my chest. If he wasn't willing to share that element of himself with me this time, then I wasn't interested in taking this any further.

His larger hand settled over mine, holding it in place against his rapidly growing flesh. "Bossy and greedy…" he commented lightly, until I squeezed gently and his eyes fluttered shut with a groan.

"*Theo…*" God, I loved it when he said my name like that. "I willingly offer every part of myself. All that I have to give, it's yours. I'm yours. For as long as you'll have me, I will be yours."

His irises glowed a deep forest green, and I could read the conviction he was feeling in them. He wasn't lying here with me because of an obligation or because it was a duty he needed to fulfill—he wanted to be here. Something inside me cracked. It was as if the last of my fears and insecurities were breaking into a million pieces as they were confronted by Farranen's sincere desire to be with me.

I nodded, not trusting myself to use words.

He wiped something wet from my cheek, and I

realized with horror that I was crying.

"Sorry—" I choked out.

"Don't." He kissed my other cheek. "Don't ever apologize for how you feel."

I didn't protest when he rolled me onto my back and feathered kisses down the side of my neck. Another tear escaped as he traced the hollow below my throat with such tender care that I let out a soft cry. All the while he continued to murmur endearments; only some of which were in a language that I understood.

His strong hands were surprisingly nimble when he popped the front clasps on my sports bra open, and the rush of cooler air against my breasts was startling and wonderful. I arched my back, watching his pupils grow as they traced over my curves and came to a rest on my pearled nipples.

I squirmed, my breath continuing to saw in and out of my lungs, waiting for him to *do* something. When I couldn't stand it any longer, I let out a ragged "*Please.*"

"Ahh, my bossy little vixen..." His tongue darted out and circled one ridged mound, then the next, sending a stroke of pleasure straight down into my belly.

I uttered a series of profanities as he brought me to the edge repeatedly, each time backing off before I could come. It was torturous, the way he knew just how far to push my body, always stopping just before the pleasure could overwhelm me.

A broken sound, part moan and part sob, escaped me as his sensual licks and sucks brought me to the brink again. "Still not naked," I panted, half hoping for a reprieve from his wicked foreplay and half hoping it would continue.

"How careless of me." His fingers slid into the waistband of my pants and slowly drew them over my hips and down my legs. Cool air assaulted my flushed skin, but I made no move to cover myself with the discarded blanket.

My plain cotton panties were a clearance bin purchase that hadn't been designed with seduction in mind. But I'd never felt sexier than I did right then as Farranen knelt next me, raking his eyes across every inch of my body, like the cure for the fae's infertility was written across my skin.

"Theo…" He swallowed harshly before reaching for his pants with shaking hands. I almost laughed at how fast he shucked them before tossing them onto the grass next to his boots.

When he leaned in to kiss me, I pulled away and reminded him, "Still not naked…"

Hovering over me, he pressed a kiss to the sensitive skin beneath my bellybutton. "If naked is what you desire…" A pulse of longing swept through me at the sight of my panties caught between his teeth as he slowly tugged them down the length of my body. How had I ever thought the pale pink discount garment wasn't sexy?

His hands, calloused from years of holding a sword, slid from my ankles to my knees, teasing the sensitive skin and urging my legs apart. I should have been self-conscious. My thighs had always caused me the most embarrassment, but the lust shining in my guardian's eyes was more than enough to chase away any lingering insecurity.

Just enough starlight shone through the snow-choked branches that I could make out every taut line of the male looking down at me, and I knew he could see every inch of me in return. I smiled, silently telling him how much I was enjoying this.

The darkness beyond the canopy of snow surrounding us provided a layer of privacy that I'd never truly felt before, not even at my isolated cabin. Nothing could touch us here in this perfect little secluded bubble.

"I believe you had one more demand that I have yet to satisfy…" He gripped himself with one hand, drawing my eyes to the only part of him that I'd been avoiding looking at. My mouth went dry, and lower down a rush of moisture bloomed. Fully erect, his cock jutted straight out of his fist like he was struggling to hold it back.

When his hard thighs nudged my knees farther apart, I eagerly opened for him. The soft skin of his knuckles grazed my core, and I arched into his touch. It had been so long since I'd shared this part of myself with anyone. I wanted to catalogue every single look and touch we shared so I could go back and relive them over and over again.

"Theo…"

He lowered himself over me with his arms braced on either side of my head. At some point his hair had come free from the leather tie, and it fell in shimmering white waves around us, adding another layer of privacy.

We both groaned when the thick head of his erection brushed up against my slick opening. The hard muscles in his back shivered beneath my hands.

"Yours, Theo—I'm yours."

He slid into me in one hard thrust, the sudden combination of pleasure and pain from being with a man, after so very long without one, wrung a cry from my lips. Farranen froze, and I dug my nails into his back. When he tensed to pull away from me, I wrapped my legs tighter around his hips and locked my ankles.

"I'm sorry—" he gasped with his face pressed against my hair.

I took a deep breath, and my body relaxed around the fullness. Tilting my hips experimentally, I gave an involuntary shiver as the base of his shaft brushed against my clit.

"More," I coaxed in a thick voice.

He hesitated, probably afraid of causing me more pain, and I arched under him, silently urging him to move. Every muscle in his body was tense as he pulled back, withdrawing from my body until I could see his face. Cupping it in my palms, I reminded him, "You said *every* part of you."

"I'm yours," he confirmed on an exhale, and I smoothed away the last wrinkle of uncertainty from his forehead with my fingers.

His lips found mine a second before his hardness slowly plunged back inside me, bringing with it a fresh wave of his magic that soothed some of the sting from being filled so completely.

"More," I gasped, unashamed of how needy I sounded.

Each thrust of his hips sent him deeper, and he unerringly found a way to drag his full length against my throbbing little bundle of nerves with every slow withdrawal.

When my limbs started to tingle and I couldn't catch my breath to warn him that I was close, I tangled my hands in his damp locks of hair so my fingernails wouldn't dig into his back. The trembling muscles in his arms let me know that he wasn't far behind.

The rhythmic slap of his hard abs meeting my softer belly became erratic, and all the air left my lungs on a scream as an exquisite orgasm caught me. Every part of my body, every single muscle and nerve ending, tightened to the point of pain, and I convulsed around the man that was still thrusting intently, drawing out the waves of pleasure that I was lost in.

A silent shudder wracked my body, and my vision started to go dark. I couldn't drag a single gulp of air into my lungs and couldn't even find it in me to care.

The weird little nugget of foreign magic that had been lying dormant inside my body uncurled in a sensual wave and reached out to embrace Farranen. I felt the exact moment his own magic welcomed it, and I shivered.

He tensed, and his harsh groan filled the air while a hot wave of his seed started to fill me. I wrapped my legs tighter around him, not wanting to lose a single drop of what he was sharing. I couldn't use it to make any babies, but it was the very essence of what made him a male, and I wanted all of it.

Feeling returned to my limbs, and I wrapped my arms around his shoulders as waves of his heat continued to fill me. When he stilled, breathing erratically and still buried in me, I whispered, "Let go, and I'll catch you." He'd used the same corny line the first time I'd had an orgasm with him, and the memory brought a smile to my lips.

He let out an uncharacteristic snort of laughter a second before collapsing on top of me. I giggled and made a sound of protest when he rolled us over so that I was no longer squished beneath him.

Chapter Eleven

"Where did the snow come from?" I asked sleepily as wet clumps of snow dripped from the trees around us. In a matter of minutes, the cool air had reverted to the normal warmth of a summer afternoon. Puddles of slush filled the glade, but the circle of grass surrounding our bedroll remained dry. I didn't bother asking why; I'd probably get a vague answer that referenced mystical mumbo-jumbo I didn't understand.

"The seasons are fluctuating." There was exhaustion in his words that had nothing to do with the large amount of physical energy he'd just expended.

My fingers slowly traced the roadmap of scars on Farranen's chest. It was still strange to see the damage that he'd suffered while he'd been imprisoned in the queen's dungeons. I used to be the one with the scars, and he'd had perfect unblemished skin. Given the chance, I'd go back to being the one with physical imperfections, because this new version of me felt like a lie.

Beyond the canopy of bright green leaves and melting snow, the sky had lightened to a normal afternoon brightness. The sudden changes in the weather and diurnal cycle were most likely another symptom of Fairie's impending doom. Poor Lief, having to shoulder the burden alone. I wished there was something I could do to help him.

My fingers continued their exploration until they

bumped against something hard, and I lifted my head to see what it was.

Holy guacamole!

A small white key lay in the hollow of Farranen's throat, tethered by a matching chain around his neck. I sat up, uncaring that I was still naked, and lifted the intricate piece of jewelry by the chain so that it dangled above my guardian's face. A green gem, inset in the head of the key, refracted the light in its many facets.

"Is this—"

He jolted upright, nearly dislodging me from his lap. "The key!" He let out a breathy laugh, and I couldn't help but stare at the open astonished expression on his face. Would I ever get used to seeing him so unguarded? I hoped not. It filled me with a giddy joy every time I saw it.

"But where did it come from?" Gently taking the dainty chain from my fingers, he held it out so the small white key dangled between us.

I shrugged and pulled a blanket around my shoulders. "I don't know." I could personally vouch for the fact that his body had been seriously lacking any form of clothing or jewelry until now. Heck, I could probably give you a detailed inventory of every freckle and scar he had without looking. I definitely would have noticed if he'd been wearing a necklace.

"Is it *the* key?" I wondered. It had to be. It looked just like the one Lief had, only it was white instead of black. I mean, what where the chances of a different magical key showing up around his neck when we were on the hunt for this one?

"Yes. I can feel the power in it," he confirmed, sounding as breathless as any woman presented with unexpected bling.

I reached out tentatively and touched it with not just my finger, but my magic as well. Recognition flooded me, and the surprised ring of my laughter filled the glade.

"It's the mystery magic!" I excitedly told my confused guardian. "The magic that jumped me when I touched the queen's body." I'd felt it tucked away inside me but hadn't been sure what it was. Apparently, it had been hibernating until Fairie chose a new ruler.

"*You're* the new king," I gasped, my mouth stumbling to keep up with my brain. "I felt it reach for you when we were—" I blushed, unable to label what we'd just done with words. I could describe sexual encounters a hundred different ways when I was writing, but I was incapable of using the phrase "making love" with the man I'd just had sex with. It was a sad thing to admit.

Farranen didn't seem to notice that my ramblings had stumbled to a halt. His eyes were on the small key, but he wasn't really seeing it.

"The dark prince sent me to kill the queen, knowing that if I was successful, I would ascend to the throne." Contemplation and resolve warred for dominance in his expression. "It would seem that Fairie has chosen me as well."

"This is great! We found the key, *and* Fairie has a new ruler." I ran my fingers through his unbound hair. "Hey—where's your crown?"

His lips quirked, cracking the grim mask that had settled over his features. "The crown is metaphorical."

Darn. He'd have totally rocked a braided updo with all his silky blond hair piled on top of his head beneath a medieval-looking crown.

"Do you feel any different?" I scanned the parts of him I could see but didn't spot anything out of the ordinary. He was still ridiculously beautiful—and naked—but he'd been that way before the key mysteriously appeared. I'm not sure what I'd been expecting, maybe some fireworks in the sky or an eighty-piece orchestra marching through the glade? This was surprisingly anticlimactic for a realm full of magical beings with a flare for the dramatic. Although, if my stoic guardian really was the new ruler of the Light Court, then it was possible Fairie was taking on some of his understated character traits. I doubted Farranen would want a parade thrown in his honor.

"I do." His soft admission pulled me from my disappointment. "Here—" He touched his chest over his heart. "—I can feel it growing. It's a part of me, like my own magic, but different."

I kept my mouth shut as he struggled to find a way to describe what he was feeling. I'd never seen him fumble for words before, and it was oddly endearing.

"I felt it claim me, but I assumed it was from our lovemaking."

He could say "lovemaking," so why couldn't I?

I reached up and fingered the key where it lay against his chest. The magic in it was familiar, and when I took my hand back, I could still feel the slow steady pulse of it. Now that I was conscious of it, I was reminded of the same awareness that I'd had of Lief's key, even when I wasn't physically touching it.

"We need to advise the dark prince of this development."

"This development?" I asked in surprise. Wasn't he even a little bit excited about his promotion? "You're the *king* now, but you look like your dog just died."

He looked back at me with resignation in his eyes. "The burdens of the crown must be dealt with before any personal desires I harbor."

"What are you talking about?" I asked in a tone that leaned heavily into flabbergasted territory. Was he saying he couldn't have a relationship with me because he was now the king? That was just...*stupid.* And not going to happen. "You are *not* dumping me just because you have a new responsibility to deal with." I narrowed my eyes fiercely, daring him to contradict me. "We'll deal with it together." I'd worked too hard to get over the hurt he'd caused by disappearing the first time—I sure as hell wasn't going to let him do it to me a second time.

To my absolute shock, a smile slid across his face, growing until it was brighter than the sun that didn't exist in Fairie. "I was suggesting nothing of the sort."

I let out a squeal when he pulled me into his arms and rolled me under the weight of his body. He was still grinning when he kissed me, firmly exorcising all thoughts of a possible breakup from my future. Far too soon, he pulled back. I knew by the open expression on his face, whatever he was going to say would be the absolute truth.

"Theodora Edwards, I am yours. Never doubt it." His smile dimmed. "Do you know how long I waited to find you?"

His question caught me off guard, and I shook my head. I still didn't know how old he was.

"Lifetimes." A tingle of magic accompanied the word; the same magic that bespoke a promise made or an offering of the absolute truth. "Theodora, my blade exists only to protect you. My body exists entirely to please you. I exist, solely to be with you."

My heart gave a happy little lurch in my chest. He wasn't dumping me. Why the hell did my suspicious brain always jump to the worst possible conclusion? I needed therapy. The good kind that was ridiculously expensive. Did Fairie even have shrinks?

"Wait—what were you talking about then? What 'personal desires' of yours will be taking a backseat to the 'burdens of the crown'?" And why couldn't he talk like a normal person instead of throwing around cryptic phrases like that?

"I was merely expressing my displeasure that on the eve of our first coupling, my aspirations of keeping you naked and well satisfied for the foreseeable future are being cut short. By now, the dark prince will be aware that the Light Court is under a new rulership, but he won't know who sits on the throne."

I assumed the throne, like the crown, was figurative. One of my hands slid down to squeeze the hard expanse of his perfectly sculpted butt cheek, and yep—he definitely wasn't sitting on a throne.

"You're not making this easy," he growled, but there was no real protest in it.

I laughed. Because it was either that or beg him for a repeat of his earlier performance. And to be honest, I still had some lingering aches from the first horizontal dance we'd shared. I wasn't ready for an encore quite yet.

"The dark prince awaits you." A small voice broke through the silence in the glade, startling a squeak from me.

In a move that defied the laws of physics, Farranen palmed the sword lying next to us and rose to his feet in one swift motion. Seeing all the muscles rippling under his skin while he held his sword in a combative position made me feel like I was in a museum, admiring a naked Greek statue exhibit. Although, with the long scars criss-crossing his torso and arms, it might be better to compare him to a Picasso painting. Actually, was there a such thing as a porno museum? Because with the wood that he was still sporting, he'd be a shoo-in. They'd probably build a special exhibit exclusively for the glorious package that was currently pointed at the intruder in our midst. I'm pretty sure there was an analogy in there somewhere as I watched him hold his sword with unwavering confidence and precision. The sharp pointy metal one—not the one I was contemplating in an obsessive way.

I grabbed the discarded blanket and tugged it into place around my body before sitting up.

"Svencer!" I exclaimed when I caught sight of the tiny ghost.

While I'd been pondering my guardian's naughty bits, he'd put his sword away and was in the process of pulling his pants on. Which was for the best, because now I could properly focus on the ghost calmly watching us.

"He'll rendezvous with you at the Light Castle," he told us, seemingly unfazed by my disheveled appearance. He was a child, so hopefully he hadn't caught on to the fact that we'd been engaged in some pretty grownup activities. I didn't want to be the one to introduce him to the concept of the birds and the bees.

"Wait—who are we meeting at the Light Castle?" Now that Farrranen was fully dressed, my brain was able to fully participate in the conversation.

"The dark prince." For a kid, Svencer was surprisingly patient while I played catch-up.

"Did he send you?" I glanced longingly at my clothes. Now that we had company, my modesty had returned with a vengeance.

"I serve Mary of the Dark Court." Oh, right.

Because she was technically his boss.

"Did she say anything else?"

"Find the guardian and the human female with ankou magic, and deliver a message to them, that's all." With one last wide-eyed look at Farranen, he gave a small bow and took off running across the glade, not bothering to dodge the trees in his path. I wondered if he was always so serious, or if he'd adopted the somber demeanor after his death.

With a sigh, I looked at the deceptively bright sky. It could literally be any time of day or night, but my body was inclined to believe that it was still sleeping hours by normal person standards.

"What time is it?" I self-consciously got to my feet, keeping the blanket firmly wrapped around myself.

"I believe it is midafternoon, possibly later given the amount of time we were—"

"Thanks!" I brightly told him, not wanting a recap of the things we'd been doing or an estimate of how long we'd been doing them for.

Approaching me carefully, like he thought I might run away, he wrapped his arms around me until I was snug against his chest. Letting out his own soft sigh over the top of my head, he asked, "Do you regret our lovemaking?"

"What? No!" I looked up to see if he was joking, but his expression was so well guarded that I couldn't tell what he was thinking.

"Did I not satisfy you?"

"Yes! I'm extremely…satisfied." I was blushing. I knew I was blushing, but I couldn't stop.

Farranen's forehead crinkled, exposing the smallest hole in his emotional armor. "Are you ashamed of the pleasure we shared?"

"Of course not!" He didn't get it. I wasn't embarrassed by the things we'd done, but talking about it was *weird.* People didn't just talk about sex. Did they? I mean, yeah, all my books had sex in them, so I wasn't unfamiliar with the adjectives and verbs that were used to describe the act, but hearing him throw the words around so candidly was shocking. "It's just…*awkward.* I'm kind of modest"—okay, I was the prissiest prude in existence—"and talking about it is uncomfortable."

Understanding replaced the worry that had been slowly inching across his face. "I apologize for making you uncomfortable. The males of my realm place great importance on being able to sexually please their female. Hearing you confirm it fills me with pride."

I blinked, and some of my embarrassment disappeared when I realized he was no different from human men and just wanted his ego stroked. It was startling to think that someone as self-assured as my guardian might have insecurities.

Every word he'd whispered, every look, and every single touch we'd shared had made me feel cherished. I wasn't beautiful, but he'd made me *feel* beautiful. He deserved to know exactly how much I'd enjoyed our time together.

Burying my face in the soft folds of his shirt so he couldn't see my flaming face, I quietly admitted, "What we just did…It was amazing. Seriously, mind-blowing."

Chapter Twelve

The gate was blown to bits, Farranen had just become the king of the Light Court, and I was daydreaming about penises.

Well, just one actually.

But still—it was time to focus on what was important: getting Lief caught up on everything that had happened.

During a brief dip in the cold stream to bathe ourselves, Farranen had pointed out that my tattoo was gone. At first, I'd been strangely disappointed that it was MIA. I'd never wanted a tattoo before, but at some point in the last few hours, I'd become attached to it. The only upside was that I had definitive confirmation that it hadn't been a mating mark. The possibility of fate deciding who I should be with for the rest of my life still freaked me out.

The three-hour trek to the Light Castle was blessedly uneventful, aside from the fact that the leaves on the trees were beginning to wither. When I'd questioned it, Farranen explained that the seasons were trying to realign themselves.

"Both realms are usually in perfect harmony, and when Earth welcomes winter, Fairie reciprocates in kind." He ran his hand down the trunk of a large tree affectionately. "The magic of the realm is working to restore the natural balance that has been lost. It will take time, but she will heal."

I didn't bother to hide my smile. He'd referred to Fairie as "she."

"Can I see the key?" I asked from where I was lying across a giant rock like a lizard soaking up warmth from the nonexistent sun. The Light Castle loomed large and imposing in the clearing ahead. Since we didn't know if the Army of Light was still inside, waiting out here seemed like the smartest choice.

My guardian tugged the small chain from beneath his shirt and lifted it over his head before holding it above my waiting hand. Even before I touched the metal, I could feel the hum of power that surrounded it. When it finally made contact, the magic uncoiled toward me. Like an old friend, it slid into me with a familiarity that was comforting.

Farranen released the chain, and it fell, pooling in my cupped palm.

I blinked, and it was gone.

"What the—" I sat up straighter and pulled my hand in until it was almost touching my nose. Where the hell had the key gone? I scanned the ground desperately. I must have dropped it.

"Theodora."

I looked up, expecting to see anger, or at least some irritation, but there was only astonishment in his eyes.

"Sorry! I must have dropped it." I fell to my knees and sifted through the small pile of leaves that was slowly accumulating on the ground.

"You didn't drop it."

I paused my frantic search efforts. "What?"

"I can still feel it." He offered me a hand and pulled me to my feet. "It has returned to you for safekeeping."

"What?" Panic had reverted my vocabulary down to a single word.

"The key is inside you."

I wanted to give him a skeptical look, but a quick inventory turned up not just my own weird blend of vampire and ankou magic, but the mysterious power that I now knew came from the key. "You're right!" I tapped my chest for emphasis. "It's right in here."

With gentle hands, he spun me to face away from him. "May I?" he asked.

"Yes." I already knew what he was asking. The cool breeze against my skin made me shiver when he lifted the back of my shirt, even though I'd been expecting it. His fingers traced the contours of the tattoo that had returned to reclaim its rightful position on my skin.

"It's achingly beautiful," he whispered before placing a kiss between my shoulder blades. "Even more so, now that we know its origins."

I would have agreed with him, but my throat was tight with emotions that I was struggling to understand. Now that I knew it wasn't a mating mark, the tattoo didn't bother me. In fact, I liked the idea of it branding me. It was a symbol of the power that I carried inside my body.

"So, how do I give it back to you?" I asked as he smoothed my sweater back into place. The soft orange fabric matched the leaves that were slowly tumbling from the branches above us. Once again, I found myself grateful for Farranen's ability to glamour my old clothing into something clean. Walking around Fairie in the same thing I'd worn yesterday wouldn't have been my first choice.

"We could employ the same methods that removed it the first time," he suggested, wrapping his arms around my waist to pull me against his chest. I couldn't see his face, but I suspected there was an extremely male grin plastered all over it.

Yeah, I'd just bet that he'd be willing to engage in some mind-blowing sex in the pursuit of retrieving the key. "Nice try," I told him with a snort of laughter.

The dark prince of Fairie arrived on a gust of wind with a cloud of orange leaves rippling past his black cloak like a wave of pumpkin-colored bats. If he was expecting applause for his dramatic entrance, he was going to be sorely disappointed.

Half a second later, Dog materialized behind him.

"Dog!" I exclaimed, admittedly louder than was necessary. I didn't even care if the whole realm heard me—Dog was back!

Every muscle in his body went taut, and then he launched himself at me. It was like getting hit by a freight train, and together we fell back in a tangle against the softness of the leaves. I was laughing like a drunk lunatic and didn't bother to reprimand him when his wet nose forced its way under my jaw and behind my ear.

"Hi, Lief." I gave a little wave to where he was watching me with a look of barely concealed affectionate exasperation. "Hey! What happened to your hair?"

A thin streak of silver cut through the dark locks, starting at his forehead and ending behind his left ear. He ran his fingers over the hair in question in a manner that I would have described as self-conscious (if it had been anyone other than the formidable dark prince).

"My sovereignty over the realm has taken its toll." It was a bland statement of fact, but the weariness in his tone told me more than the words ever could have. And now that I was looking, there were fine lines around his eyes that hadn't been there before.

The wind chose that exact moment to sweep through the trees, causing another wave of leaves to fall around us. The men brushed the stray foliage from their broad shoulders while I fought the urge to roll around in them.

"The castle is deserted. I suggest we continue our conversation inside where we're less likely to be overheard," Lief proposed before turning and heading toward the waiting shelter with a haughty arrogance that I was used to by now.

Farranen pulled me to my feet and laced his fingers through mine as we followed.

****

The massive wooden front doors opened for us, even though the place appeared to be deserted. Maybe they had some sort of sensor and opened for everyone like the ones at the Shop 'n' Save did. Or maybe they recognized the two males. Either way, it was spooky but cool. Nobody spoke until we were safely within the sturdy walls of the castle and the doors were firmly shut behind us.

The last time we'd been here, all the color had been leached from the building. Now, as I stood gazing around the large foyer, the pale stone had regained some of its previous luster. The ribbed ceilings high above us had delicate gold veins creeping through the pale gray stone, matching the veins in the black marble floors.

"The Light Court has a new ruler. I felt them ascend a few hours ago." Lief's normally pale eyes were bright with hope. "I've had the ankou send out a number of ghosts to see if anyone has word on the identity of the new monarch. I've also asked—"

"Found him," I interrupted before Lief could completely brief us on his wasted efforts. The confused look on his face gave way to jaw-dropping disbelief when I pointed a finger in Farranen's direction. I may have taken a small amount of satisfaction in shocking the unflappable dark prince.

My guardian dipped his chin in a brief nod and gave the dark prince a smile that could almost be described as a smirk. Almost, but not quite—Farranen didn't smirk.

"You?" Lief sounded like he'd been punched in the belly until he broke into a laugh. "Of course, it would be you!" He pulled Farranen into one of those back-slapping hugs that men use to cover their affection for each other with.

"And you found the key?" he asked once the male bonding session was concluded.

"The key found me," Farranen informed him, with obvious pride in his voice.

Damn it. I'd been hoping I could avoid giving a recap of certain parts of our adventure since we'd parted ways with Lief. Just the naked parts really. Was a little privacy too much to ask for? Apparently, it was.

My guardian filled Lief in on the finer points of our journey, beginning with our failed search and ending with the discovery of the key. I was eternally grateful when he glossed over the intimate bits.

"May I see the mark?" Lief asked, trying unsuccessfully to hide the hint of eagerness in his voice.

I sighed and turned around so Farranen could lift my sweater. My bra was white, so I figured Lief could see through it easily enough, and if he couldn't, that was too bad because I wasn't taking it off in the middle of the castle foyer. Baring my back in front of multiple people was already pushing the limits of my comfort zone further than I wanted to.

"*Resplendent…*" Lief breathed, and some of my self-consciousness disappeared.

I jumped when his cool fingers touched the warmth of my skin, but I didn't pull away. He was close enough that his magic brushed up against mine in a lazy wave, and I was able to pick out the exact thread of it that emanated from his key.

He lowered my sweater back into place, and I turned around to face him.

"You're wearing your key." Without meaning to, I laid my palm flat on his chest where the key was hidden beneath his dark shirt. The magic beneath surged up to meet mine. The last time I'd seen his key, the magical signature emanating from it had been nulled when it was in contact with his skin. So why could I feel it now?

Lief's eyebrows climbed his forehead, bringing them closer to the new silver streak in his hair. "You shouldn't be able to sense my key at all."

When I shot a curious look at Farranen, he shook his head. "I am unable to feel his key."

I took a step back, once again feeling like the biggest freak in the room. Dog butted his head against my hip, and I absently ran my fingers through his fur.

"So why are we back at the queen's castle?" I asked, just to steer the topic of conversation away from any further discussion regarding my unexplainable ability to sense both keys. "Wait—it's *your* castle now!" I turned to my guardian and realized by the soft smile on his face that he'd just come to the same conclusion I had.

"Yes, it would appear that I am once again welcome in the Light Castle," he mused.

My heart sank a tiny bit at the sadness in his voice. I'd forgotten that once he'd been labeled a traitor, he'd been kicked out of the castle that he'd called home. And now that the gate was gone, he'd lost the ability to return to his cabin in my realm. My poor guardian had essentially been homeless until Fairie had elevated him to king.

"I should like to visit my old quarters," he stated sedately.

"Lead the way." Lief gestured toward the vastness of the empty castle with a flourish.

Subtle differences teased at the edges of my awareness as we passed through the abandoned hallways. Little things, like the once-crimson carpeting on the massive staircases that had previously faded to a dull gray, was now a rich green. The tall arched windows, previously topped with stained glass images depicting orgies or demons hunting women, now were wooded landscapes.

And the paintings on the walls...At first, I didn't realize that the artwork had changed as we walked past the expensive-looking works. They were generic scenes; beautiful landscapes portrayed in every season. They could have been created from any number of places on Earth or in Fairie. But as we continued down the hallways, I began to recognize the settings. The first to jump out at me was the shoreline at Tamarac Lake, where I used to swim in the mornings. A pale orange denoted the setting of the sun against the smudges of a pink and purple twilight sky. The second, a path winding through the woods to the lake, was where I'd been attacked by Lebolus and incidentally met Farranen. At the third, I stumbled to a halt, just so I could stare. The hawthorn tree that held the gate proudly stood against a background of dark sky and shining stars. Every single branch and leaf had been expertly captured by the artist, down to the smallest knot of bark. The perfection was literally breathtaking.

"Exactly as I remember it," Farranen whispered from behind me.

"Who did this?" I asked, still staring at painting. If I

reached out, would the leaves feel just as velvety as they looked?

"Fairie."

For once I didn't have a snarky reply to his vague answer. In a weird way, it actually made sense. She knew he wouldn't want the bloody images of torment and suffering that Safeena had enjoyed.

When we reached the wooden door to his room, it looked no different from any other in the hallway. It opened without protest, and I followed the two men inside.

****

"Do you remember the vision we shared?"

Lief's question caught me off guard, and my brain took a few seconds to catch up and kick out an answer. "Yes. It was me, kneeling in a white dress."

"The mark on your back, that we assumed was a mating mark, was actually the key." Speculation and unspoken knowledge swirled through the blue facets of his eyes.

Oh, fuckerdoodle. I had a hinky feeling that I wasn't going to like where this conversation was going.

"Yeeees…" I drew the word out to stall for more time.

"Your human eyes were unable to see the entirety of the mark, but I could."

My forehead wrinkled. What was he getting at?

"Theo, your mark, while beautiful, is incomplete." He stepped closer, his expression earnest.

Farranen must have sensed my discomfort, because he came over and wrapped an arm around my waist. I leaned into him, trying to let go of some of the apprehension that was coiling through me. Lief was usually blunt to the point that he came across as crass;

the fact that he was building up to something wasn't good.

"What do you mean, 'incomplete?' " I asked, hating how suspicious my voice sounded in the vast room.

"The key is faultless, but in my vision, there were blossoming herbaceous plants and vines intertwined with it." He took another step closer, and I leaned farther into the strength of my guardian.

"So, there are flowers missing from the mark?" Well, that didn't sound too dire. I wasn't big on flowers, so maybe Fairie had taken my personal taste into account when she branded me.

"Essentially, yes. I believe they were meant to represent another power."

"What power?" Panic tightened my throat, making the words come out hoarse. I didn't want another power taking up residence in my body. Yes, I'd come to love my ankou and vampire magic, as well as the nugget from Farranen's key—but I had no desire to add to the mix. It was already dangerously close to overcrowded inside me.

Lief reached beneath the dark folds of his shirt and pulled out his key, sliding it over his head. He took a single step closer, forcing me to tilt my head back so I could maintain eye contact. His magic brushed up against mine, tasting like the fresh snow on a cold winter morning. There was nothing aggressive about it, but having two huge males right up in my personal space was intimidating in a wow-look-at-those-grizzly-bears-in-their-cage kind of way. I knew they wouldn't hurt me, but it was still alarming.

He captured my hands with one of his, the one that wasn't holding the key.

"Take my key," he murmured, his eyes imploring

me with a stark desire that was uncharacteristic of the dark prince. For him to let me see how badly he wanted it, made me rethink my resistance.

The tingle of anticipation wafted from my silent guardian, letting me know that he wasn't opposed to the concept. I opened my clenched fists. I trusted these two males more than anyone else in the world, so if they thought this was a good idea, then I was willing to try.

Behind Lief, Dog gazed up at me with wariness in his amber eyes, but he gave me no indication that he thought I was about to make a mistake.

I nodded at Lief, and his answering smile chased a few more butterflies from my tummy.

"I'm not sure how to do this," I told him hesitantly.

"Perhaps, if you were in a high state of arousal—"

I gave the dark prince my strongest glare, one that would have made a weaker man cry. "That's how the key came out, not how it went in," I told him in a clipped tone. The jerk. His smirk said he was enjoying my discomfort immensely.

Not wanting to hear any other innuendo that referenced my new sex life, I reached up and grabbed the dangling key. It disappeared as soon as Lief released it, startling a soft gasp from both of us.

The new magic rolled through me, intrusive at first, but eventually settling down until it came to rest nestled up against the slumbering mass of Farranen's key. I let out a breath that I hadn't known I'd been holding. Magically speaking, I felt stuffed, like I'd eaten too much. Emotionally, I felt elated; having Lief's magic inside me was like discovering that your favorite book had a sequel.

"I can still feel it." Lief was looking over me to where Farranen stood with his arm still wrapped protectively around my waist. "I can still access it—" His eyes widened. "There are two keys!"

Despite my joy, I rolled my eyes. Hadn't we already established that I was holding both of the keys?

Lief backed away from us with too many emotions flitting across his face to count. "I feel the power from *both* keys." His pale eyes bounced between Farranen and I. "I shouldn't be able to feel yours."

I barely heard my guardian's sudden intake of breath, but I felt his chest expand next to me.

"You're right." I gave him an inquisitive glace when his face tilted down toward mine. "The key should only be detectable to the one who wields it, but I can feel them both here." He rested his hand over the soft fabric of my sweater. "I believe I could draw from them both if I desired."

"Draw from them?" I asked, already suspecting I knew the answer but wanting to hear it confirmed.

"The keys hold the magic that supports the realm. The rulers of each court use that power, shaping it however they see fit. For me, the leader of the Light Court, to be able to draw from the power of the Dark Court is a very dangerous thing."

"Dangerous how?"

"It blurs the lines between the courts, giving one ruler the opportunity to cripple the opposing ruler's court. Should I be of the mind, I would be able to draw the full extent of both keys' power. The imbalance could do permanent damage."

"But you would never do that," I protested. If we'd have been talking about Safeena getting her greedy paws on both keys, I would have said, hell yes, she'd be willing and eager to try something so clearly underhanded. But I had absolute faith that Farranen would never intentionally harm Fairie.

"Nor would I," Lief solemnly affirmed.

I smiled. "I know." The dark prince was an imposing figure, all dressed in black with a hard jaw and raw determination oozing from every pore, but under all that severity was a good man who would never put his realm in jeopardy.

"So, does this gig have a name?" I looked expectantly at both men. "Should I be calling myself 'the key keeper,' or 'the two kings' power smuggler,' or maybe a 'magical storage unit'?"

Lief gave me a wry grin. "It would be best not to refer to your new guardianship at all. The fewer people who know about the key's new location, the better."

Oh, right. I'd forgotten that the key's hiding spot needed to be kept secret.

"Wait—why can't anyone know where the keys are? I thought you two were the only ones that can use their power?"

"If they were to be stolen, we would no longer be able to access the power needed to maintain the realm's health and stability." The determined lines on Farranen's face let me know that he wasn't about to let anyone walk off with either of the keys.

"I can draw from my key when it's not physically on my person, from as far as half a mile away," Lief told Farranen. "I would imagine the same will apply now that it is under Theo's guardianship."

I scrubbed my hands over my face, suddenly overwhelmed by all that had happened today. Not the sudden death of my six-year celibacy (because I was a hundred percent a-okay with that), but the discovery of Farranen's governance over the Light Court, as well as the fact that I was the new guardian of two incredibly powerful objects.

If I stopped to think about it, it was just…crazy. None of this should have been possible. Yet here I was, standing with two fae and a shifter who would literally lay down their lives to keep me safe and happy. The two lumps of power resting inside me gave a slow thrum, as if they could sense my affection for them too.

"May I see it?"

Lief's tentative question pulled my attention back to reality, and I gave him an embarrassed grin. "Sorry, what?"

"May I see the mark?"

Oh, right. Now that I had them both, he'd want to know if they matched what he'd seen in his vision. I turned and presented Lief my back. His touch was gentle as he lifted my sweater and when he didn't immediately say anything, I prompted, "And?"

When nobody answered me, I risked a glance over my shoulder.

Both men stared, mesmerized by whatever they saw on my back. The unconcealed awe that shone in their dazed eyes was so utterly foreign to see directed at a woman like me. I bit my lip and tried not to squirm or say something snarky.

Chapter Thirteen

While Farranen and I had been busy traipsing all over Fairie and learning to hone my ankou magic, Lief and Dog had made the fifty-mile journey to the gate and back. I already knew Dog was ridiculously fast on four legs, but Lief must have been just as fast (since they'd managed to cover so many miles in just a few days).

Unfortunately, they hadn't found any trace of whoever had destroyed the hawthorn tree. If it was a fae, they'd have to cross back over into Fairie sometime. The fae couldn't survive without replenishing their magic. I didn't know exactly how long a fae could survive away from Fairie, but I started feeling weak after only a few hours. All the iron on Earth, combined with the lack of magic, would drain a fae's magic and eventually they would die. Immortal didn't necessarily mean unkillable.

I was sad to hear that Lief and Dog were returning to the gate immediately, but not entirely surprised. Nobody was going to sleep easy until the threat that Gus posed was dealt with. Assuming that Gus was behind the bombing. But what would he stand to gain by rendering the gate inoperable? I'd thought he was fully committed to the queen's insane plan to kidnap females of various supernatural races and turn them into breeding mares for the fae. Did he have an ulterior motive that I wasn't aware of yet? Was his end goal really as simple as repopulating Fairie?

My boots echoed hollowly on the marble floors of

the foyer, reminding me how empty the castle was.

"When will everybody return to the castle, now that it's under new management?" I asked.

"Once I make my presence known, word will spread quickly," Farranen stated plainly, like it would be no big deal to announce his inauguration to an entire population.

Knowing his matter-of-fact approach to pretty much everything, his accession speech would probably go something like "I am Farranen of the Light Court. I will be your new ruler. If you have any comments or questions, please direct them to someone else." Yeah, my man would tolerate the spotlight, but he'd never bask in it.

I'd been admiring the beauty of the detail in the vaulted ceilings, and when I realized I'd fallen behind, I hurried to catch up to the males, who were already waiting outside for me. As soon as I stepped through the threshold of the door, it disappeared.

Letting out a sharp gasp, I turned to find that not only had the doorway disappeared, the entire castle had as well. "What the…" There wasn't a strong-enough expletive to complete that thought.

The two capable, knowledgeable fae who hailed from a magical realm and should have been able to explain what the heck was going on looked as dumbfounded as I felt. Next to them, Dog let out a little whine.

"Um, guys? What happened to the castle?" Maybe I was being pranked? Because Lief and Farranen were such huge pranksters. Yeah, that probably wasn't the case.

The flat cobblestone road beneath my feet ended exactly where the castle had been, like someone had taken a chainsaw and cut it off. I took an experimental step onto the grass that filled the now-empty field, but nothing happened. My first theory, that the castle was invisible rather than completely gone, was a bust.

As silent as a shadow, Dog moved to put himself between me and the open stretch of grass. His eyes were alert as he scanned the surrounding forest while continuing to sniff the air.

I turned back to the men and was surprised to find that they'd spread out, each facing a different direction with their swords in hand, like they were expecting an ambush.

"It's possible the realm's magic became too depleted to maintain the castle's existence." The lack of confidence in Lief's tone wasn't inspiring any hope I had of this being an accident. Weird things, like entire castles disappearing, never ended up being a random coincidence.

"But she just finished redecorating it." Updating the carpets and paintings seemed like a pretty extravagant use of Fairie's magic just for her to eliminate the whole castle an hour later.

Nobody answered me, but I hadn't really expected them to.

After a few awkward minutes of listening to the trees shed their leaves, it became evident that we weren't under attack by a hoard of zombies or a pack of tibbers, and Lief and Farranen put their swords away.

"Dog and I will return to the gate and continue our search," Lief announced with his usual amount of haughtiness.

Dog padded over to where the dark prince stood. I ran my fingers through his silky fur as he brushed up against me, my heart aching at the thought of him leaving, but it would be selfish to hold him back.

His beautiful yellow eyes met mine, showing me a mosaic of emotions. Determination to finish what he'd started. Excitement. Sorrow that I couldn't go with him. And finally, a promise to return.

I gave him an encouraging smile. Lief needed him, and I was pretty sure Dog needed to be needed. The toothy grin he gave me proved that I was right.

"Do you want your key back?" I asked Lief, thinking that he would want it on him in case there was some sort of showdown with any unsavory characters they were able to track down. Not that I didn't think he couldn't handle any potential asshats on his own, but having a magical key that literally retained half the realm's power in his back pocket wasn't a bad idea.

"It must remain in Fairie, and it may prove necessary for us to visit Earth to find the culprit." He stepped closer. "I leave it in your care, Theo, as there is no other I would trust to safeguard it."

"It will be safe with me, I promise." The vow slipped out before I could stop it. There was no harsh snap of magic to seal the pledge, but it wasn't really necessary. Lief was fae and would have known if I lied.

With one last thoughtful smile, Lief offered me a quick bow and turned to where my guardian had knelt in the grass and was talking in a low voice to Dog. My furry friend bobbed his head like he was agreeing with whatever Farranen was saying.

"Merry meet," Lief told Farranen before sharing a look that probably meant keep-Theo-in-line. Or possibly don't-let-Theo-lose-my-key-because-the-Dark-Court-will-be-screwed-if-she-does. Or maybe it was more of a I-have-nothing-to-say-so-I'll-just-make-a-mysterious-face look. I was a writer for goodness' sake. Why were the men in my life always using cryptic facial expressions as a form of communication? It was annoying.

"Merry part," Farranen answered, giving Lief his own enigmatic look. I didn't bother contemplating what it could mean.

The dark prince made his departure with Dog trotting close behind, and I followed them with my eyes until both shadowy figures were out of sight.

"So, where to now?" I'd been harboring some pretty naughty thoughts about how we'd pass the time once we had the castle all to ourselves, but it looked like that was no longer an option.

"The Dark Castle." He slid an arm around my waist and pulled me flush against his body, startling a small gasp out of me. "But first—" His firm lips pressed against mine in a delicious kiss that ended way too soon. "—you needed to be kissed."

My entire body protested when he took a step back, and I gave him a dubious look. "I *needed* to be kissed?"

"Yes; you needed to be kissed, just as much as I needed to kiss you." He shot me a playful smile that made my heart squeeze a little tighter in my chest. I'd never seen him this lighthearted before. Was it because he'd become the king? Or could it be from…being with me?

Shoving aside that uncomfortable thought, I forced myself to ask, "Why are we going to the Dark Castle?"

"We should confirm its existence. The Light Castle's disappearance was likely due to the crown changing hands, but I'd like to see for myself that all is well in the dark prince's court."

Well, that made sense. Although, if another giant castle was missing, I'm not sure what could be done about it.

****

I wanted to shake my head at the ridiculousness of hunting for a misplaced castle, but with the sheer number of ridiculous things I encountered on a daily basis, I'd end up dislocating my neck.

This wasn't the first time I'd made the trek from one castle to the other. It was a fairly easy walk; the cobbled road had been worn smooth by thousands of years of use, and the wall of massive trees on either side protected us from the full brunt of the cold autumn breeze. With their leaves now completely shed, the trees' tall, twisted branches clawed at the sky overhead. At the rate the seasons were changing in Fairie, it would be full-blown winter in less than a day or two.

Farranen pulled my dirty sweatshirt from his pack and glamoured it into a dark green cloak that matched his own. It was gloriously warm and sinfully soft, just the way a cloak should be.

After fifteen minutes of walking, something in the distance caught my attention.

"What's that?" I pointed through the trees. It looked like a tall round building. Oh! Maybe Rapunzel lived in Fairie. If so, I totally wanted to meet her.

My stoic guardian whispered under his breath. "…can't be."

"What is it?" I cursed my puny human eyesight and squinted toward the structure in the distance. It could be anything from a tall skinny rock formation to a rocket ship about to be launched into space.

"It would appear that Fairie has indeed relocated the Light Castle." The wariness in his face didn't match his words. Shouldn't he be happy to locate his missing home?

"That's the missing castle?" That wasn't right. The misplaced castle had four large square towers that connected the outer walls, not a tall skinny round one.

"Let's find out." His determined stride ate up the distance between us and the building that was rapidly appearing from behind the trees. And despite his assurance that it was the Light Castle, it soon became clear that I'd never seen this castle before. There were definite similarities; they both had gothic elements reminiscent of mid-sixteenth-century Earth architecture.

Intricate carvings wound around flying buttresses that were multiple stories tall. Over a dozen gabled peaks rose to varying heights, nestling together to create a stunning roofline. The dark material they were made from reflected the rapidly darkening sky.

As we got closer, I could see that some of the tall narrow windows topped with stained glass were scenes of wooded landscapes, identical to the ones that I'd just seen in Farranen's castle minutes ago. I couldn't be sure, but the rest looked a lot like the ones from the Dark Castle.

The walls themselves were made of large blocks of marbled stone with every shade of gray represented, the colors swirling into white before dipping back to black. The massive, interlocked stones rose high above the road, broken up by smaller inset windows and wide balconies. Six round towers of varying heights climbed toward the cloudless sky, all reminding me of my favorite fairy tales—the ones that always ended with happily ever after.

But it was the drawbridge that truly made the castle a masterpiece. The wooden platform, which was currently wide open, lay across a large moat full of flowing water, bridging the road and castle. I wasn't sure where the current was coming from since there didn't seem to be any rivers or streams nearby to feed it.

Nobody challenged our approach, and I stopped with my boots an inch from the thick slab of wood that led over the water.

"Now what?" I gave Farranen a quizzical look, but he was busy studying the fortress with cautious eyes.

"It appears empty." He didn't actually say it *was* empty, just that it *appeared* empty. I sure was getting the hang of fae-speak.

Little tendrils of magic wafted through the air, beckoning us forward, and I attempted to brush them away. "It's welcoming us," I pointed out.

"Yes." He clearly hadn't decided if this was a come-to-my-table-said-the-spider-to-the-fly situation.

We could stand around all night debating the origin of the new mysterious castle, but I'd rather do it from inside the safety of the castle walls, rather than out in the open with twilight rapidly descending around us. I took a single step onto the wooden drawbridge, and when it didn't immediately burst into flames, I went half a dozen more until Farranen grabbed my elbow and pulled me back.

"Theodora! We don't know what's in there."

"Are any of the fae powerful enough to create an entire castle while simultaneously stealing another one?" I demanded irritably. I was tired, and the meager dried meat that I'd eaten hours ago hadn't been enough to fill my belly. I was eager to find out if the new castle came with a fully stocked kitchen before testing one of the beds.

"No," he answered confidently.

"Then this clearly isn't a trap constructed by one of our enemies. It had to be created by the realm herself." I had complete faith that if Fairie was going to plunk a brand-new castle down in front of us, with the drawbridge wide open in invitation, then she wanted us to check it out. "Please?" I added.

His indecision cracked under the weight of my beguiling gaze. Or maybe he just saw the wisdom of my words. Whatever the reason, he relented with a half smile that looked as tired as I felt.

"As my lady wishes," he murmured, with all the enthusiasm of a man headed for the gallows.

We crossed the bridge, which was at least forty feet long but only fifteen feet wide. I walked carefully, staying in the dead center of the plank since it was a ten-foot drop into the murky water below on either side, and I had a penchant for stumbling at inopportune moments.

We reached the other side of the drawbridge without incident, and the vastness of the foyer lay before us. The torches on the walls, fancier than the ones from the Light Castle's basement, sparked to life as soon as my boot stepped on the tile floor.

I froze, staring at the pale green slab that glimmered as if unmined diamonds were embedded in the rock it had been carved from. Next to it waited a pale purple tile, equally veined with shimmering flakes. Beyond, I could see the entire room was a checkerboard of green and purple tiles, each about four feet wide. Something tickled at the back of my brain…

Above us, the stained-glass windows watched over the room, while stars twinkled into sight outside, highlighting the beauty of the glass and chasing away some of the shadows in the foyer. Oddly enough, it was the window depicting an image of a white flower twined around a sword that finally shook free the thought that had been taunting me.

"This is the new Light Castle," I breathed. I'd seen that same white rose and sword image in the foyer, just before the original castle disappeared.

"Yes, I surmised that might be the case."

I tilted my head back, taking in the large chamber and picking out more and more details that made me think of my stoic guardian. And for every carving and design element that reminded me of Farranen, I found an equal number that hinted at Lief's presence.

"But it's the Dark Castle too." Excitement filled my belly at solving the mystery. "I'll bet that Lief's castle disappeared when yours did. Fairie consolidated them into one." The rightness of my deduction settled over me, and a faint pulse of the castle's ambient magic brushed against mine. Whoa—did Fairie just agree with me?

I couldn't read past the contemplation on Farranen's face. "That's…possible," he finally admitted. "In the entirety of our written histories, there have always been two castles. What changed?"

I looked at him in disbelief. "*What changed?* The crazy-ass queen that was poisoning the land died and you took over—*that's* what changed! Can't you feel it?" I sank to my knees and placed my palms on the marble floors, letting my magic seep past the stone to connect with the ground below. "She's healing." I glanced up to where he was watching me with an unreadable expression on his face. "She's healing because you and Lief are working together to take care of her."

He sighed, the sound so human that I smiled. "You see far more than you should."

I rose to my feet and gave the grand room one last look, seeing it for what it truly was—a beautiful blending of the two strong males who carried the weight of the realm on their shoulders.

Then, not bothering to wait for my guardian, I marched through the foyer and into the hall beyond. If Fairie truly sent the castle as her way of saying thank you, then there should be cake in the kitchen. Because nothing said thank you better than cake.

Chapter Fourteen

For two solid days, Farranen and I explored.

And, no, I don't mean we delved into the hundreds of rooms in the mystical new castle.

When we weren't sleeping, we explored each other.

Now I knew exactly what parts of his body to touch when I wanted him to shudder, how far I could assert my dominance before he took back control, and if I was feeling brave, I knew how to coax out a ragged groan that always ended in a curse. Until now, I hadn't known he was capable of cursing.

I'd learned when to anticipate the fascinated look that crossed his face with every bossy demand I made. When I scraped my fingernails over the sensitive skin on the back of his knees, he laughed. Knowing that my big strong guardian was ticklish was charming in a way that words couldn't compete with. I discovered the salty taste of him on my tongue turned me on faster than anything else could.

And there wasn't a place on my body that hadn't been worshiped by the man that I was slowly becoming addicted to.

That thought always threw my head into a tailspin. Being addicted to an immortal being was a dangerous thing. And stupid. Realistically, the best I could hope for was a decade or two before I aged enough that he'd no longer want me. Still, the knowledge that this was temporary hadn't stopped me from enjoying every single minute I spent under his knowing gaze and talented hands.

Since Farranen's new room had its own massive ensuite, the only times we'd ventured out was a few infrequent trips to the kitchen for food. The supply of firewood next to the hearth never seemed to go down, even though we kept the fire stoked day and night.

When we weren't making use of the massive king-size bed, there were three bookcases lined with hundreds of books to choose from. Earlier that morning, I'd woken before Farranen and spent a few minutes browsing the titles, surprised to find that half were in English. I immediately recognized some classics, like Shakespeare, Austen, Bronte, and Steinbeck. But it was the collection on one of the middle shelves that made me do a double take. Six books, all historical romance paperbacks from the Blushing Hens Press, written by Erin Bjorgum.

A blush crept along my cheekbones, tingling as it made its way down my face to my neck. Erin Bjorgum was my pen name. The last half was a little nod to my Norwegian roots, and as for the first half—well, Erin was the most boring, generic woman's name I could think of.

I had no idea how some of my books had appeared in Fairie, and honestly, I didn't care—as long as Farraren hadn't already stumbled upon them. Because the thought of him having easy access to the many sordid encounters I'd written about made me want to crawl into a hole and hide. And if Dog or Lief ever got their hands on my books—yeah, that hole better be on the other side of the planet and at least a mile deep.

To prevent anyone from discovering the paperbacks, I had tucked them behind some of Hemingway's work.

Now, freshly showered, I finished pulling on a shirt

over my sports bra, both items courtesy of Fairie. When we'd located the suite intended to be Farranen's personal chambers, the wardrobe had been filled with clothes for both of us. The shirt I was currently wearing was dark green and had a picture of a tooth with wings on it that I was pretty sure was supposed to be the Tooth Fairy. I wasn't sure if the realm was mocking me or trying to be cute, but I found the notion hilarious.

"Theodora." The previous lighthearted banter in his voice was gone, replaced with a seriousness that instantly made me leery. "It is unlike the dark prince to go so long without any form of contact. I need to ascertain his and Dog's whereabouts and see if they have need of my help."

Inwardly, I sighed. Our honeymoon had to end sometime. I'd been hoping it wouldn't be quite so soon. Instead of demanding that he stay, I said, "When do you leave?"

His arms were two solid anchors as they pulled me into the warmth of his embrace. "Now."

I thought he'd say that. And part of me was glad that if Dog or Lief were in trouble, he was prepared to drop everything and ride off to their rescue. The other part of me, the selfish part that was ruled by my hormones and libido, wanted to tie him up and—yeah, you get the picture.

Releasing me, he bent down and tugged his boots out from under the bed. I didn't bother trying to pretend that I wasn't staring.

"I could come with you," I pointed out, once he'd turned around and I was no longer distracted by the glorious sight of his firm backside.

"No. It's safer for you here." There was a finality to his words that made me think his transition to king was well underway.

"But you might need the key," I suggested. And I might need someone to keep me warm at night. Ugh, it was pathetic how quickly I'd come to depend on his presence in my life.

"I won't chance anyone else getting their hands on it." I heard the unspoken "or you" that he left out.

"What am I supposed to do while you're gone?" Seriously, didn't he know me at all? I wasn't the type to sit around and do nothing. It's not even like I could binge-watch some TV. Every time I went down to the massive kitchen, there was freshly prepared food waiting. Baking a cake for myself would be a waste of time. Not to mention insulting to whoever was actually doing the baking.

"Perhaps you could see to it that the new inhabitants are satisfactorily settled."

"New inhabitants?" The castle was empty as far as I knew.

"Many of the former Dark Castle's occupants have found their way here." The tiny wrinkle in his forehead suggested that he thought our new roommates were common knowledge.

"What? How do you know that?" The only time he'd been out of my sight was when I excused myself to use the ladies room.

"Fae hearing," he explained with a shrug.

My jaw dropped. There had been other people—people with *magically enhanced hearing*—in the building while we'd been naked and tangled up in the sheets. Loudly, I might add. An entire bucket of ice wouldn't have cooled my flaming face.

I sat down heavily on the bed, and Farranen immediately knelt in front of me. "I must go. Promise me that you'll stay out of trouble."

I hated promises. They always had a way of coming back to bite me on the butt. But I knew he wouldn't leave until I agreed, so I nodded.

"Be careful," I told him, when all I really wanted to do was beg him not to go.

With one last chaste kiss, he strode out of the room without looking back.

****

An entire flock of dragons could have moved in, and I doubt I'd even be aware since the castle was so freaking big. Did Fairie have dragons? I'd have to ask the guys when they returned.

As I wandered the halls, I decided I was sick of calling it "the new castle." I was a creative-minded writer. Surely, I could come up with something fitting for an enchanted stronghold meant to represent the joining of two segregated courts.

Ahead of me, a tall figure turned the corner and saluted me with "Merry meet, Theodora!"

"Hey, Daph." I gave Daphorus of the Light Court a little wave, relieved to see that he was fully dressed. His navy-blue cloak swirled around his over-polished boots when he came to a stop in front of me. Tiny clusters of red gems were fastened between embroidered silver leaves along the collar, shimmering like drops of blood in the light from the row of windows next to us.

"It is a true honor to be welcomed… ah, here." At least I wasn't the only one unsure what to call the new castle.

"The Shadow Palace." The name slipped out before I could stop it, hanging in the air for a few seconds before it settled over me with a sense of belonging. Yeah, there was no better way to describe the massive structure than as a palace of shadows. Just as the darkness of a shadow couldn't exist without the light that cast it, Fairie couldn't exist without Farranen and Lief to support her.

Daph's sapphire blue eyes crinkled. "Indeed, it is a true honor to call the Shadow Palace home."

"So, you've moved in?" I wasn't sure how I felt about temporarily having roommates. Some unique challenges had emerged when Dog and Farranen had moved into my cramped cabin. Coexisting with any of the eccentric fae was sure to be a struggle for someone like me, who was used to living a solitary lifestyle.

"Surely, my lady. My brother and I have located our accommodations and are elated at the aggrandizement. They are most sumptuous, truly."

Huh. It looked like Farranen wasn't the only one to get an upgrade to his personal suite. The T'Holly brothers had served as undercover agents for Lief during his attempt to overthrow Safeena, and I was genuinely happy that their loyalty was being rewarded.

After a few more minutes of small talk with the quirky fae, I politely excused myself so I could continue my exploration of the huge castle.

****

My reconnaissance mission filled the rest of the day, and once I realized the sky outside was dark, I made my way back to Farranen's room. Despite only seeing half the castle, I'd discovered a massive library, a healer's chamber (complete with Eddy, a talented healer from the Dark Court), way too many guest rooms with the beds fully decked out in clean bedding, something that would pass for a chapel, and a room that had large basins carved into the rock floor filled with scalding mud that let out an occasional bubble or hiss of steam. They were either for implementing torture tactics, or for spa purposes. I was leaning heavily toward the torture theory, but there was no way in hell I was sticking a single toe in the bubbling muck just to test my theory.

The grumbling of my belly reminded me that I should eat something, and a shower would have to happen before I retired for the night, but I was too wound up to do either. Restless fingers of anxiety were dancing down my spine, and I found myself pacing back and forth from one end of the room to the other. How was I supposed to relax knowing that the men I cared about were out there, possibly facing any number of the horrific situations that my imagination was coming up with? And how had I let myself get talked into staying home? You'd think by now that they'd know I get into ten times more trouble without adult supervision.

If Fairie had cell phones, I wouldn't be standing here stressing over the unknown. Even a freakin' telegram service would be sufficient—

I came to an abrupt halt in the middle of the room. There wasn't any internet or phone service, but I had something even better: unlimited access to every single spirit that was on the other side of the veil. And there were a ton of them.

Why hadn't I thought of this sooner? I could send a ghost to check on the males—except, if they weren't okay, if something had gone wrong and they were in trouble, would they tell me? I already knew the answer to that. When Farranen was being tortured by the Army of Light, he'd refused to tell me where he was being held so that I couldn't get hurt by trying to rescue him. Stubborn fae.

I didn't need a messenger so much as a spy.

My feet started moving again, this time carrying me to the table where a pale loaf of bread and a pot of sticky-looking jam were waiting. I'd need all the energy I could get to pull off the plan already forming in my head.

Since my only grave-reaping experience came from creating Vanessa, Harvey, and Safeena, my knowledge on the subtler nuances of the subject was somewhat limited.

In this particular situation, a ghost that was invisible to everyone but me would be the best choice, but I wasn't sure if I could go back to creating tangible ghosts (in my head, I'd started referring to my flawed ghosts as tangible ghosts, and normal ghosts as traditional ghosts).

Since Harvey and Vanessa likely needed more time to recharge, I decided to use Svencer since he was super fast; the sooner I knew everyone was okay, the better.

One of the biggest differences I'd noticed was that I'd used a lot more magic to pull the tangible ghosts through the veil. When I pushed my magic into them, it was kind of like stuffing a turkey: I'd just filled the vessel as full as I could by cramming magic wherever it fit. With the queen, I'd concentrated the magic into a tiny little pinprick, forcing all the power into a single point within the spirit.

After I finished filling myself with the soft bread slathered in sweet jam, I took a seat on the shaggy black rug, with my back resting against the foot of the bed. I experimentally pushed my magic out to weaken the veil. It was slightly easier than last time, but still left my limbs shaky from the effort.

Immediately a few shimmering forms came into view, hovering around the edges of my vision. I took it as a good sign that there were spirits here, and my heart sped up at the thought that I was really doing this by myself. The last time I'd summoned a ghost, Farranen, Harvey, and Vanessa had been there to coach me through the process. This time I was completely on my own. The prospect should have scared me, but all I felt was determination. I was going to do this.

"Svencer of the Light Court, come to me," I called.

A spirit materialized in front of me, and I had to swallow a surprised squeak. Dang, those darteen fae were fast.

I was proud that my hand didn't tremble when I extended it in his direction. The instant his fingers came in contact with mine, I mentally pictured floodgates opening. My magic surged outward in a rush, just like when I'd accidentally created Vanessa and Harvey.

Bright blue eyes blinked at me from an expressionless face.

"Hi, Svencer." I lowered my arm and gave the small ghost what I hoped was a friendly smile. "Would you do a favor for me?" At his solemn nod, I reached over and poked him in the shoulder. He was just as solid as a real boy, and I couldn't hide my grin. I'd created a flawed ghost—but this time it was on purpose.

Chapter Fifteen

Without any breeze, the entire realm felt like it was holding its breath. The familiar chill promised that winter was coming. From the wide stone balcony, I waited as the day slowly faded into night. Until Svencer completed his recon mission and reported back to me, I wasn't going to be able to sleep.

I huddled a little farther into the thick cloak that I was bundled into.

"I located the dark prince and the shifter northwest of the dungeons."

A shriek lodged itself in my throat at Svencer's sudden arrival, and my fingers gripped the cold railing like it could save me from whatever new threat had triggered my fight or flight response. Good Lord, the darteen were not only fast, they were deadly quiet too.

"Thank you, Svencer," I told him, hoping he could hear me over the sound of my heart knocking against the wall of my chest. "Did you find Farranen?"

"Yes, he is following their original trail and should rendezvous with them soon."

A relived breath escaped me, deflating my entire body. Thank goodness everyone was okay. I pried my fingers off the railing and shook my hands to get some feeling back in them.

"That's great. Thanks for checking on them for me." Now that I knew there was nothing to worry about, I could take a shower and get some shut-eye. Maybe I'd wander down to the kitchen to see if there was any cake.

"He's being followed."

I blinked in surprise, like maybe I'd heard the little ghost wrong.

"Who's being followed?" All the fears that Svencer's return had allayed came rushing back, nearly knocking me over with their intensity.

"The king is unaware that shadows stalk him." Something flickered in his guileless blue eyes, scaring me more than his words had.

Shadows were stalking Farranen? What did that even mean? And why the hell didn't Svencer start with that? Maybe I should have been more specific with my questions. "Are the shadows going to hurt him? And what about Lief and Dog? Are the shadows stalking them too?" I was going to shake the answers out of my newest ghost if he didn't start spitting them out.

"I don't know. I was unable to ask them." Right, because none of the fae could see him. Damn it, maybe I should have made a regular ghost after all. I needed to warn the men, but there was no way my slow ass was going to get to them in time. I looked down at the ghost patiently waiting for me to act like the grown-up here.

"Svencer, if I return you behind the veil, and then pull you back so everyone can see you, do you think you could warn the king about the shadows before they get to him?"

He shook his head, and I dug my fingers into my hair in frustration. "Why not?" I demanded, uncaring if I was being rude. Getting info out of the kid was like pulling teeth.

"The shadows have likely already caught up to him." The starstruck glow Svencer had been rocking the first time he'd met Farranen was nowhere to be seen, replaced with a dejected acceptance that caused my heart to splash down into my stomach. It landed like a brick next to the small bit of hope I'd been holding onto.

Svencer had to be wrong. A bunch of shadows wouldn't be able to get the upper hand on my man. He'd fought numerous fae who had crossed the gate unsanctioned and returned them to Fairie without breaking a sweat. He'd survived months in the queen's dungeons and lived to tell about it. Farranen was no victim. The man was deadly with a sword and more resourceful than any other fae in the realm. He was literally *immortal*. What threat could a bunch of shadows possibly be to him?

Still…I'd feel a lot better if he knew what he was walking into.

I'm not sure how long I stood there staring off into the darkness beyond the castle, but Svencer was still waiting when I finished silently debating my options.

The quick little darteen wouldn't make it in time, but maybe there was another way. After all, this was Fairie, a magical realm, that might have some magical solutions I was unaware of.

"We need to warn the king. What's the fastest way to get a message to him?"

His eyes narrowed and lost focus for a few seconds before a grin lit up his face, making him look more like the child that he was. "The dragillian fae are even faster than the darteen; they can create holes in time."

" 'Holes in time'? Like, time travel?" Just when I thought I'd already discovered the absolute coolest of the fae's gifts, Svencer went and blew my mind. The concept of time travel was a little bewildering to me, but if I could get a message to Farranen faster, then I'd be happy to enlist the help of a dragillian.

"They can't actually travel through time; they merely jump from one hole to another so that they can reach their destination sooner."

That sounded pretty darn good to me. "Great, where can I find one?"

A lock of blond hair fell across his eyes as he shook his head. "The dragillian have all died out."

I let my head fall forward until it was resting on my chest. Of course, they were all dead. It was just my luck—

My head popped back up as a metaphorical light bulb smacked me upside the head. So what if they were all dead? I could just yank one of them through the veil and send them to warn my guardian.

Ignoring the look on Svencer's face that said he'd clearly beat me to that conclusion, I turned and went back inside so I could create another ghost without freezing my butt off.

The fire had died down in the hearth, so I tossed a couple of logs in before settling down on the shag rug. Still chilled from being outside, I kept my cloak on.

"Do you know the names of any of the dragillian?" I asked the ghost that had followed me inside. I doubted there was a way to summon a spirit based on what type of fae they were; or if there was, it was beyond my abilities.

After a moment of thoughtful contemplation, Svencer nodded. "Call Sepian. He was the strongest, as well as the last of his kind."

Okay, then. I rubbed my hands together to get some warmth back in them—and inadvertently did a terrible impersonation of a stereotypical antagonist in a sci-fi novel—before concentrating on the veil. The memory of pulling Svencer through a few hours ago was fresh in my mind, and it didn't take nearly as long to force my magic up against it.

A handful of shimmering forms slid into view, hovering on the other side of the weakened veil as they silently watched me. I ignored them, knowing any old spirit wouldn't do.

"Sepian, come to me," I called.

Nothing happened.

I glanced over at Svencer, but he looked just as confused as I felt.

Maybe the spirit I was seeking hadn't heard me. "Sepian, come to me!" I demanded, more forcefully than I'd intended.

A glimmer of movement across the room caught my attention. I didn't so much see it with my eyes, as I felt it with my magic, as if the power I was expending had just brushed up against a polar opposite and was being repelled. I focused on the spot again, and the same resistance shrugged away from my magic.

"Sepian, come to me!" The command shot out of me like a bullet aimed straight at the stubborn spirit that was resisting my efforts to drag him through the veil. I gritted my teeth. If this came down to a battle of wills, there was no way I was letting a centuries-dead fae beat me.

I extended one balled-up fist toward the spirit across the room, before opening my fingers and yanking with my magic. A small thread of power recoiled painfully back into my body, but the remainder latched onto the thing that was squirming in my grasp. Again, I made a grabbing motion that my magic mimicked. The reluctant spirit shot across the room and slammed into my outstretched arm.

As soon as we made contact, I lost the tenuous hold I had on my magic, and it exploded out of me. Like a runaway freight train, it slammed its way into the spirit, before the remainder ricocheted back into me.

My cry, born partly of surprise and partly of pain, was lost in the unhuman roar that rattled the stone walls and ceiling.

Bright eyes, the same shade of yellow as a safety vest, glared at me—but there was nothing safe-looking about the man standing over me. His handsome face, complete with a hard jaw and strong nose, was framed by long black hair. Light from the fire behind me reflected off the thick glossy locks, giving them an auburn tinge that some women spent hours in the salon trying to replicate. The soft waves cascaded over his shoulders and hung across his bare chest, where his dark nipples played peek-a-boo with me. Farther down, his washboard abs were covered in a giant rippling tattoo that looked like green scales.

I snatched my hand back, shocked speechless by the sheer size of the seven-foot-tall ghost. Why the hell hadn't Svencer warned me that the dragillian were giants? A little heads-up would have been nice.

With his thick arms fisted at his sides, Sepian continued to glare down at me, so I quickly scrambled to my feet.

"Why have you summoned me?" His deep voice assaulted my eardrums like thunder, and I cringed.

"Sepian? I'm Theo." Now that the introductions were out of the way, I tried to remember the phrase that Mary had used when she'd asked Svencer to serve her. "Will you serve me—"

Sepian's huge hand shot out and wrapped itself around my throat, effectively cutting off my words as well as the air that I needed for breathing. I kicked, trying to nail him in the shin, but his arms were about eight miles long, and I couldn't reach any part of him. My hands clawed at his forearm, but he didn't loosen his hold.

That's when I realized my mistake. When I'd ripped him through the veil, I'd lost control of my magic and instead of creating a traditional ghost like I'd intended, I'd made another flawed one. As evidenced by the fact that his ghostly hand was slowly squeezing the life out of me. Gah, what a stupid way to die. Killed by my own ghost. Since Svencer and Sepian would be the only witnesses to my murder, I doubt anyone else would ever know what happened.

Just when the buzzing in my ears was starting to drown out the sounds of the fire, along with Svencer's tiny voice, the hand around my neck abruptly let go. I fell on the floor in an ungraceful heap like a pile of discarded laundry.

"You *dare* to summon the king of the Dark Court?" He spoke softly, but the thick thread of warning in his voice was clear.

The *king* of the Dark Court? Oh good Lord, Sepian was one of Fairie's long dead rulers. I let out a harsh gasp. That meant—oh, crap. Harvey had given me some history lessons, one of them about how Lief had come to wear the crown—by killing the former king.

The same king that was currently eyeing me like he wasn't sure if I'd be tasty, but he was going to take a bite regardless.

****

As a woman who'd never spent a lot of time around children, I can admit that I'd never grasped just how manipulative they could be until I had the privilege of watching Svencer work his wiles on the former king of the Dark Court.

Maybe he'd felt somewhat responsible since he'd been the one to suggest that I summon a homicidal spirit. Or maybe he was just as concerned about Farranen as I was. Either way, Sepian had lost most of his indignant rage at being summoned like a cheap whore to service the cock of every man with a shiny coin in his pocket. His words, not mine.

After my newest ghost had stopped throttling me, Svencer had thrown his tiny body across mine. With his skinny arms wrapped around me, he'd pleaded with the former king not to hurt me.

The look on Sepian's face had downgraded from murderous psycho to grumpy bear.

Now that he wasn't hell-bent on killing me, Svencer was explaining to him, "Dark times have fallen on Fairie, my lord. The new king of the Light Court is in danger."

Sepian scoffed. "If he needs the help of a ghost, then he's not strong enough to lead his own court. Let it play out—the stronger fae will prevail and rise to the throne."

"He's not up against another fae!" I cut in. So far, I'd been silent, since my throat was raw, but I couldn't hold my words back any longer. "There are shadows stalking him!"

"*Shadows?*" Derision dripped from his deep voice, and I wanted to smack him. Why did all the males in Fairie have to be so closed minded? Couldn't he just take my word for it, and help me get a message to Farranen?

Sitting in my lap with his arms around me, Svencer told us, "They look like shadows, but they reek of foul magic. They're nothing that belongs in Fairie." He topped it off by letting a big fat tear roll down his cheek. The kid had some mad acting skills. At least, I assumed he was acting, since he'd always been so unemotional in the past.

161

That seemed to get Sepian's attention. His eyes narrowed as he contemplated what we were asking. "What would you have me do?" Apparently, his desire to protect the realm was greater than his hatred for me.

I tightened my arms around the tiny ghost. It was actually kind of nice holding onto him. His hair smelled like soap and the outdoors, and the green velvet of his jacket was soft beneath my fingers.

"I summoned you to warn the new king about the shadows, but I did it wrong, so now I'm the only one that can see you." Admitting my failure should have rankled more than it did, but I was too tired to feel much of anything right now. Making two ghosts in less than a day had left me exhausted. It would be a while before I had enough energy to attempt another summoning, and who knows what would happen to Farranen, Lief, and Dog in the meantime. It might already be too late.

The heat from the fire was adding to my lethargy; I'd have to sleep soon. I would've taken off my overly warm cloak if I could have done it without dislodging Svencer from my lap.

"*You* can warn the king!" Svencer suddenly exclaimed, startling both me and Sepian. I wanted to smirk at seeing the big guy jump but didn't want to risk breaking the unspoken truce that had sprung up between us.

I looked down at the face of the excited little ghost, not understanding what he was getting at. "That's what I've been trying to do." He was smarter than I assumed most children were, so I shouldn't have to explain that an overweight woman in her thirties with endurance issues wouldn't be able to cover that amount of distance in a timely fashion.

"The dark king can escort you there in seconds." His

162

blue eyes blinked hopefully.

It took a few seconds for my poor tired brain to latch onto the notion, but I realized the idea had merit. My eyes traveled over the shirtless expanse of Sepian's chest, silently evaluating his physique. Would he be able to carry me? It was possible. I mean, Lief and Farranen had both lugged my heavy butt around when the occasion called for it, and this guy was bigger than either of them.

"Do you think you could hold me long enough to do your 'hole in time' thing?" I fought the urge to squirm while his chartreuse eyes flickered across my entire body. I was fully aware that I'd just left myself wide open to comments regarding my weight.

A snort slipped out of his nose, followed by a small tendril of smoke. "It would require minimal effort to carry a dozen of you. You alone aren't even worth mentioning."

It wasn't exactly a compliment, but I smiled anyway.

"Great! Let's do this," I told them. The longer we waited, the greater the chance that the mysterious shadow things would make a move on Farranen.

Svencer climbed off my lap, and I stiffly rose to my feet. I was still feeling the effects of being manhandled by Sepian. "Do I need to bring anything?" I asked the dragillian.

He shook his head, before holding out his hand in invitation. I took it after the slightest hesitation, his cool palm a welcome addition next to my overheated skin. Feeling like a cow being led to the slaughterhouse, I followed him outside. The wind had picked up while I'd been inside, and it greedily grabbed at my cloak and loose hair.

"Where is the new king?" Sepian's voice echoed in

the cavernous space of the balcony before getting sucked over the edge and disappearing into the dark void beyond the railing.

"Between here and the west gate."

His dark eyebrows rose in a universal gesture of *and?*

"West of the dungeons," Svencer supplied helpfully.

The massive ghost in front of me rolled his eyes. Which was kind of comical. And much better than him trying to choke a more specific answer out of me.

"Do you have an object of his that I can use to track him? Something that he greatly values?" His narrowed eyes implied that I should find something quickly.

But Farranen wasn't really the sentimental type that held onto physical mementos. It's not like he kept a scrapbook of all the battles he'd won. He prized his sword, but he'd taken it with him. Of course, he valued me, but I doubted that counted. The only other thing that I could think of was the key to the Light Court. But if I pulled it out, then I'd have to explain the how and why behind it being in my possession. I wasn't worried about word getting out that I was carrying one of Fairie's most powerful artifacts around—its not like either of my newest ghosts could tell anyone. I just didn't want to play twenty questions and delay our departure any further. Every instinct I had was screaming at me to get to Farranen. It might already be too late.

Screw it, I thought. It was past time to get moving.

"Yes, I have something that he values. But I want you to promise that if I show it to you, you won't ask any questions until my friends are all safe." I had no idea if a ghost would be bound to any promise he made, but it didn't hurt to try.

"Very well," Sepian calmly conceded, shocking the

heck out of me since it didn't really fit with his bossy-king-in-charge persona. I'd been expecting a bit more bartering.

"Okay, then." I made a fist and extended it away from my body. I closed my eyes and nudged the little nugget of power inside me that represented the key to the Light Court. Slowly, it undulated, as if it was waking and stretching. I bumped it again, pushing with my own magic to guide it toward my outstretched hand. It slowly gained momentum, like a ball of molasses that was rolling downhill. When it reached my palm, it solidified in my fist in the familiar shape of a key. I grinned and opened my hand.

Sepians handsome bronzed face paled a few shades, but his cantankerous expression never wavered.

Chapter Sixteen

Now that we were about to ride off into the night at warp speed, a swarm of bats had taken up residence in my belly. And not just any normal bats, they felt like big nasty vampire bats that were trying to devour me from the inside out.

"So how do we do this?" I asked, genuinely curious despite my fears.

Sepian tossed his hair over his shoulder before answering me. "I will shift, and then we will create a hole to jump through."

Before I could even begin to consider what that might entail, he closed his eyes and his body began to change. At first it was subtle; he sprouted a few inches taller and his shoulders widened. Then the tattoo on his torso began to ripple. The green and aqua colors of each individual scale began to reflect the starlight, their iridescent colors becoming more pronounced until I realized that they'd become actual scales, layered over his body like armor. I was just about to reach out and see if they were as hard as they looked, when a giant pair of wings unfurled from his back.

I bit back a gasp as they arched out behind him. The outer part was black with sharp talons at the peaks. A delicate dark green membrane connected the strong black ropes of muscle that ran along the top. Smaller talons grew from the bottom edges.

"Holy shit!" I exclaimed. "I *knew* it! There *are*

dragons in Fairie!"

My poor brain came up with a hundred questions in the same amount of time it took to blink. Could he breathe fire? I'd thought it was weird when a small bit of smoke had come out of his nose—

I squealed when Sepian plucked me up like I weighed no more than a toddler, cradling me to his chest before he leapt up onto the balcony railing. We were only two stories up, but the ground was lost in the darkness, and it felt like we were posed on the edge of the Grand Canyon.

"Wait—"

The wind stole my protest as Sepian stepped out into space, and we began to plummet to what was assuredly our deaths. Over his shoulder, his massive wings snapped out to their maximum width and immediately filled with air. My stomach jerked in response as our descent turned into a glide. With a powerful surge, the muscles in his wings bunched gracefully as they pumped a few times to lift us even closer to the stars overhead.

My eyes adjusted to the darkness, and I could make out the forest below. The air was even colder up here, and I buried my hands in the folds of my cloak to keep them warm.

I was flying.

Now that the initial shock had worn off and I was able to shake off the fear that Sepian was going to drop me, I enjoyed the feel of the wind pulling at my hair. The stars seemed even brighter as we rose higher and higher. Below, the individual roads that bisected the forest blurred and then disappeared completely.

I was *flying*. I couldn't wait to tell Dog about it.

"Here we go." The unusual note of glee in Sepian's voice should have clued me in that I wouldn't like what was going to happen next.

We stopped climbing and for a few seconds just hovered in the same place. "What—"

His lush lips split into a fierce grin that had my stomach doing a terrified backflip.

We dropped.

The massive ten-foot wings that had been holding us hundreds of feet above the ground stopped flapping and folded in tight against Sepian's back. I shrieked as we started to freefall. My hands fumbled out of my cloak and clutched at his shoulders for dear life. Oh, dear God, we were going to die. I must have really screwed up when I summoned him and created a suicidal ghost. Dog and Farranen would spend the rest of their lives wondering how I'd ended up splattered on the forest floor.

We tipped forward so we were falling headfirst. My eyes watered as the ground rushed toward us, but I couldn't look away. So, this was what it must feel like to be a bug, staring down a windshield that was coming at it at a hundred kilometers an hour.

Directly below us, the air began to warp and bend, reminding me of the portals that Lief and Safeena had used. Mist coalesced, leaking outward from the center. Horror coated my tongue as we shot straight toward the hole, and I would have screamed if my stomach hadn't been lodged in my throat.

A bright flash of light enveloped us when we smashed into the mist, and for a few seconds I couldn't see anything. When my vision finally returned, I was relieved to see Sepian's wings were once again open as we glided along the air currents. Below, the tops of the trees were so close I could probably touch them if I was brave enough to let go of the male carrying me.

I craned my neck to peek over his shoulder, but there was no sign of the weird misty portal we'd fallen through.

"Hold out the key so I can use it to track him."

I tugged on the chain that was hanging around my neck and pulled the key out from beneath my cloak, keeping a tight grip on it. Dropping it would be a really bad idea.

"Now what?" I asked, sounding more suspicious than I meant to. My trust was stretched pretty thin at this point (thinking I was falling to my death probably had something to do with it). I was hesitant to let him get close to Farranen's key. As a former king, he'd be familiar with what the key was capable of and how to wield its power. I doubted there was a single history book in Fairie that could predict what would happen if a broken ghost got hold of one of the keys.

"Now I use my second sight to track its owner." He blinked, and I let out a startled little squeak when I saw that his eyes had changed. A thin membrane covered them, and the chillingly bright yellow irises had expanded to block out all of the white. His pupils had narrowed horizontally and stretched vertically, so now they resembled serpents' or goats' eyes. Or dragon eyes.

I bit my lip as he scanned the ground below while occasionally glancing at the key where it danged at the end of its chain. Every so often he would adjust his course, like he was following a trail.

Knowing he needed his concentration for the task of finding Farranen, I kept a lookout for Lief and Dog, or any of the shadow creatures that Svencer had identified as a threat. With the stars providing the only source of illumination, I didn't spot any insidious shadows lurking in the sleeping forest. Although, it was dark enough that if we'd passed a herd of Tyrannosaurus rexes, I probably wouldn't have seen them either.

Sepian's wings slowed, and I looked down to find a cheery campfire burning next to a small cottage. The tight knot of worry in my chest loosened a smidge at seeing all three of the males I'd been worried about. As we descended on the cozy scene, three identically shocked sets of eyes rose to acknowledge me. And their faces…Oh, man, I wanted to giggle at their disbelief, but since they couldn't see the dragon carrying me, I didn't want to freak them out anymore than I already had. Descending from the sky like a cackling mad woman wouldn't do anything to reassure them that I was there to help.

Dog was the first to move, lunging past the fae like his pants were on fire—even though he was on four legs and not wearing any pants.

Sepian landed soundlessly and lowered me to my feet before telling me, "I must go." His usual bronze coloring had faded to a pasty white, and even his dragon scales were looking lackluster. Until now, I hadn't thought about how much energy he'd been expending on my behalf.

"Thank you," I murmured, hoping he just needed to recharge and wasn't leaving for good. Yeah, he was a bit ill-tempered, but I liked having him around. I was no ray of sunshine myself most days.

The dead king winked out sight, and I turned back just as Dog's furry body collided with mine. His excitement was contagious, and I laughed as his wet nose inspected every part of me. When he finally backed up enough for me to stand, I brushed off the dried leaves and dirt clinging to my cloak. Before I could finish, a strong pair of arms caught me around the waist and once again I was lifted off the ground and enveloped in a hug that was so snug, I couldn't even inhale.

I sighed; every part of the warm body pressed up against me was familiar. From the hard chest crushed against my face, to the fresh scent of cinnamon and pine, my soul recognized every part of this man.

My fae. My guardian. Farranen.

I squeezed a little tighter with my arms, silently telling him how much I'd missed him and how worried I'd been.

Oh, crap—I'd almost forgotten why I was there. I squirmed until he loosened his embrace.

"What are you doing here?" Green eyes, bright in the surrounding darkness, peered down at me with a mosaic of emotions shifting through them. "How did you…" His gaze shifted up to the sky for a moment, like he couldn't even begin to describe how I'd arrived like a wicked witch without a broom.

"Perhaps we should continue this conversation around the fire," Lief commented, reminding me just how cold I was.

After we were settled around the warmth of the blaze, and Lief had tossed an armful of dead branches into the flames, I tried to fill them in on what I'd learned.

"I just wanted to know that you guys were all right, so I sent Svencer to check up on you."

Dog harumphed from where he was lying next to me, and I cringed. I'd probably insulted his manliness by implying he couldn't take care of himself and the dark prince.

Farranen shared a glance with Lief before saying, "I didn't encounter any ghosts on my journey."

"Nor did we," the dark prince added.

"Yeah, you wouldn't have been able to see him." I

was so busted and regretted my decision to use Svencer as a spy, rather than a messenger. I continued in a rush, "Anyway, he saw that Farranen was in danger, so I came to warn you."

"What danger?" The teasing smirk was gone from Lief's face, replaced with an alertness that filled me with relief. Sepian had blown off my concerns about the shadows, and I'd been anxious that the two current kings would as well.

"Svencer saw shadows following Farranen." Okay, it did sound kind of stupid when I put it like that. "He said they reek of foul magic and don't belong in Fairie." Which still wasn't helping to drive home my point about them being dangerous. If I'd had more energy, I would've put my storytelling skills to use and found a way to make them understand that the shadows were bad news. But it was already past my bedtime, and combined with the fact that I'd just created two ghosts, I was dead tired. No pun intended.

Lief rose to his feet in one fluid movement, scanning the clearing around us. "Are they here now?"

I shrugged. "It's possible." I wasn't even sure what to look for. Any number of monsters could be lingering in the darkness of the woods that surrounded us, and we'd never be any wiser. I could call one of my ghostly companions, but I knew most of them were still recharging. And honestly, if the shadows hadn't attacked by now, maybe Svencer had been wrong about them being dangerous. Maybe they'd just seen the new king and been following him out of curiosity.

I jumped when my guardian gently pulled me to my feet and guided me over to where his makeshift bed was waiting. "Dog will take the first watch, while you and I get some much-needed sleep."

Since my body was inclined to agree, I didn't protest when he removed my cloak and used it to cover us. It didn't take long to get comfortable on my side with his warm body spooned up against me. Before I could submit to my exhaustion, Farranen whispered next to my ear, "Of all the fallen stars I've wished upon in my lifetime, none have brought me what my heart most desired until tonight."

He was wrong. I didn't get here on a falling star. I rode here on a dragon.

****

Despite the fact that I had spent the whole night sleeping on the hard frozen ground, I woke feeling well rested. It probably had something to do with the fae that kept me warm all night. And when he'd left to take his turn keeping watch, Dog had draped himself across my feet. Seriously, the guys in my life knew how to spoil me.

It turned out that the cottage we were camped next to was above the vacant dungeon where Farranen had been imprisoned after standing up to the queen. Neither of the men had wanted to spend the night inside, since this was where I'd died just over a month ago. I didn't blame them one bit. As soon as I'd made the connection in my head, I was ready to put some distance between me and the site of my murder.

In my haste to get to my guardian as fast as possible the night before, I'd neglected to consider a few practicalities, such as food and clothing. Making the journey to the Shadow Palace with an empty belly and wrinkled clothes wouldn't kill me, but it sure wouldn't be enjoyable either. Thankfully the men had more than enough provisions to go around—probably due to the fact that Dog was traveling with them.

"What's the plan?" I asked Lief as I accepted a piece

of dried meat from him.

"It should take the better part of the day to reach the new castle."

I froze with the food halfway to my mouth. "But what about the shadows?"

I looked to Farranen, but he casually lifted a shoulder as if to agree with the dark prince's disinterest regarding the hypothetical danger.

"So, what? We're just going to skip home through the enchanted woods like Little Red Riding Hood and pretend we're not being stalked by the Big Bad Wolf?" I shot Dog an apologetic look for the insensitive comparison. "Svencer said the shadows are bad news."

My guardian put down the chunk of bread he'd been holding and took my hand, interlacing our fingers together. "Theodora, I assure you the dark prince and I have no plans to disregard your concerns. If these shadows truly are a threat, it would be unwise to prolong our return home. Given the choice, it would be best to deal with them from the safety of the castle."

I nodded slowly, seeing the wisdom of his reasoning. Whatever the shadows were, it would be harder to deal with them from our exposed position in the middle of nowhere. We were lucky they hadn't tried anything hinky already.

Once we finished eating, the males packed up and were quickly ready to go—and not a moment too soon. I'd already jumped at a few of the darker spots in the woods that turned out to be nothing more than normal shadows.

"Did you figure out who blew up the gate?" I asked Lief as we started walking. When Mary and I had tried to rescue Farranen, we'd snuck through the trees to avoid getting caught. The cobblestone road was much easier to traverse.

"There was no sign of—"

The dark prince had his sword out before I even realized he'd stopped walking. My guardian grabbed my arm, tugging me behind him as a low growl rolled out of Dog's throat.

Fifty yards ahead of us, a figure waited in the middle of the road.

Chapter Seventeen

"Is that—"

"A shadow," Farranen grunted, confusion evident in his voice.

The smoky black thing was vaguely humanish and hovered a few inches off the ground. Until now, I hadn't fully grasped the seriousness of the situation that Svencer had been trying to impart. It was literally *made* of *shadows*. There was no similarly shaped object nearby or a light source that could cast such an obvious configuration.

My guardian took a few steps forward and drew his sword, the sharp metal giving off a low whine as he pulled it free.

Lief's boots scraped against the road as he slowly turned to survey the entirety of the forest surrounding us for threats. "There's another one behind us," he calmly stated.

I spun, and sure enough, another one of those shadow things was blocking the direction we'd just come from.

"Funny, I was expecting a little more of a challenge to hunt down the illustrious new king of the Light Court." A shiver ran down my spine as Gus's voice thundered out of the woods. Hostile bitterness rebounded off the solid trunk of each individual tree in the forest.

I turned to face the fae who had been hiding behind a thick mushroom-covered tree we'd just passed. Magic rolled off the gray knight in a thick oily wave, and my own magic recoiled at the wrongness of it. Gone was the taste of cedar and metal that I'd always associated with the asshole, replaced with something rotting and foul. I should have picked up on the telltale prickling of another fae's magic sooner, but I'd been too focused on listening to Lief's tale of not being able to discover who bombed the hawthorn tree.

Outwardly, Gus hadn't changed. The same gray shirt with gold buttons was immaculate, as were his black pants and boots. The velvety black cloak he wore was open, making me think he must have been waiting a while and had undone it to get comfortable. His long dark hair was uncharacteristically disheveled, but other than that one small change, he looked like he was ready to wine and dine some little old ladies at a high-society event.

"It's a shame," he continued, as though we were discussing nothing more pressing than the weather— weather that he wanted to strangle with his bare hands. "I'd been looking forward to crossing swords with an opponent worthy of my blade. Sadly, your ragtag band of misfits will have to suffice."

A scowl settled into place on my face, as comfortable and familiar as the post-coital glow I woke up wearing most mornings (but not this morning, because that would have been awkward with Lief and Dog there).

"It would appear the rumors are true, and the guardian succeeded in taking the bitch's head."

I kept my glower in place, using it like armor to hide my surprise. I hadn't really thought about it until now, but most of the fae would probably assume that Farranen had risen to power by using the traditional method of assassinating the current monarch. Gus didn't know that my guardian had been handpicked by Fairie herself. Or that I was the one who had done the evil deed.

"What do you want, Gus?" I asked, with as much flippancy as I could muster, while I subtly glanced at the males around me. Lief and Dog hadn't taken their attention from the two shadows that were still blocking the road in both directions. Farranen only had eyes for the fae who had just unsheathed his sword and was prowling closer to where we stood. The sight would have been enough to have me backing up, if not for the three strong males encircling me.

His smile was a hard slippery thing as it snaked across his face. "The crown to the Light Court."

Right. Of course, the evil-smelling bad man wanted to control half the realm. Some days I felt like I was living in a poorly written fantasy novel.

I let out an exaggerated sigh without taking my eyes from the huge male. At some point, he was going to attack, and I wanted to be ready when he did—even if all I could do to help was get out of the way. "We both know your 'mating' to the queen was a sham, and now that she's dead, you have no claim to the throne."

His lips peeled back from his teeth. "I wasted months planning for the day I would take her head and become Fairie's rightful ruler."

What? Gus had been planning to kill the queen? That was…not surprising actually. It was selfish and underhanded, exactly the kind of thing a worm like him would concoct.

And I hadn't missed the way Gus had said, "Fairie's rightful ruler." She had two rulers, and I was betting that Gus' diabolical plan involved getting rid of Lief too.

The anger simmering in my belly reached white-hot

levels that even the newly discovered forges run by the dwarves in the basement of the palace couldn't compete with. Maybe psychogenic atrophy was sexually transmitted, and Gus had picked it up boinking the queen? That would explain why he was so out of touch with reality. His plan to rule both courts had more holes than a pair of fish-net stockings. Even I, a mere human, knew that the realm needed two rulers. I'd seen firsthand what the strain of supporting both had done to Lief in just a matter of weeks.

"*Enough.*" Power radiated in the single word, leaving no question as to who currently wore the crown to the Light Court. "Any attempt you make to annex my sovereignty will end in your death. Surrender now."

Gus came to a halt, no more than fifteen feet away from my guardian. His cocky frown said more than any words could have; surrendering obviously wasn't on his to-do list.

"Why did you blow up the hawthorn tree?" I demanded, hoping to distract Gus from the bloodlust that was gathering in his eyes. It would take nothing short of a miracle to make it out of here without spilling any blood, but I was determined to try.

He laughed. The asshat actually laughed, like the destruction of the magical gate was comical rather than tragic. "A mistake on my part. I set the jars of chemicals in the doorway, but the trip-line snagged and set off the explosion prematurely before the guardian crossed back to Earth."

My magic snapped angrily, trapped within the confines of my body but wanting to lash out at the fae in front of me.

"How did you get back to Fairie without the gate working?" I asked, even though I knew there were other gates. I wanted to see how long I could keep him talking. Because talking was preferable to finding out what his shadows were capable of.

"I used another gate and made sure the dark prince wouldn't be able to track me here." He leered at my shocked look. "Yes, I know exactly how attached the heartless dark prince has become to the human female with fae magic. The whole realm knows. And that misguided affection will be his downfall." His hard eyes shot to my left where Lief stood, fully aware that the dark prince could hear every word.

Not happening, I silently promised. And why the hell had he called Lief heartless? The dark prince was a freakin' teddy bear.

Before either of the men could offer a retort, Gus lunged toward Farranen and screamed, *"Now!"*

The harsh clang of swords clashing filled the air, and I stumbled backward so I wouldn't get caught in the path of the deadly blades. I kept backing up until I was off the cobblestone road with my back firmly pressed against the bark of a thick tree.

The fighting was intense and far too fast for my eyes to keep up with. Farranen and Gus were locked in a dance, seemingly oblivious to anything else going on around them. A slash of blood on Gus's bicep and a ragged tear on the thigh of his pants proved that my fae had already gotten in a few hits. The fallen gray knight continued to throw taunts at his opponent, but Farranen, with his emotionless mask back in place, just ignored them.

I didn't know much about sword fighting; was Farranen toying with him? I couldn't tell. When I'd seen them fight in the basement of the dungeon, Gus had easily bested my fae because he'd been wounded with only a hunting knife to defend himself. Now that they were on even ground, so to speak, shouldn't Farranen have the upper hand?

While the majority of my attention had been on monitoring the man attempting (and failing) to assassinate my guardian, I was still able to keep an eye on the shadows that were tormenting Dog and Lief. The weird shadow things were incorporeal most of the time, like when the dark prince slashed through them with his sword, but sometimes they were able to take on a physicality that let them strike at their adversaries. They didn't seem to cause any permanent damage, but after a minute or two I realized they were gradually herding Lief and Dog away from the rest of us.

Before I could call out a warning, Farranen's blade carved a path across Gus's chest, splitting the fabric of his shirt and the skin beneath. The gray knight's furious roar was cut off when my guardian did a neat spinning kick that knocked Gus on his butt. A fat drop of blood fell from the tip of the blade when Farranen leveled it with Gus's throat.

From his prone position, Gus shouted, "*Take her!*" and icy cold hands clamped down on both my arms. I cringed and flailed my limbs to break free. Twisting around, I found two shadows holding onto me. Like the others, they were the same size and shape as real people, but their black bodies were semi-transparent, and I could see the wall of trees through them. It was like they were made from a cloud of diesel exhaust that seemed to float a few inches above the ground.

I shrieked, a shrill mixture of desperation, outrage, and fear, and the sound rose above the scuffle the others were locked in. Three sets of eyes flew to where I was being held.

Farranen let out an exclamation of furious denial, and his sword that had been swinging toward Gus, stilled. Lief must have recognized this new vulnerability for what it was and tried to push his way past the shadow he'd been wrestling with.

"Nobody moves, or she dies," Gus bellowed, effectively freezing all three of my friends in their steps.

I fought harder to wrench myself from the solid grip of the shadows. The longer they hung on, the colder the skin on my arms grew. What the hell were these weird creatures? If I didn't know better, I would have said they were ghosts, based on their insubstantial appearance. They felt like fae but in a really horrible, warped way. The steady rhythm of their magic continued to brush up against my own, making me feel sick to my stomach.

Gus got to his feet with none of the cocky confidence from a minute ago. I was glad to see he'd been knocked down a peg or two. His left hand probed at the wound on his chest, staining his fingers with blood.

"Drop your weapons," he ordered, while taking a few cowardly steps back.

My eyes locked onto Farranen's, silently pleading with him not to comply. The *thud* of his sword hitting the ground was unmistakable, followed a few seconds later by Lief's. His jaw clenched, as if he was holding back words.

"Should any harm befall her, my lack of weapon will matter not. Once I've destroyed every single thing you've ever loved, I will take your life with my bare hands." Softly spoken, without any emotion or infliction, my guardian's declaration was rife with possession and promise.

The rapidly beating lump of muscle in my chest warmed, helping me to forget about the pain from the shadows' icy grip.

Gus's face blanched, making his pale skin even more noticeable next to the bright splash of blood soaking his ragged shirt. Still, I had to grudgingly acknowledge his bravery—or maybe it was stupidity—when he raised his sword and pointed it at the king of the Light Court.

"I can run you through right fucking now, and you won't move a muscle because if you do, my minions will tear her apart faster than either of them—" He gestured to where Lief and Dog were silently seething. "—can get to her."

"Then it would seem that we're at an impasse," Lief called. "Because the second any harm comes to Theo or her companion, the shifter will rip you apart." He smirked, in true dark prince fashion. "Have you ever seen how fast a shifter can hunt down his prey? I've never had the pleasure of seeing Dog in action. I wonder if he'll go for your throat? Or perhaps he's in the mood for evisceration."

My stomach rolled at the crude visual Lief's congenial words inspired.

But it was true; while the men had been forced to give up their weapons, Dog hadn't relinquished his teeth or claws. Dog *was* the weapon.

Gus's dark gaze bounced back and forth, like he couldn't quite figure out how he'd lost the upper hand. I wanted to give him a cocky grin, but that seemed a little premature since I was still caught in the shadows' freezing grip. If they truly had the power to tear me apart as Gus claimed, there was no point in antagonizing their master.

The severity of the situation must've finally gotten through his fat head, because the false bravado drained out of him faster than the blood dripping from his wounds. With one last angry scowl, Gus tucked tail and retreated into the forest on the other side of the road. I was slightly disappointed that he didn't even try to get the last word by dropping a corny line with a stereotypical vow foreshadowing future retaliation.

A low growl emanated from Dog's chest as he tracked Gus's movements with narrowed eyes. Next to me, the shadows remained motionless, and nobody else dared to move. Was he just going to leave them here with us? Were we free to go? This was the most confusing hostage situation I'd ever been in.

"To me!" The distant call of Gus's voice came from the woods, and immediately I was released. The four inky shadows darted across the road and into the trees in the same direction their leader had taken.

"Well, that was intense." I rubbed my arms. A chill lingered where I'd been held, despite the thick cloak I'd been wearing. The flawed ghosts I'd created were chilly to the touch, but these suckers were hypothermic on a glacial level.

Farranen moved faster than humanly possible, seizing me in an embrace that was wild and desperate and exactly what I needed. "Did they hurt you—"

"I'm fine." My hands were shaking as they explored his body. There wasn't a hair out of place, but I couldn't stop touching him to reassure myself he was uninjured.

"What were those *things*?" Lief mused as he sauntered over, also bearing no outward ill-effects from his scuffle. With his disheveled hair and black cloak billowing in the breeze, he looked like the cover model for a gothic romance novel that any single woman would be happy to co-star in. And probably a few married ones too.

"Wraiths," I told both males, figuring it would be easier if they had a name. "And did you feel the magic coming off Gus? Something was wrong with it. It's like it was infected or tainted—"

A shrill *twang!* echoed through the air, and Lief lunged toward Farranen and I, knocking us over. He grunted and fell to his knees on the road next to us. I detangled myself from the man holding onto me and gasped at the arrow sticking out of the dark prince's shoulder.

Chapter Eighteen

"Lief!" Panicked disbelief washed over me in a wave, and I crawled closer.

"It's not that bad," Lief told me when he caught my stricken gaze, but the thin sheen of sweat coating his sallow skin begged to differ.

I wanted to help, but I knew it would be a bad idea with the way his right arm hung uselessly at his side. The metal shaft was embedded in his shoulder with the sharp end sticking out six inches in front of him. A small smear of bright red blood coated the tip.

Dog's enraged howl cut through my shocked silence. It was a pledge of pain and suffering to be doled out, offered on the dark prince's behalf. Muscles rippled beneath his fur, and he tensed to launch himself in pursuit of the bastard who had tried to take us out from what he must have considered a safe distance—which was an epic mistake. There was no safe distance when it came to evading Dog's keen senses.

"No! The coward has already retreated farther into the woods." The order was every bit as entitled as a king's command should be, and my shifter heeded it without hesitation.

Dog's ears twitched as he confirmed the truth of the statement.

"The bolt was meant for the new king," Lief murmured wearily as he knelt with his eyes shut.

I scooted closer and gently took his good hand in

mine. When my magic ventured up his arm, the power from his key stirred and reached for him. Any other time, I probably would have found it odd how it had a mind of its own, but right now I was just thankful that it seemed to know that it was needed.

"The bolt is iron," he calmly pointed out, probably for my sake since everyone else seemed aware of the fact.

"What do we do?" My gaze bounced between the two fae. While I doubted the wound would kill an immortal, it sure couldn't be comfortable.

"We need to remove it." Wrapping strong arms around the dark prince from behind, Farranen effectively caught him in a bear hug that would have been adorable if not for the torment twisting Lief's face into a grimace.

"We need to get the iron out." Green eyes, filled with acceptance, were grim when they met mine. "I should be able to hold him while you pull it out."

"What? Me?" What if I ended up hurting him more? I looked to Dog, hoping he'd jump up and volunteer to be the one to pull the bolt out, but he was pacing along the edge of the woods that Gus had disappeared into. If the wraiths returned, they wouldn't get past him unnoticed.

"While I can handle small amounts of enchanted iron, the bolt is raw iron, and there will be rather unpleasant consequences if I hold it directly." I wondered if he was referring to the iron handcuffs he carried around for when there were unsanctioned crossings at the gate. He'd never had a problem with them.

Another tremor went through Lief, and his molars ground together as a small groan tried to escape his lips. With one last squeeze, I pried my hand out of his and pushed my hair back from my face.

"Okay." I took a deep breath. "What do I do?"

"Pull the shaft straight out," my guardian advised.

I nodded, even though nobody was looking at me.

I could do this. Lief needed me to do this. Dog gave me an encouraging whine from across the road, which I appreciated.

Wrapping my hand around the metal shaft, I leaned across Lief's bulk, trying to figure out how to yank the thing straight through without causing any more damage. After trying a few different positions, none of which gave me enough leverage, I muttered a curse. As carefully as I could manage, I swung my leg over Lief's outstretched legs until I was straddling him.

"If I knew this was all it would take to get you—"

"Shut up," I told the man that was trapped between my legs. The injured jerk.

I planted one hand in the center of his chest and ignored the doubts beating at the back of my brain. At first the shaft resisted, like it was perfectly happy in the new home it had made for itself in Lief's shoulder. *Screw that.* I pulled harder, relieved when the metal slid out another inch. Lief let out some agonized sounds that had guilt pooling in the back of my throat. My lips formed an apology that was lost under the harsh sound of his labored breathing. Taut muscles in his neck and forearms quivered as Farranen continued to hold him immobile.

With a disgusting sucking sound, the bolt slid free, and I barely caught myself before I toppled over backward.

A thin trickle of blood ran down Lief's chest, before disappearing into the black fabric of his damaged shirt. After several deep breaths, he opened his eyes. The pale blue was filled with strained gratitude, holding me in place for a few seconds before they slid shut and his head lolled to the side.

****

It was near dusk when we finally made it back to the Shadow Palace.

Lief had denied Farranen's offer to carry him, so we were forced to maintain a pace that a geriatric amputee would have been able to beat. Dog and I kept a wary eye out in case Gus made a second attempt to eliminate either of the rulers of Fairie, but our journey was uneventful.

I already knew from the previous day's exploration that Eddesta, one of Fairie's most talented healers, had found her way to the castle and her healing chambers were set up on the main level of the castle.

Once Eddy was satisfied that Lief was resting comfortably, she waddled out of the room, leaving Farranen and I alone with the sleeping prince. Dog was AWOL, probably off investigating the massive building and marking his new temporary territory.

"Will he be okay?" I quietly demanded from where I sat next to the bed. Lief was able to draw from the key's power without any physical contact, but I wanted him to know he wasn't alone, so I kept his hand in mine.

Inside my chest, the key to the Dark Court was no longer as dormant as it had previously been. I suspected it was because Lief was drawing from its power. The warm tingle was a pleasant distraction from the thought of Gus and his wraiths.

Farranen had taken up a position along the wall, standing with his feet slightly apart and hands loosely by his sides, like he was ready to intercept anyone that came through the door. An ugly streak of Lief's dried blood marred the perfect white of his shirt, reminding me that even immortal beings could be hurt.

"Yes, it will take more than an iron arrow to kill the dark prince." The rhythmic *tic, tic, tic* of his jaw let me know just how he felt about someone shooting iron arrows at the people he cared about—even though he'd been the likely target.

"How was he able to use an iron arrow?" As soon as I voiced the question, a memory from the night I killed Safeena resurfaced. *My lover had a special pair of gloves made so that he might wield it in the human realm...* At the time, she'd been talking about using a gun I'd discovered tucked in with her unmentionables. Was it possible he still had the gloves? He hadn't been wearing them when he'd ambushed us on the road, but I hadn't exactly frisked him. Then again, he hadn't had the crossbow or arrows with him either.

"I don't know." Frustration laced his words, the angry kind that usually made a person foolish.

"Damn it, I just remembered Gus had a special pair of gloves made so he could hold a gun. He must still have them," I tiredly explained.

"And the iron arrows?" he pondered.

"They wouldn't be hard to get from any sporting goods store," I speculated. We already knew he'd spent some time on Earth, so it wouldn't be too farfetched to assume he'd brought back some goodies that weren't available in Fairie. He'd probably stashed them in the woods before ambushing us, since I'd have known if he'd tried to hide them with glamour.

"What about the wraiths? Where did they come from?" he continued, echoing my own thoughts.

They sure as heck hadn't come from any sporting goods store. A cold lump of ice settled in my chest, making each beat of my heart painful. The creatures had felt fae to my magic, but in the most twisted, warped sense of the word. I told my guardian as much, and his eyebrows slanted down as he contemplated my words.

"It is possible that they resonate as fae because they were created by one of us." He didn't sound entirely convinced, and neither was I. But without any other brilliant conjecture regarding their origins, the subject was dropped, and only the sound of Lief's steady breathing filled the room.

How in the hell had Gus eluded Dog and Lief? He must have one heck of a hidey hole. And what would have happened if he'd somehow succeeded in killing Farranen? Fairie was finally beginning to heal, but after centuries of steadily declining, it would probably take just as long to restore her to her former glory. In her current weakened state, I doubted the realm would survive whatever devious plans Gus had.

A knock on the door echoed throughout the large room, startling a gasp out of me. The familiar buzz of fae magic resonated from the hallway, without any of the oily wrongness that had accompanied Gus and his shadows.

Before Eddy had left, Farranen had covered Lief in a layer of glamour that rendered him invisible to most—meaning that anyone who knew he was in the bed would be able to see him. Those who were unaware that he'd been injured and was recuperating in Eddy's room, would only see an empty bed. It was incredibly brainy, and not something I could have come up with. Since Eddy, Dog, and I were the only other ones that knew where Lief was, we were the only ones that could see him. If anyone with nefarious inclinations came looking for him, they'd be sorely disappointed.

I stood, putting myself between Lief and the door—just in case.

"Enter," Farranen called out, filling the single word with as much haughtiness as Lief would have used. I'd be lying if I said that his new position of power didn't look good on him.

The T'Holly brothers entered, and for once they weren't sporting the jolly smiles that I'd come to expect. The seriousness of our situation suddenly hit me. This was bigger than Lief getting injured. This was an attack on the leader of their court. It was no wonder they looked like they were gearing up for a fight.

"My lord." They both executed a bow in perfect synchronization with their blue cloaks sweeping across the stone floor. When they stood, I caught the glint of metal at their hips. I'd never known the eccentric brothers to carry a sword. I'd always assumed that the role they played was in more of an information gathering and spying capacity, rather than actual combat.

Daph spared a single glance to where Lief lay, before focusing on my guardian, giving no indication that he'd seen anything other than an empty bed. "The castle is secure, and its residents have been alerted to the danger."

"Good. And a census of those now living under its roof?"

"Two hundred and eighty-six. Would you like a break down of the types of fae and which courts they belong to?"

"That won't be necessary."

Two hundred and eighty-six fae were living in the Shadow Palace? This place must be bigger than I'd thought. Responsibility settled heavily across my shoulders; how were we supposed to keep almost three hundred fae safe while Gus was running around and shooting at us with iron arrows? It was too bad the Army of Light had jumped ship and thrown their lot in with Gus.

"Hey!" I exclaimed. "What about the queen's—I mean, Farranen's army? Isn't it their job to protect the new king and his castle?"

Across the room, one of the logs in the hearth popped, filling the air with a tiny shower of sparks.

Three sets of eyebrows furrowed as the men contemplated my words. Farranen was the first to speak.

"It's likely that word of my ascension has reached them by now." He slowly nodded. "At the very least, they should have sent an emissary to confirm or deny my claim."

"So where are they?" I demanded, taking a few steps closer to the men. "They weren't with Gus, so maybe they bailed on him." Or maybe Gus had ditched them? If they'd returned to the Light Castle, only to discover it was gone, where would they have gone? But hundreds of other fae had found the new Shadow Palace, so why hadn't they? Gah, so many questions with not nearly enough answers was making me cranky.

The muscles in Farranen's jaw hardened. "They've either become traitors to their court or have fallen victim to those who would seek to weaken me."

Neither of those options sounded good to me. Maybe they'd just hopped a plane to Hawaii and were taking a vacation? Yeah, even I wasn't naïve enough to believe that. The few fae that I knew who had once been a part of the Army of Light had been hard-core soldiers who wouldn't desert their realm in the midst of so much uncertainty.

"I'll leave within the hour." My guardian turned his hard green eyes on the T'Holly brothers. "You two will oversee the castle defenses in my absence."

"My lord, the honor would be…" The brothers' rambling faded to background noise as Farranen's words replayed in my mind, smacking me upside the head with their meaning. He was planning a solo rescue mission to find the Army of Light—which was the absolute stupidest thing I'd ever heard him say.

I opened my mouth, effectively cutting off Daph's gushing acceptance of playing boss while Farranen was gone.

"*No*. There's no chance in hell you're going out there by yourself!" I took six more steps, getting right up in Farranen's face so he'd be forced to see all the fear and determination in mine.

His eyes narrowed, never leaving me, even when he addressed the two males that were watching us with rapt expressions. "Find Dog. I'll meet you in the foyer in thirty minutes."

Their over-polished boots didn't make a single sound on the stone floors as they beat a hasty retreat through the door.

Chapter Nineteen

I planted my hands on my hips, while mentally strapping on every single piece of emotional armor that I owned.

"Theo—"

"*No.*"

"I must—"

"*No.*"

He sighed. "I know—"

"*No.*"

He sighed again, and this time the weary sound was accompanied by a half smile that I didn't trust one bit. When he pulled my rigid body into an embrace, I wanted to push him away, but if he really was about to embark on a mission that was likely to end in his death, then I was going to spend every last second we had together with my arms around him.

"This isn't the first time I've forgotten how tenaciously loyal you can be," he murmured against the top of my head.

"Then stop doing stupid things that are likely to get you killed, and I won't have to keep reminding you," I grumbled.

He exhaled, and I felt his exasperation in every fiber of my being. "The soldiers in the Army of Light are a part of my court, and until I know differently, they are my responsibility."

"Can't you send someone else?" Good leaders

delegated, right?

"Who would I send? The only fae in my court with any experience are missing."

"What about the Dark Court?" I pulled back so that I could look up at his face. "What about those who supported Lief when he was working to overthrow Safeena?"

I'd met a few of the dark fae in Lief's temporary war camp last month when I'd been forced to pose as his consort. It was a memory that I'd been trying to forget until now, since it involved me spending most of my time dressed like a hussy.

"Yes…" Speculation filled his eyes, brightening them and filling me with hope. "There were many in the Dark Court who were instrumental to the success of the rebellion, whose allegiance transcended the court they were born unto, and fought to do what was needed for the realm as a whole."

I held on a little tighter to the soft white fabric of Farranen's shirt, as relief made my knees weak. If he took some of Lief's supporters with him, he'd be infinitely safer—or maybe he wouldn't have to go at all.

"But the dark prince has already stationed those with battle experience in the Fallow Woods next to the dead lands."

My mouth fell open. *Seriously?* He couldn't have started with that unpleasant little fact? "Why? Fairie is finally on the mend, so why are the dead lands still a threat?"

"They're not. The attack on the weeden fae was shocking and unacceptable. The dark prince felt it was necessary to protect the helpless members of his court by sending his strongest warriors to defend them until he's certain the danger has passed."

Dang, I'd almost forgotten about the attack on the weeden fae. My gaze shot to where Lief was sleeping across the room, and my stomach flipped at the sight. What would Fairie do without him looking out for all the weaker fae?

"Theodora."

The husky tenor of his voice dragged me out of my melancholy thoughts, and I forced my eyes to meet his.

"I must go."

I wanted to yell and scream and cling to him like a toddler with separation anxiety, but I just nodded. "How many are in the Army of Light?" I asked softly. I had no idea how long he'd spent working alongside the soldiers in the queen's army before becoming the guardian of the gate, but I had to assume he knew most of them. If they were in trouble, and there was even a small chance he could bring them home, I couldn't blame him for trying. I'd have done the same thing if I was in his shoes.

"There were seventy-five, but some were lost due to skirmishes during the uprising. I'd estimate sixty-five remain."

Ten of the Light Court had died during the movement to dethrone the queen? I wondered if he was counting Harvey. Losing so many immortal beings was shocking. Still, an army of sixty-five soldiers when there were twelve hundred fae in the Light Court, seemed like a pretty small number. I hadn't realized that there were so many normal citizens here without any combat training. With the company I was keeping these days, it was no wonder I'd assumed that all fae were sword-wielding veterans.

I lifted myself onto my tippy toes, stretching as high as my body would allow, and Farranen leaned down to meet me halfway. Our lips met, and I infused the kiss with as much affection and trust as I could. He was the king of the Light Court and didn't need my permission to embark on this super-risky mission, but I wanted him to know that, despite my fears, I supported him all the way.

Inside my chest, the little lump of magic that represented his key uncurled toward its true owner, and I nudged it with my own magic. It wouldn't do him any good if it stayed with me.

One of us finally ended the kiss—probably him, since I was content to remain canoodling for the foreseeable future—and the expression on his face warmed me all the way down to my toes. Affection, fierce and possessive, radiated from the harsh set of his jaw, while his eyes roamed across my face like he was trying to memorize every part of me. All traces of the stoic unfeeling warrior he'd been when we met were gone, replaced with raw passion and determination.

Was his determination in regards to finding his missing buddies? Or, possibly, was it because he was intent on returning home so we could continue exploring whatever was growing between us? We hadn't discussed what would happen once Gus and his wraiths were dealt with, but I hadn't forgotten that he'd used the L-word. Did that mean that we'd go on courting indefinitely, until I aged to the point where he no longer wanted me?

I stepped back, letting my own impassive mask fall into place. "You have the key?" I asked, just to derail my thoughts from the cycle of relationship insecurities that my brain was caught in.

"Yes," he affirmed, pulling the chain from beneath his shirt to show me the small white key.

I ignored the flash of compassion that brightened his eyes.

"I'll take care of Lief while you're gone," I stated, looking over my shoulder to where the dark prince slept. We both knew there wasn't anything I could do to aid in Lief's recovery. If someone saw through the glamour hiding him, I would be less than useless in protecting him. It was painfully obvious that I was changing the subject, but thankfully my guardian didn't call me out on it.

****

I didn't go down to the foyer to see Farranen and Dog off.

It was cowardly. And shameful. But the prospect of saying goodbye felt like I would be putting one more nail in the proverbial coffin, and I refused to consider the fact that they might not survive whatever was waiting for them outside the palace walls. Because living without my guardian or shifter wasn't possible. They would complete their risky mission and then come back to me. I couldn't live with any other outcome.

My eyelids felt like they were made of sandpaper. I was exhausted, but I didn't return to the room I'd been sharing with Farranen.

Even though it was well past my bedtime, I wasn't comfortable with leaving Lief by himself. Eddy had already retired for the night, with promises to check on him first thing in the morning.

Stuffing a few pillows between my back and the uncomfortable chair, I wiggled around until I found a semi-comfortable position where I could prop my feet up on the bed while still holding Lief's hand.

The silence of the castle settled around us, and I wished I'd brought a book so I could read out loud to the comatose prince. I had a number of passages memorized from my own writing, but there's no way I was about to recite any of the steamier scenes conjured from my imagination to the biggest playboy in Fairie.

****

Magic tingled throughout my body, no longer dormant. The intensity of it stole my breath, and then it lunged toward Lief like a zombie pouncing on a big juicy brain.

I opened my eyes and was shocked to find I was no longer in Eddy's healing room. The wall of cabinets that held the meticulously organized medical supplies were gone. The small tea cart was no longer parked in the corner of the room—and the room itself was also missing.

"The *fuck?*" I sat straight up, ditching the last vestiges of sleep that had been clinging to me.

Walls made from irregular-sized rocks were held together with a mortar of dried mud. A crude fireplace dominated the wall in front of me, the hot coals hidden beneath the ash providing the only illumination in the dark room.

My feet slid off the bed, sending up a puff of dust as they landed on the hard-packed dirt floor. The ruffled white bedding looked absurd in such a dingy setting, and my gaze bounced around wildly as I tried to figure out where the hell I was.

"Theo?" Lief's hoarse voice sounded as confused as I felt, but the sudden realization that I wasn't alone filled me with relief.

The dark prince struggled to sit up and when I met his gaze in the near-darkness, I let out a strangled shriek. His pale blue irises were completely black. When his left eyebrow rose inquisitively, I whispered, "Your eyes are doing that freaky all-black thing again."

"Again?"

"Yeah, like when I got yanked into your vision of me in the glade." I sucked in a breath at what I'd just said. Holy crap, Lief was having another vision, and since I'd been holding his hand, I'd been unintentionally invited along for the ride.

He must have come to the same conclusion, because his fingers tightened around mine. The last time, he'd warned me we had to maintain physical contact so I wouldn't get lost in the vision. Since I had no desire to wander through this weird place for the rest of my life, I tightened my grip too.

Now that I knew the super-spooky setting wasn't real, some of my fear turned to curiosity.

"Where are we?" I whispered, hesitant to disturb the heavy silence.

"Let's find out, shall we?" Lief scooted out from under the covers, and I averted my gaze when I realized he was naked from the waist up—but not before I caught the way the stark white bandage on his shoulder stood out against his tanned skin. He moved with all his former grace and fluidity, so I had to assume his injury wasn't a problem here.

I stood, and as soon as Lief joined me, the bed behind him disappeared. A quick glance behind me confirmed that the high-backed chair was gone as well. "Neat trick," I commented.

Without the extra furniture taking up the majority of the room, I was able to see that the only items remaining were a small cot and a crudely made table and chair. A single pot rested on the scarred table, and whatever substance filled the bottom of it had congealed into something that resembled moldy gravy. I didn't risk giving it a sniff test. Some things are better left to the imagination.

A sudden scream cut through the silence, causing me to jump, and Lief pulled me behind his body without letting go of my hand. Which totally dispelled my theory that nothing could hurt us here. Or maybe it was just an intuitive reaction for him.

Without any windows, the only way to find out what was happening outside was to open the door. Was it even tangible? I had no idea what the rules for interacting with a vision were.

Another blood-curdling scream ripped through the air, and goose bumps broke out all over my body. It sounded like someone was torturing a stray cat.

"Whatever the vision is trying to show us is happening out there." Lief nodded toward the door, and I got the impression he was leaving it up to me whether we lingered in the rickety old hut or went outside.

"Then let's check it out." I didn't bother trying to hide my apprehension. Lief was having a vision for a reason, and I wasn't going to be the one to hold him back from learning whatever he needed to, just because I was a weenie.

Before I could chicken out, I stepped in front of Lief and tugged him toward the door. When I reached for the round doorknob, it slid right through my hand.

Lief chuckled, and I shot him a dirty look. The jerk.

Before I could comment, he walked through the door, which didn't freak me out nearly as much as I expected. I must be getting acclimatized from all the time I'd spent around Vanessa and Harvey. Taking a deep breath, I followed.

The second I passed through the door; I regretted my decision to leave the tiny hut.

There were bodies everywhere. Not the walking, talking kind—the dead kind.

Corpses in various states of decomposition were strewn around the forest like someone had hired the devil himself as a landscaper.

I clapped my free hand over my face as the overwhelming stench of death crawled up my nose.

Lief let out a string of profanities that I never would have thought to combine and pulled me toward the closest pile. I really, *really* didn't want to get any closer, but Lief was being shown this macabre scene for a reason.

My restless magic hummed within the confines of my skin, recognizing the shroud of death surrounding us and wanting to reach for it. I put every single ounce of self-control I had into keeping it firmly locked away. Strangely enough, I hadn't felt anything from his key since I'd arrived in the vision.

Lief knelt, fixated on one particular face. Sightless eyes stared back at him, unfocused and milky. Bloated skin, an ugly mottled blue, was undamaged with one glaring exception: a gaping hole in the left side of his chest. His shirt was covered in so much blood I never would have known it used to be pale gray if I hadn't recognized the style of the garment as belonging to the traditional uniform of the Army of Light. A single gold button had somehow escaped all the gore and remained just as shiny as the day it had been sewn on.

"Wervern," Lief murmured softly. "His name was Wervern. He hailed from the Light Court."

Before I could push some sort of response past my numb lips, Lief stood and tugged me toward another body. "Banshaa of the Light Court." Names fell from his mouth, as fast as he could identify the poor fae that had met their end. Some were beyond recognition and unnameable. The one thing they had in common: they all hailed from the Light Court and wore the uniform of the Army of Light.

Another shriek, weaker than before, sliced through the ominous air. Lief and I exchanged a troubled look before following the direction the sound had come from.

Most of the bodies we came across were lying abandoned on the ground, but a few were strung up against the large, twisted trees. I was no expert, but the chains holding their wrists in place looked like iron—the raw, unenchanted kind.

All the hairs on the back of my neck stood straight up.

"Do you hear that?" Lief cocked his head in the direction we were already facing. "It sounds like chanting."

I didn't hear anything, probably because of my pathetic human ears, but I trusted whatever his senses were telling him.

We continued past a few more bodies that weren't as ripe as the previous ones. I hadn't been counting, but I'd estimate there were at least forty dead fae here—wherever here was.

Above us, the sky was black, but I didn't think it had anything to do with what time of day it was. It almost felt like we were in a massive underground cave, but that wasn't possible since we were surrounded by trees and brush. Granted, they were all dead; but at some point, they had to have had access to sunshine and water to grow to such large proportions. No, it wasn't a ceiling of rock that blocked out the sky and smothered any signs of life on the ground. So, what was it?

"The magic that lingers in the air…" Lief murmured as we crept along, taking care not to step on any of the bodies. "It's familiar."

"And wrong," I added, still appalled by the dark oily power staining the air around us.

"Yes, but I know I've felt it before. It covers everything like a film, yet the land itself is void of magic." He stopped to peer down at the body of another fae, his face a jumble of grief and regret.

"Gus and his wraiths have the same oily feel to their magic." The ugly blend of fetid perverted magic left me feeling nauseous just from coming into contact with it.

Lief made a noncommittal noise in the back of his throat, as we made our way around another large tree. I stepped carefully, unsure if the aboveground roots were solid like the ground or intangible like the door to the hut had been.

Ahead, another body chained to a tree came into view. And judging by the sporadic twitching that it was doing, the fae was still alive. A shriek wheezed out of him, so much weaker than the first few screams that had led us here.

The back of my throat burned with unshed tears. My ankou magic recognized the tang of death that clung to the male, digging its claws in deeper with each shallow breath that stuttered from his struggling lungs. What could possibly kill an immortal being?

The poor fae had his back to us, so it was impossible to get a glimpse of his face. Long dark-blond hair hung down his back, obscuring most of his dirty gray uniform. I couldn't see any apparent injuries, but that didn't mean that they weren't there.

Lief pulled me through the trees, circling around to the left until the injured male's tormentor was revealed. A snarl worked its way out of my chest.

Gus.

Finding out he was behind the heinous scene wasn't

really a shock, but the force of my anger as it ignited in my chest was startling. I'd never been a violent person, but right at that particular moment in time, I wanted to rip Gus's head off and punt it as far as it could go. My hands were literally shaking with the need to put an end to the threat that he represented. He'd hurt Lief and killed all the soldiers that were strewn around the forest like trash, and in my book, those crimes alone had earned him more than a slap on the wrist.

My eyes shot to Lief, and judging by the harsh lines bracketing his black eyes, he was harboring some pretty violent fantasies of his own.

Completely ignoring me and the dark prince, Gus continued to chant. Which was expected since this was a vision.

"What's he doing?" I don't know why I was still whispering; it wasn't like Gus could hear me.

Before Lief could answer, the chanting reached a crescendo, and Gus plunged his hands into the chest of the dangling fae. I uttered a scream of denial as the gray knight lifted his hands, clasping a dark lump of flesh. Ribbons of blood ran down his arms, splattering the already wet ground, adding to the gore I'd naïvely thought was mud.

The hard muscles of Gus's jaw unclenched, and he opened his mouth to reveal sharp, pointed teeth that would have looked more at home in the mouth of a piranha than a fae. Then he ceremoniously lifted his bloody prize toward his—

Lief spun me away from the gruesome sight, pulling me flush against his chest and holding me in place with his free arm. "Don't look, Theo." For once I didn't mind Lief using his I'm-a-bossy-jerk voice to order me around. I gladly squeezed my eyes shut, but it didn't do anything to shut out the wet squelching sound of flesh being torn. And then—*oh God,* then came the audible crunching that could only be chewing.

The dark prince's grip tightened, and he muttered something unintelligible next to my ear, drowning out the repulsive sounds that surrounded us. I took a deep breath, and the scent of freshly fallen snow calmed a few of the agitated butterflies that had taken up residence in my belly.

Chapter Twenty

"Damn it, Theo! Wake the *fuck* up!"

I jolted upright in the uncomfortable high-backed chair. My heart galloped in my chest like I'd been sprinting for the last three days straight, and adrenaline left a metallic taste in my mouth. Sudden brightness assaulted my eyes, and I squinted while holding up a hand to shield my face.

"Damn it, Theo! What the fuck is *wrong* with you?" Under Vanessa's snide anger, I could hear a thin layer of apprehension. Had she been worried about me?

Blinking rapidly until the pretty brunette standing over me came into focus, I took a deep breath to calm my racing heart. "What happened?"

Hazel eyes narrowed as she leaned in even closer. "Harvey and I could feel your distress. You were terrified, and when we showed up to save your butt, you were just lying here *sleeping*." She spat the last word out like the penalty for anyone caught napping should be the electric chair.

I looked over at the bed, where my hand was still clutching Lief's. His skin was pale, his breathing slow and even, but he didn't seem any worse for wear from what we'd just witnessed.

Unease from the vision we'd just shared was still coursing through my blood, and I unwound my fingers from his. If there was even the slightest chance that he was going to have another vision, I didn't want to risk getting dragged along for the ride.

"Lief had a vision and I got sucked in," I told Vanessa, then looked past her to where Harvey was scanning the room, his indigo eyebrows furrowed.

"Oh! Sorry, Lief is right here." I pointed at the bed and tried not to snicker when Vanessa and Harvey jumped in tandem. It must have looked like Lief appeared out of nowhere.

"Anyway, in the vision, Gus was killing soldiers from the Light Court."

"Could you tell where they were?" Thank goodness for Harvey's practical nature. He was taking Lief's sudden appearance in stride, unlike Vanessa, who was still gawking.

"Some kind of spooky forest, but it was really dark." I stood and stretched some of the kinks from my body with a wince. The high-backed chair really wasn't meant for sleeping in.

"It's the middle of the night, Theo. *Of course* it's dark out," Vanessa pointed out with a level of sass that I'd never be able to achieve. Apparently, she'd gotten over her astonishment.

"The dark prince's visions aren't concurrent." Harvey crossed his arms and leaned back against the stone wall. "From what I've heard, his gift provides insight on prospective events to come."

"In English, Harvey." Vanessa twirled a long piece of hair around her finger, looking pissed off and bored at the same time.

"I think Harvey's trying to say that Lief's vision was of the future, so the time of the day the vision occurred in doesn't matter."

Harvey confirmed my interpretation with a brief nod.

"Hey!" I exclaimed, suddenly catching onto the implications of what he'd said. "That means he hasn't killed all those fae yet!" Although, it was probably safe to assume that some of the murders had already taken place based on the degree of decomposition to a number of the bodies. Still, it might not be too late to save a few of Gus's victims.

The brief prickle of fae magic announced that we were about to have a visitor right before the door opened. Harvey immediately straightened and reached for his left hip, presumably for the sword that he used to carry. I quickly grabbed Lief's sword from the corner and put myself between the bed and our new visitor—which turned out to be a useless gesture since it was just Eddy.

"Hey, Eddy." I greeted her with a curious smile, since I'd been under the impression that she'd retired for the night and wouldn't check on Lief until morning. The lemon-colored nightdress and matching sleeping cap she wore suggested that she wasn't finished getting some much-needed shut-eye.

"My lady." She dropped into a surprisingly coordinated curtesy. "I'm afraid the Shadow Palace has new residents who are in need of my services."

I smiled at her use of the castle's new name—until the rest of her words sank in. *New residents?* Very cool. I wondered who had moved in.

Eddy stepped aside, and a dozen pixies filed into the room.

Only twelve inches tall, the small fae had pale, nearly translucent skin that sharply contrasted their brightly colored hair and eyes. Even though they normally resided in the grassy fields near the Fallow Woods, they dressed like they were planning to spend a night out at a high-class dance club. As a single unit, they came to a halt in front of me and bent at the waist, bowing low enough to give me a good view of the iridescent wings on their backs.

I let out a little squeak of surprise. That was super weird. The first time I'd met them, they'd agreed to help me find where Farranen had been imprisoned and distract the male guarding him. And by "distract," I meant they literally went Hannibal Lecter on his ass. But there hadn't been any bowing. Maybe it was because we were in a palace instead of an empty field? I really needed a manual on fae etiquette.

The leader of the little band of pixies, Karista of the Dark Court, straightened, and the others followed in her wake like a colorful wave of pink and purple soccer fans. The male closest to her put an arm around her shoulders, pulling her into the protection of his body—which set off all kinds of warning bells in my head. The pixies were a matriarchal group, with the males subservient to the females. The fact that she was leaning on him for support was worrisome.

"The pixies thank you for your hospitality," Karista announced softly. Thin lines bracketed her pink eyes, making her look anemic and weak. What the hell was wrong with her?

"There's no thanks needed. The Shadow Palace is for everyone," I told her automatically. Quickly scanning the rest of the group, I was relieved to see that the others looked no different from the last time I'd seen them. At least they weren't all suffering from whatever was ailing their leader.

"My lady, I humbly request privacy so that I may perform my duties." Eddy's big hands wrung nervously, and I realized that she was asking me to leave so she could take care of Karista.

"Oh! Sorry—of course!" It was the middle of the night, and my brain clearly wasn't firing on all cylinders.

The pixies parted ranks, clearing a path between me and the door that I quickly scrambled through.

"I hope you feel better soon, Karista!" I called over my shoulder before firmly shutting the door. Dang, what had happened to the fierce little female?

Harvey and Vanessa were waiting in the hall and fell into step with me as I made my way back toward Farranen's empty suite.

"Did you catch all that?" I asked, my voice echoing off the stone walls in the empty hallway.

"They were stinkin' *adorable,* like little dolls," Vanessa said. I didn't bother to tell her that they had teeth sharper than a shark's and could rip through flesh in seconds.

"Karista appeared indisposed."

The small amount of concern in Harvey's voice only compounded my own worry. Immortal beings could get sick; many of the older fae suffered from psychogenic atrophy, a condition that led to the loss of brain function. Their erratic behavior eventually led to their demise— either by their own actions or by the hand of another. Just as Farranen was forced to kill Lebolus, and I'd inadvertently shot the queen. I wondered if there was a whole spectrum of germs in Fairie that plagued the immortal beings, just as humans suffered from the common cold and flu.

Deciding it was best to leave Karista's medical diagnosis to the healer, I let my feet guide me toward Farranen's room as sleep beckoned.

****

After several exhausting hours of tossing and turning, I still couldn't get the images from Lief's vision out of my head.

I wanted to march back downstairs and hear his interpretation regarding what we'd witnessed, but it was still the middle of the night and I doubted he'd be awake.

Since it wasn't possible to lull myself into a comatose state by watching TV, and I wasn't the type to take up needlepoint or knitting, I decided to do something to alleviate some of the unease that had settled in my stomach after witnessing the dastardly activities Gus had been engaged in. Some ghostly reconnaissance was in order.

When I was finished making the bed I'd slept in, I called to Harvey and Vanessa, and they appeared as quick and silent as lightning.

"Can you guys check on Lief and Karista? I don't want to go down and disturb them, but you guys can peek in and report back to me."

Harvey took up a position next to the door and gave me a single affirmative nod, but Vanessa jammed her hand on her cocked hip. "You want us to be your glorified peeping toms?" she asked, clearly appalled by the thought.

"Essentially, yes," I confirmed, after a moment of thought.

Her swift smile held no warmth. "Fine, but if I have to be a creeper, I call dibs on the scrumptious dark prince. Harvey can check on the pixie."

"Fine with me," Harvey told her. "It wouldn't be the first time you've observed the dark prince without his knowledge."

My mouth fell open as my two ghosts winked out of existence. Vanessa had been lurking in the shadows and spying on Lief? That was all kinds of messed up. Not that I could really blame her. I'd caught myself staring at the handsome male too many times to count. Of course, I'd rather give myself a pedicure with a chainsaw than admit that embarrassing fact out loud.

With that unpleasant thought hounding me, I headed into the bathroom to shower.

Out of all the wonderful features in the Shadow Palace, the lavishly appointed ensuite was my favorite. Like Farranen's personal chamber, the large room was designed with his tastes in mind. The floor was tiled in large simple squares that had an abrasive texture, which was absolutely genius, as I'd be a lot less likely to slip and fall. The walls were covered in a smaller version of the white marble, only smoother. The cupboards were made from dark wood, contrasting nicely with the countertop that looked to be cut from a giant slab of green quartz with uncut gemstones embedded in it. Every single one of my hair and makeup products could easily fit on less than a tenth of it. Gold faucets that were probably worth more than my entire cabin rose elegantly above the sink.

I stripped off my Tooth Fairy shirt and sports bra, momentarily shocked by the large amount of blood that covered them—until I realized it was Lief's. There was no laundry hamper, so I tossed them in the corner knowing they would be gone the next time I came in here. I hadn't seen any sign of a housekeeper or maid, but every time I left Farranen's room, even for just a few minutes, I'd return and find the place spotless. The next ghostly assignment I'd have for Harvey and Vanessa would involve staking out my guardian's chambers to see who was coming and going when I wasn't around.

Shucking my yoga pants and panties, I balled them up, planning to toss them too, but a streak of blood caught my attention, and I hesitated. It was the bright crimson of fresh blood, rather than the hours-old dried blood from when I pulled the bolt out of Lief's shoulder. A closer inspection showed that it was smeared across the crotch of my panties.

What the hell?

"Oh my *God*—"

Vanessa's exclamation of horror startled a shriek out of me, and I jumped a few inches into the air. I clutched the dirty clothes to my chest and whirled around to face my traumatized ghost. "Vanessa! You scared the crap out of me!"

"Good God, Theo!" She scrubbed her hands across her face like she was trying to exfoliate her eyeballs. "I'm never going to get the sight of your pasty white butt out of my head!"

Yanking a fluffy white bath towel off the shelf, I quickly wrapped it around my body. "You could have knocked!" Being caught off guard always brought out my inner shrew, and because I also happened to be naked, my mood catapulted straight into incensed bitch territory.

"How the hell was I supposed to knock? I'm a ghost, *remember?*"

Okay, at least I wasn't the only one with a stick up my butt.

I took a deep breath and held it while I mentally counted to ten. Since I was the one with a pulse, it was probably my responsibility to suck it up and be the better woman. "Vanessa, I'd really like to take a shower to wash off all the dried blood." I was extremely pleased with how civil I sounded.

"Be my guest." Vanessa flopped down on the closed toilet, seemingly no longer bothered by my nudity. Which made me think her distress had been greatly over-exaggerated. I mean, she'd seen my naked heinie after Gus had killed me and hadn't lost any sleep over it. Lord knew the girl was a drama queen.

I narrowed my eyes at her before marching over to the bathroom door and hollering, "Harvey, I'm naked and taking a shower. Don't come in!"

"He left to recharge," Vanessa informed me with an innocent smile.

"Oh." I wanted to talk to him about what I'd seen in Lief's vision. Whatever Gus had been doing to the poor fae soldier's body was magical in nature, and I was hoping that Harvey, with his centuries of experience living in a magical realm, would be able to help me figure out what was going on.

The shower was as large as the entire bathroom in my cabin, complete with a large bench and multiple shower heads. While the rest of the room was mostly white, the entire stall was tiled in black with gold trim, giving it the illusion of a cave. Four small lights recessed in the ceiling flicked on as soon as I turned on the water.

"The dark prince was still sleeping like a baby," Vanessa smirked. "A big sexy baby with lips that would be perfect for—"

"Thanks for the update," I told her flatly. I had no desire to know what she'd like to do with any part of the dark prince's anatomy.

In one coordinated move, I dropped my towel and stepped into the shower stall while sliding the frosted glass door shut behind me. It was rather smooth, if I do say so myself.

"Why did Harvey need to recharge?" I had to raise my voice to be heard over the sound of the water falling around me. I had no idea what kind of water heater the Shadow Palace was equipped with, but it already had two thumbs up from me. It didn't seem to matter what temperature I set the dial to, the water always came out two degrees below scalding, just the way I liked it. Even the time Farranen and I had spent over an hour under the spray together, the temperature hadn't fluctuated.

"He stayed while you were asleep, in case those weird shadows came back. We decided to take shifts so you'd always have someone with you."

Harvey had watched my back while I was sleeping? And Vanessa was keeping me company while I showered because she didn't want me to be alone? A warm buzz filled my chest, having nothing to do with the water temperature. A year ago, I didn't have anyone; now I had two dutiful ghosts, an overprotective shifter, and multiple fae that all cared about me. It was a sobering thought.

I cleared my throat awkwardly. There was something I'd been needing to say to her. "I didn't get a chance to apologize for asking you to leave when I brought Safeena's ghost through the veil." Saying it out loud sucked, but I'd hurt Vanessa's feelings, and she deserved to have that acknowledged. "So, I'm sorry."

"Whatever, it's not a big deal." Her flippancy was one hundred percent fake, but I didn't call her out on it. Vanessa used her I-don't-give-a-crap attitude as emotional armor, the same way I used sarcasm.

"It's a big deal to me." I squirted some shampoo into my hand before massaging it into my scalp. "I know you didn't have any say in becoming a ghost, but I'm really glad I got to meet you."

Silence filled the steamy air, and I wondered if maybe I'd gone a little overboard with my honesty and scared Vanessa away, until she finally spoke.

"I really wanted to kill that cold bitch for you."

"I know," I told her, meaning every word.

Later, I'd consider the possibility of bringing Safeena back through the veil as a corporeal ghost, just so Vanessa could rough her up. It was the closest I could get to providing her with some apparitional therapy.

Chapter Twenty-One

By the time I finished showering and had braided my wet hair, I was starving.

I quickly dressed in some black leggings, a white tank top, and a dark green sweatshirt that had a yellow smiley face with bloody fangs on it. Was Fairie mocking my vampire magic? Or maybe just poking fun at the UV-challenged in general? I had no idea, but I was tickled by the hideous graphic.

As an extra precaution, I tied a few knots in the strap of Lief's borrowed sword until it was tight enough to stay in place on my back. It looked ridiculous, with its massive length sticking out above my shoulder, but at least I knew it was safe. Leaving it downstairs where anyone could waltz off with it wasn't an option.

Vanessa had disappeared—at my insistence, and with much grumbling about prudish women—when I'd started to get dressed.

Someone had left a tray of assorted meats and cheeses on the massive wooden table, so I sat down to fill my nervous belly. What was taking Farranen so long? What if Gus caught him by surprise? Even with Dog for backup, I didn't like the idea of my guardian getting anywhere near Gus and his polluted magic. Now that I knew he didn't have the strength of the Army of Light supporting him, I felt marginally better about Farranen and Dog confronting the gray knight.

The sudden *creak* of a door opening behind me was

louder than a gun going off, and I shot to my feet and spun around.

Gus stood on the threshold of the doors to the balcony, with his long dark hair blowing in the breeze. His hard eyes landed on me, and he smiled. There was nothing friendly in the ugly twist of his lips.

My stomach cramped, the breakfast I'd just devoured seemingly no longer content to stay where it belonged, as his oily magic washed over me. The pristine gray shirt and pants he wore were identical to the ones he'd worn yesterday, with no sign of the injuries he'd sustained at my guardian's hand.

"You damaged my minions," he accused with a sneer.

I blinked at the strange allegation. *His minions? What the hell was a minion?*

Gus's lips thinned; apparently, he found my ignorance irritating. "The fae that I have remade into superior beings, the next step in our evolutionary journey."

What, now? I didn't have to bother feigning my confusion for the sake of pissing him off.

"To me!" At the sound of Gus's words, four wraiths drifted into the room from the balcony.

I uttered a silent curse and backed a few more steps away from the table. So, this was how Gus had snuck into the castle—he used the shadows as his own personal magic carpet to lift him onto the second story balcony.

"So, you brought your friends back for round two? I can't promise that there will be anything left by the time I'm done with them." I had no idea if my bluffing would set off Gus's lie-detector, but I wasn't going to stay silent while he tried to cow me. A smarter woman would have run from the glower he gave me. Instead of tucking tail and heading for the hills, I chose another option. I called my ghost.

"Harvey." I didn't have to shout, or even raise my voice, but Harvey immediately appeared between me and the intruders that were currently letting all the warmth out of the room. I doubted they'd humor me if I asked them to shut the balcony doors. The seasons in Fairie were still correcting themselves, and the temperature outside was a brisk five degrees, making it feel like it was late autumn. My sweatshirt and bare feet were proving to be sadly inadequate in the rapidly cooling room.

My ghostly merdain fae took in the entirety of the situation with a quick sweep of his indigo eyes, and his jaw hardened. "I apologize for not arriving sooner; I was unaware of your distress."

I shrugged. "I wasn't really feeling much distress. It'll probably come as soon as he tries to kill me. Again." If I freaked out every single time someone snuck up on me, I'd be living in a perpetual state of panic.

Gus's eyes shifted from side to side, probably trying to figure out who the hell I was talking to. I was content to let him wonder. Maybe if he thought I was bonkers, it would garner me some empathy. Yeah, probably not.

"Check the room," he ordered the wraiths, and the four shadowy figures darted around the room to check in the wardrobe, behind the armchairs next to the mantle, and under the bed. When they finished poking their noses where they didn't belong, they rushed back to where Gus was waiting with his hand held out to the side. One by one, they brushed up against his outstretched palm before taking up their previous positions behind their master. The suspicious lines that were already carved into the former gray knight's face deepened.

Harvey and I watched the weird exchange before he asked, "What's the plan, Theo?"

I really wished I had a good answer for that—one that was stunningly brilliant, yet easily executable, and would ultimately result in me walking away from this encounter without a scratch. Needless to say, I didn't have one of those, so once again I'd be relying upon my underwhelming improvisation skills.

"What do you want, Gus?" When he opened his mouth to answer, I cut him off. "If you're hoping for another chance to get your grubby fingers on the crown—the crown that belongs to the new *king of the Light Court*—then you're out of luck. He isn't here." I didn't try to hide the pride I felt when referring to the man I was courting.

While I'd been initiating a round of verbal sparing with Gus, Harvey had moved closer to where the wraiths were hovering. He reached out and stuck his hand inside the inky darkness of the most solid one. I did my best to school my face into some sort of neutral mask, but seeing Harvey's blue hand disappear into the misty void was weird.

Gus smiled, the movement infinitely scarier than any threat or denial he could have used to rebuff my observations. I backed up a few more steps, recalling the sharp teeth he'd had in Lief's vision, even though they appeared normal at the moment. Maybe he'd glamoured the sharp piranha fangs into normal teeth? Or maybe the sharp ones had been glamour?

"You're right. I'm not here to waste time sparring with the king." Sparring? That was a really interesting way of saying Farranen would kick his ass.

I scoffed. He hadn't stopped by because he was looking to be BFFs with the new king of the Light Court.

"He's not lying, Theo." Harvey stopped poking at the wraiths and walked toward me. "I would sense if he was."

Oh, crap. The fae could sniff out a lie from a mile away; if Harvey said Gus was telling the truth, I believed him.

To further his point, Gus unsheathed his sword from his hip and pointed it at my chest like he was about to unknowingly slice and dice his way to the key that remained inside me. "My minions were quite adamant about what they saw last night."

Gus had used his shadows to spy on Farranen and I? Oh, God, what else had they witnessed that was supposed to be private?

"That's not all they had to report," he drawled, watching my face for a reaction. I didn't give him one.

His dark eyes wandered lower, raking over my body with an intensity that was nearly tangible. It was like having live electric eels slither across my skin, and I fought the urge to shudder. "You know, you're not really my type," he continued.

Thank goodness for that. I'm pretty sure Gus's type involved women that had long legs, perky boobs, were bat-shit crazy, and enjoyed foreplay that involved torture and maiming.

"But the dark prince's taste in females has never been very discerning."

I rolled my eyes. Really? He was worse than the popular girls in high school, trying to insult Lief because he was interested in someone that didn't fit their definition of attractive—wait, did he say *the dark prince?* I was courting Farranen, not Lief.

Oblivious to my bewilderment, Gus continued to monologue like a lame evil villain in a children's cartoon. "Imagine my shock when I heard you bore the prince's mark."

His words were conversational, but I didn't miss the hard glint in his eyes. The dude was fuming, and all that pent-up anger was pointed squarely at me.

My heart sank even further when the meaning of his words was finally able to pierce through the fog of confusion surrounding me. He knew about the tattoo on my back.

"He thinks you're mated to the dark prince." Harvey moved closer until he was standing directly in front of me. His hands were cold when he gripped my shoulders, pulling my attention away from Gus's rant. "He knows the key to the Light Court is with the king, but not that the second one remains with you."

I nodded. The wraiths must have caught me saying goodbye to Farranen last night. He'd confirmed that he was taking the key with him, and my tattoo must have been visible enough for the minions to mistake it for a mating mark.

Looking past Harvey, I interrupted Gus's tirade outlining exactly how he felt about pathetic humans receiving a highly sought-after, ultra-rare mark that only the fae were worthy of.

"How did you know Lief gave me the mark?" I mean, the logical assumption should have been that it came from my guardian. The guy had gone head-to-head with the queen in order to release me from being her breeding mare; and I'd literally died trying to rescue him in return. That alone implied that Farranen and I had some affection for one another. Of course, if the minions had only caught the tail end of our goodbye, then they would have missed the searing kiss he'd given me.

Harvey turned, so we were both now facing the giant

male, who was currently flipping his sword from hand to hand.

"Are you denying that the dark prince has marked you?" Gus twisted his wrist, swinging the sword through the air in an arc that was a clear challenge, before catching it with his other hand. Which was overkill if you asked me since he didn't really need the long blade to intimidate me.

"I'm not denying it." But I also wasn't agreeing with it. "I just wanted to know how you knew it was Lief's mark. If it said 'Property of the dark prince,' I'd get it, but it's just a bunch of vines and flowers." The longer I kept him talking, the longer Farranen had to return to the castle—hopefully with the Army of Light at his side. And where the hell were the T'Holly brothers? They were in charge of the Shadow Palace during the king's absence. I was seriously going to demote their asses the next time I saw them.

"The dark prince's line has a very distinctive color associated with their markings," he sneered, like I was an idiot for not knowing. Maybe I was; the whole concept of different bloodlines and family trees was pretty darn confusing.

"So, back to my original question: what the hell do you want? You didn't break in just to congratulate me on the new ink on my back."

"Theo…" Harvey cautioned. Maybe he had some insight as to what Gus had dropped in for? Because I sure didn't.

"Where is the dark prince?" Gus growled.

"Why don't you ask your shadows?" I countered.

"They've been over every inch of this castle, and there's no sign of him. If I didn't know about your mating, I'd be inclined to believe the iron bolt I shot him

225

with was on target."

Confusion replaced a little of the confident cynicism that I'd wrapped around myself like a shield. What did our fake mating have to do with anything? And the glamour that was concealing Lief must be doing its job; without it he would have been a sitting duck.

"True mates are irrevocably bound for life; if one dies, the other does too," Harvey explained from next to me.

What? That was news to me. And just one more reason I had no desire to become mated. But that still didn't explain—oh, crap. I forced my eyes to meet Gus's smug gaze. He was going to kill me, believing that Lief would then die too. I backed a few more steps away, not stopping until my toes were on the shaggy black rug that extended from beneath the bed.

"This is your last chance to tell me where the dark prince is hiding." Gus lifted the sword, pointing it directly at my chest, where my heart had begun to pound.

I couldn't tell him that Lief wasn't my true mate without revealing that I was holding one of the most powerful magical items in Fairie inside my body. He had me backed into a figurative corner, and the harsh grin on his face said he knew it.

A quick glance across the room confirmed what I already suspected. I was closest to the door, but Gus was faster.

"Even if you kill Lief, you won't take his place." I'm pretty sure I was past the point of being able to reason with the delusional fae, but if there was even a small chance I could solve things with words, I had to try. "Only someone from the Dark Court can wear its crown."

"I am well aware how the totalitarianism in my

realm works and have no intention of taking the dark prince's head."

"He's not lying." Harvey tilted his head to the side and stared at Gus like he'd suddenly developed X-ray vision and could see straight through to the thoughts in his skull.

"What about his heart?" I demanded. "Or any other part of his body that would result in his death?" Now that I'd caught on to how the whole telling-a-lie-without-actually-lying thing worked, I was able to hear what wasn't being said.

Gus rolled his eyes, and I had to stifle a giggle. Annoyed teenage girls rolled their eyes, not malevolent villains that dripped with dark oily magic.

With a long-suffering sigh, Gus growled, "If the dark prince is dead, Fairie will just appoint another from the Dark Court. Now that I've found his weakness, I'll be able to control the throne through him."

Extortion? That's what this all came down to? This guy was no criminal mastermind. He was just a bully with delusions of grandeur, but no legitimate means to achieve his goal of becoming the top dog in Fairie.

It was actually kind of ironic that Gus was hoping to use me to get to Lief, since his plan would be a lot more effective against Farranen. But I certainly wasn't going to be the one to enlighten him. Not that I thought he'd succeed—with either of the males. There was no chance of my death kicking off a chain reaction and killing either one of them, since there was no true mating.

"Now, if I've satisfied your curiosity, we should be going." With a mocking bow, Gus slid his sword back into the sheath at his hip.

Now I was the one to roll my eyes, galled to learn that he'd been waving his sword around just for show. If

I hadn't already seen him naked, I'd have accused him of overcompensating for a lack of greatness in other areas.

"Take her."

Two wraiths floated over and grabbed my arms. I shivered. Their hands were like ice cubes wrapped around my biceps. I squirmed, trying to dislodge their grip, but nothing I did stopped them from dragging me out onto the balcony and then tossing me over the railing.

Chapter Twenty-Two

To say that I was feeling bitchy was a vast understatement, but I couldn't think of a better word to adequately describe the furious cauldron of emotion that was seething in my belly. I doubted such a word had even been invented yet.

My freefall from the balcony had lasted only a second or two but had been filled with so much terror that my entire body was still shaking from the adrenaline overload. The wraiths had slowed my descent for the last couple of feet and gently set me on my feet. Aside from the bruising on my biceps, my body was none the worse for wear. My attitude on the other hand…Yeah, I was no picnic to be around right now.

Gus led the way across the drawbridge with his minions dragging me in his wake. And why the hell was the drawbridge down? I thought the castle was supposed to be on lockdown?

In a rather ballsy move, Gus sauntered down the cobblestone road like he was out for a morning stroll, without a care in the world. His blasé attitude toward kidnapping only served to further sour my mood. After all the females he'd successfully kidnapped from Earth, he wasn't afraid of getting caught here. The cocky bastard.

Harvey kept pace beside me, and the wraiths silently trailed a few paces behind us.

The breeze picked up, tossing the freshly fallen

leaves on the road. With my bare feet, I was grateful for the small amount of cushioning they provided.

Gus, no longer feeling as chatty as he had been in the palace, ignored my multiple demands to know where we were going. Thankfully Harvey was familiar with the landscape, even after Gus led us off the road and into the woods.

"There are a number of different fae that reside this way, mostly of the lower classes."

Well, that was kind of interesting; I hadn't known there was any sort of hierarchy to the different types of fae. Actually, now that I thought about it, I remembered Farranen referring to the T'Holly brothers as coming from an elite bloodline.

"We just passed the site of the previous Dark Castle," Harvey continued, sounding like a tour guide. "If we continue in this direction, we'll reach the Wild River in a few more hours."

I knew from my previous adventures that the Wild River was bordered by a series of steep rocky hills (that really deserved to be called mountains) on one side, and flat grasslands on the other.

My dread grew with every step we took. Where the hell was Gus taking me? He said he wasn't planning on murdering me, but there was still a huge gray area regarding bodily harm that wouldn't technically kill me.

"He let you keep the sword," Harvey observed, echoing some of my own surprise.

I nodded, wincing as I stepped on a hidden rock.

"I believe the glamour the king used to hide the dark prince extended to his belongings," Harvey mused. "The pixies seemed unaware of it too."

Again, I nodded, because I didn't want to appear to be talking to myself. And it made sense that Farranen had wanted to keep Lief's things hidden. If anyone searching for him had found his sword or cloak lying around, then the cat would have been out of the bag.

By now it had to be well into the afternoon hours, and my stomach cramped painfully in hunger. Gus and the wraiths seemed unaffected by our grueling march through the dense forest, but Harvey was looking a little ragged around the edges. His pale blue skin no longer shimmered with the same level of intensity as it previously had, and the dark blue hair that hung above his shoulders was lackluster and limp.

"Go recharge," I whispered.

He shot me a small smile and opened his mouth to protest.

"*Go,*" I told him, quietly but forcefully. He'd be able to find me wherever I was once he was recharged. I didn't know what would happen if he completely drained himself, and I wasn't selfish enough to find out.

He winked out of view without another word.

****

The sky was just beginning to fade into twilight when our destination became obvious.

After we'd crossed the stone bridge that spanned the rushing river, the dead lands came into view. Gus led us toward them with mindless determination, ignoring my protests when my feet grew numb from the cold and my stomach hurt so much, I had to hunch over to alleviate some of the pain. Needless to say, my mood had gone even further downhill.

Not long after Harvey disappeared, Vanessa showed up. She took one look at the wraiths hovering behind me, then the broad expanse of Gus's back in front of me, before falling into step next to me.

"What the hell, Theo?" she hissed, but there was no

real incrimination in it.

I narrowed my eyes. She was going to have to be a bit more specific if she wanted an answer.

"I can't leave you alone for two damn minutes," she grumbled.

I gave her an incredulous look. How was any of this my fault? I was contemplating exactly which hand gestures and facial expressions I'd use to convey my innocence, when the forest in front of us disappeared.

I knew we'd been approaching the dead lands, but in the growing shadows of dusk, I'd lost track of where they began. The giant wall of darkness rose above me, blocking out the trees and sky, and I was forced to acknowledge just how extensively they'd subjugated this part of Fairie.

The inky blackness had swallowed everything it touched. The last time I'd seen the dead lands, they'd been in the process of claiming the grassy hills near here. Now, the hills were completely gone, and they'd taken a part of the forest too. Any trees caught with their limbs touching the void were already shriveling in on themselves. None of the typical sounds of life could be heard from within the gloom.

When I got close enough to feel the absolute absence of magic that radiated from the dead lands, my feet stopped walking. My entire body protested the wrongness of getting closer to the magic-less space. We were still a good twenty yards away, but my skin was crawling like I was bathing in a tub full of maggots and battery acid.

"I'm *not* going in *there.*" I crossed my arms.

When Gus turned back to scrutinize my sudden defiance, I lifted my chin. Anything that went into the dead lands didn't come back out—so I wasn't setting a single foot in there.

He spun back around and called out, "Bring her!"

Two of his minions immediately latched onto my arms and dragged me toward the vast wall of death. I screamed and thrashed, slicing my feet on the roots and rocks that stuck out of the grass, but it didn't slow the wraiths down.

Gus shot me one last smug leer over his shoulder before disappearing into the darkness with the two remaining wraiths in his wake.

Vanessa snarled something obscene under her breath, giving me about a second of warning that she was about to do something really stupid, then the weight of her body crashed into my back. I staggered, nearly going to my knees, only the freezing grip of my captors kept me standing.

"*Aaah!*" I grunted. For someone who regularly liked to tease me about my size, Vanessa was no lightweight herself. Wrapping her long legs around my waist, and her arms around my shoulders, she clung to my back like a koala bear that had just tried caffeine for the first time.

While the two shadowy figures had been strong enough to drag my one hundred and sixty pounds around, they proved to be no match for Vanessa and my combined weight. Top heavy from the ghost on my back, I lurched back and forth on my feet while the ghosts tried to rip my arms off.

Draining them was an option, but I didn't want their dark nasty magic inside me if I didn't have to.

Deciding that the dead lands might be the better alternative to having both my shoulders dislocated, I opened my mouth to tell Vanessa to get off, but Gus choose that exact moment to step back out of the darkness.

His eyes widened when he saw what appeared to be two wraiths unsuccessfully trying to lead a short woman toward him. "What sorcery is this?" he demanded. His steps were angry as he marched toward me, and I gritted out a strained smile when he came to a halt ten feet away. Was he scared to get closer? The small sliver of uncertainty that I caught in his dark eyes suggested he was.

I clenched my jaw against the taunt that was on the tip of my tongue. Enraging him wouldn't be in my best interest. Satisfying, yes; but not at all productive.

Gus let out a determined growl and unsheathed his sword.

Uh oh, was the last thought I had before he swung the huge blade directly at my head.

****

An entire rock band had taken up residence inside my skull. And not a very talented one either.

I slowly cracked my eyelids open and immediately regretted the small movement. My stomach lurched, and I rolled onto my side just in time to throw up. I heaved a few times, but the meat and cheese I'd had earlier had already been digested, so there wasn't anything in my belly to eject.

Once I was confident that I was done yakking, I slowly sat up and looked around.

What I'd first assumed to be a cave was actually a sky-less forest just like the one I'd seen in Lief's vision. My heart beat a little harder behind my ribs. We were in the dead lands. Like, *in* the *dead lands.* How the hell was I still alive?

Dead trees twisted artlessly upward, their branches clutching awkwardly at those of their neighbors. The dirt beneath my fingertips was as void of life and magic as the moon was. All the typical sounds of the forest were absent; absolute silence filled the air around me.

But the worst part, the part that filled me with the most terror, was the bodies. The smell hit me first, far stronger than what I'd experienced in Lief's vision. It was the festering of an infected wound left to rot in the sun, combined with the sharp tang of blood and old meat. If my stomach hadn't already been empty, I probably would have thrown up again. Despite the dim lighting, I could pick out a number of corpses strewn around the small clearing. Thankfully, not quite as many as I'd seen in the vision, but enough to make my heart hurt. All these poor fae hadn't deserved to die.

A figure stepped out from behind a tree, and I let out a relieved breath when I realized it wasn't Gus.

"Theo?" Harvey quickly knelt next to me on the hard ground, running his gaze over my face like he couldn't quite believe I was alive. His fingers were gentle as he probed at the back of my head. I winced when he found a lump next to my ear. "You have a concussion," he told me, confirming what I'd already deduced.

When Gus had swung his sword at me, I'd assumed his goal was decapitation. A concussion was all right with me if it meant I got to keep my head.

"What happened?" I asked, as Harvey helped me to my feet.

"Gus hit you with the flat of his blade to knock you out. Then his shadows dragged you here."

"Is Vanessa okay?" The last time I'd seen her, she'd been clinging to my back like an octopus.

"Yes, she expended a lot of energy and needed to rest. And she lost her vision."

I looked up in surprise as I continued to brush dirt

off my pants. "Vanessa's blind?"

Harvey shook his head. "I suspect her human eyes are unable to pierce the darkness of the dead lands."

"That doesn't make sense," I objected. "My human eyes are working just fine." Sure enough, the longer I looked around, the more my sight seemed to adjust to the darkness. When I'd woken up, I'd only been able to see a few feet in front of me, but now I could make out the outline of twisted trees that were twenty feet away.

His indigo eyes widened in revelation. "You're right."

If we hadn't been in such a dire situation, I would have been insulted at how surprised he sounded.

"We need to get out of here," I suggested. The magic in my body was churning apprehensively, urging me to get as far from this place as possible. And the longer we lingered here talking, the more it felt like it was weakening. I performed a quick internal inventory. The weird blend of vampire and fae magic inside me was present and accounted for, but the friendly buzz of Lief's key was missing.

Panic made my movements clumsy as I spun around. "Check my back!" I told Harvey. He must have heard the urgency in my voice, and he quickly lifted both my shirts. "Is Lief's tattoo gone?"

Damn it! I should have known I wasn't up for the responsibility of babysitting his key. What was going to happen to Fairie? She never should have chosen me as the guardian of the keys. Farranen still had his, so theoretically he could support the realm until I was able to find the key I'd lost. Hopefully. Had it slipped out of my grasp while I was unconscious? Oh God, what if Gus found it?

"It's still here." Harvey's calm voice cut through my

consternating thoughts, beating back some of my dismay.

"It is?" If he was messing with me, I was going to pull a page out of Vanessa's book and acquaint his freshly healed balls with my knee.

"Yes."

The stoic merdain fae really wasn't the type to joke around, so if he said the key was still safely stashed inside me, then I believed him. The fact that I couldn't feel it was worrisome, but something I'd have to wait to deal with later.

"I've been watching Augustus since I arrived." Harvey tugged my shirts back into place and took me by the elbow, leading me into the woods. "He's currently in a small cabin behind us."

The windowless stone hut from Lief's vision, most likely. Was this where Gus had been hiding out the whole time? And how was he still alive? Maybe Farranen and Lief were wrong about the dead lands being a death sentence to the fae. If so, they should be renamed the in-between lands, or the lands-that-won't-kill-you-but-sure-are-no-place-to-book-a-vacation.

"Harvey? How am I still alive? I thought the dead lands killed anything they touched."

"I believe humans are exempt."

Yeah, I doubted many humans accidentally wandered into Fairie to test the theory.

"What about Gus?" Not to mention the fae that he'd been snacking on had been alive when he brought them here. But I hadn't told Harvey about Lief's vision yet, so I didn't bother bringing them up now.

I ducked under a low-hanging branch while Harvey contemplated my question.

"Honestly, I'm not sure how anyone would be able

to survive here for more than a minute or two. Your presence is explained easily enough, but for any of the fae…It shouldn't be possible."

A thick root, the same color as the dirt, tripped me, and Harvey caught me by the arm before I went sprawling. "Thanks," I told him, absently. The whole concept of Gus being in the dead lands was hinky. "How much farther?" I asked, temporarily letting the subject drop.

The forest around us was becoming denser, and more than once I got snagged on one of the prickly thorns of the many bushes. Without realizing it, sometime in the last few days I'd gotten used to pulling magic from the world around me while I was in Fairie. Now that I was in an environment that was completely devoid of magic, the empty feeling was stifling. Was this how Earth felt to the fae? If so, I was going to be in for a world of hurt when I got back home. *If* I ever got back home.

"I'm not sure. Vanessa accompanied you for the journey through the dead lands. I only arrived an hour before you woke up." Harvey wrapped his hands around my waist and lifted me over a fallen log that was in my way before he neatly stepped through it.

I nodded my thanks before I caught what he wasn't saying. "Vanessa stayed with me while I was unconscious, even though she couldn't see anything?" That was really…loyal. And slightly shocking. But mostly just sweet. "Hey—if you've never been here before, how do you know which way home is?"

The chagrined look he gave me would have been cute if I hadn't just caught onto the fact that he might be leading me farther into the dead lands. "I have an excellent inner compass. I'm confident we'll find the edge of the dead lands if we continue in this direction."

Him being confident wasn't the same as him being a hundred percent absolutely certain, and my lips parted to tell him—but a thin metal arrow whizzed past my ear and lodged itself in a tree to my right with a sharp *crack.*

I let out a startled shriek as Harvey yanked me sideways, and Gus's voice filled the sudden silence.

"Leaving so soon?" Amused condescension dripped from his mocking words, and I slowly turned around to face the asshat that had just tried to shoot me in the back. Dark oily fae magic crept across the space between us, and I fought the urge to cringe. I had to assume that from such a short distance away, he'd meant to hit the tree rather than me. So, he probably didn't want me dead. Yet.

"I don't know how you got out of those chains, but the only place you're going is back with me. We can do this the easy way—" His lecherous smile was probably supposed to be charming. "—or the hard way," he finished, taking another self-assured step in my direction. God, the jerk was cockier than a bag full of dicks.

The easy way or the hard way? What a cliché pile of bologna. We both knew I wasn't going to make things easy for him. I had absolutely no inclination of heading back to the revolting little clearing where I'd already witnessed him eating another man's heart.

When I didn't say anything, his conceited humor faded into annoyance, and he leveled his reloaded crossbow at my chest. The guy was worse than a woman with the way he kept changing his mind. Was he planning on killing me or not?

I opened my mouth to call him out on his lack of commitment to follow through on a death threat, but Harvey cut me off.

"Sassing him is not in your best interest." He scurried through a large tree to where Gus was standing and waiting for my predictably snarky retort so I could see both males at the same time without having to turn my head.

"What should I do?" I aimed the question at Harvey, but Gus answered.

"That way. Move it," he ordered, gesturing back the way we'd come from.

"Do it," Harvey urged. "Your compliance will lure him into a false sense of security that we can use to our advantage. And he doesn't know about the sword yet, so let's keep it that way." Thank goodness I had the tactical-minded ghost to talk me through my standoff with Gus.

With a resentful sigh, I walked back toward the dilapidated cabin and the piles of bodies that surrounded it.

Chapter Twenty-Three

Something that Gus had said was bugging me. Well, *everything* Gus said was disturbing, but one thing stood out from the rest of his predictable do-what-I-say-or-else ultimatum.

I don't know how you got out of those chains.

What chains was he talking about? When I'd woken up, I'd been lying on the ground, but I hadn't been chained up. Actually, I did recall seeing a pile of metal chains lying at the base of one of the dead trees, but I hadn't thought anything of it at the time. Had I somehow gotten myself free of the chains without knowing it?

My foot caught on another aboveground root, and I went sprawling on my hands and knees. I spit out a few choice words and awkwardly got to my feet.

Gus let out a guffaw. "Humans are so inept. Not to worry, that won't be a problem for much longer." His bawdy chuckle scraped across my nerves like a dull knife.

What the hell was that supposed to mean? Was it a poorly concealed way of saying I wouldn't be alive much longer? Or was he just messing with me? Gah, what I wouldn't give for an archnemesis that shot straight from the hip rather than playing head games that kept me guessing.

I continued on, this time paying more attention to where I was stepping—until I caught sight of my feet. My *booted* feet. My eyebrows rose so high that it was a miracle that they didn't fly away. I'd been barefoot when Gus had dragged me from the Shadow Palace, so where the hell did the boots come from? I seriously doubted the slightly too-big footwear was Gus's doing.

Harvey must have sensed my confusion, because he caught my eye and smiled. "I discovered that I was able to remain corporeal if I maintained physical contact with you, as did the boots."

I looked down as he stepped through a thick shrub covered in thorns, and sure enough, his pale blue feet were bare. And webbed. Which momentarily shocked me, but shouldn't have since he was a water-loving merdain.

Shooting him a grateful smile, I made two fists and held my wrists together, hoping he'd be able to interpret my unspoken question. My charades skills were sorely lacking, but he seemed to understand.

"Yes, I was able to manipulate the chains that were in contact with your skin." His bright blue eyes were twinkling with obvious pride, and my own pride grew in response. My somewhat timid ghost was practically glowing with self-confidence. I shot him two thumbs up.

The smell of rotting bodies let me know that we'd nearly reached our destination. Harvey and I really hadn't gotten very far before Gus had tracked us down. I sure hoped Harvey had a plan, because letting myself get dragged back to Gus's cabin of horrors at arrow-point went against every instinct I had. Still, I trusted my faithful ghost, so I didn't stop until I was standing in the exact spot where I'd woken up.

I turned and crossed my arms across my chest while raising my eyebrows challengingly.

Harvey took up a position on my left side. "He doesn't know about the sword. If he turns his back or gives you an opportunity, draw your blade. Go for the head or heart."

My jaw dropped, and I spun to stare at him in disbelief. "*That's* your plan?" I whispered in shock, no longer caring if Gus thought I was talking to myself. Seriously? *Duel* with *Gus?* Had Harvey even *met* me? There's no *way* I could ever best the gray knight in a sword fight.

My stomach cramped even harder, and it had nothing to do with hunger. History has taught me that I don't do well with sharp pointy objects. After being stabbed in the belly on two separate occasions, I already knew exactly how this would end.

Looking a teensy bit guilty, and a whole lot determined, Harvey raised his hands in a placating gesture. "You'll have the element of surprise. If your aim is true, you should be able to slay him in a single blow." His use of *if* and *should* were not inspiring.

I remembered that I had an audience and glanced over to where Gus was watching me with perplexed amusement on his face. He probably thought my rising hysteria was in response to his perceived scariness. With a low chuckle, he spun on his heel and bent to prop his crossbow against the trunk of the closest tree. When he reached for the coil of chains that had been abandoned on the ground, my stomach crawled up into my throat. If he chained me up—again—I'd be completely helpless.

"Draw your sword," Harvey ordered, and the authority in his voice compelled me to obey. This was a hard side of the calm, yet nervous ghost that I'd never seen before.

I slid Lief's sword out, somewhat awkwardly, since the shoulder holster was intended for a left-handed user. It was lighter than Farranen's, and the leather-wrapped handle was too big to hold in a single hand. Wrapping both my sweating palms around it, I took four large steps toward Gus's vulnerable back.

Nausea filled my belly. I really, *really* didn't want to have to kill another fae. The guilt I carried around over all the supernatural creatures that I'd already killed was a heavy load, and it would only get heavier if I did this. But if it came down to him or me, I was going to choose me.

In a move that I'd done thousands of times chopping firewood, I brought the blade straight up in the air and then back down. I aimed directly at his thick neck that was hidden beneath a curtain of black hair, as he finished gathering the chain into his hands. The low whistle of sharp metal parting the air was nearly drowned out by my harsh exhale as the blade dropped.

The hard cords of muscles in his shoulders tensed a fraction of a second before he threw himself to the side, avoiding the blow that would have gone straight through the unprotected nape of his neck. The blade still managed to catch a piece of his left shoulder, cutting a path down to his shoulder blade as he rolled with the sudden momentum. Bright red blood wept across his ripped gray shirt, disappearing into the fabric, and making it cling to his taut back.

"What—" His startled exclamation ended as his eyes roved over my offensive stance, as if he was just seeing me for the first time. His gaze never wavered from mine, even as he unfolded himself back to his massive height. His right hand prodded at the skin that had been split open by my blade. Eyes, dark with sudden rage, broadcasted the world of pain that was coming my way.

I swallowed hard. I hadn't taken his super-fast fae reflexes into account. I was human, and therefore expected him to move like a human—but he was fae. A really fast, really deadly fae that I'd just pissed off.

The loaded crossbow was suddenly back in his big hands and once again came up to point directly at my chest. "You're going to regret whatever sleight of hand you're playing at."

I kept the sword tip pointed at the ground, so it wouldn't be so obvious that I was holding a weapon. It probably looked like I was practicing putting with an imaginary golf club. Subconsciously, I reached for my magic, happy to feel it bubbling beneath my skin. Lief's key remained unresponsive.

"I need you alive for what's to come," he smirked. "But you'll still meet the requirements if I take some fingers and toes."

I couldn't decide what was worse: being kept alive for a mysterious torture session in the near future, or the thought of losing a few digits. I kept my head high and shoulders back, even though I was vibrating with fear on the inside.

I'd nearly forgotten about Harvey until I felt his ghostly presence behind me. His right arm reached out and gripped my shaking hands, steadying them, while his other hand rested on my shoulder.

"Do you know how to dance?" His breath was cool against the top of my head, but I didn't mind. His hard chest was pressed up flush against my back, more reassuring than any words would have been.

"Yes," I answered, trying to figure out what his question was leading to.

"Then follow my lead."

He took a step forward, and I was forced to take one too or get knocked over. The hand on my shoulder guided me to the left, then the right as we made a number of seriously awkward steps that would have belonged in a beginner's ballroom-dance class, while Harvey murmured directions in my ear. Twice I tripped over the borrowed boots that were too big for my feet. With the number of dead trees clogging the forest around us, we were confined to a space of about fifteen by twelve feet.

Gus laughed, the sound little more than air grating through his vocal cords. "Your inadequate attempt to divert my attention from the ceremony won't work."

I tuned out his taunts, focusing instead on Harvey's voice as he continued to guide me.

"Three quick steps straight ahead, then aim for his neck. Be light on your feet, and keep your arms loose so I can guide the blade." Raw determination oozed from Harvey's voice, bolstering my own. I didn't bother to point out that women my size were physically incapable of being light on their feet.

"What ceremony?" I asked, hoping to keep Gus talking. Talking was so much better than brawling. Even with Harvey for backup, I was going to get my butt handed to me.

"The ceremony in which I create another minion in my army." Smug satisfaction rolled across his arrogant face, slanting his eyebrows as his gaze turned pointed.

I snorted, amused that he was referring to his four wraiths as an "army." Aside from acting as glorified thugs, they didn't seem like the brightest soldiers. Speaking of which—where the heck had his sneaky little minions slunk off to?

"Theo…" Harvey's reluctant warning rumbled through his chest, and the hand resting on my shoulder tightened. "He's referring to you."

"What are you talking about?" The words, which were meant for Harvey, slipped out before I could stop them.

Gus, assuming that I was talking to him, opened his big mouth to launch into a predictable monologue regarding his nefarious plans to rule the world. I cut him off as the implications of Harvey's comment hit me.

"Oh my God! You're going to turn *me* into one of those messed-up things?" It all made sense now; the mysterious "ceremony" he'd mentioned was probably what I'd been forced to witness in Lief's vision. And if that was true, it meant that the wraiths he'd already created were former soldiers in the Army of Light.

I stared at Gus, waiting for him to get to the punchline, or deny the scenario that my overactive imagination had come up with. He just stared back, looking slightly perturbed that I'd stolen his thunder by figuring things out for myself.

No way in hell, I thought fiercely. There was no way in hell I was going to let Gus turn me into one of those things with tainted magic. I narrowed my eyes, letting all my determination and objection to his plan leak into my gaze. I hadn't forgotten the part of the ceremony that would involve him ripping out my heart and eating it. As much as I complained about the size of my body, I wasn't ready to live without it.

And it seemed to me that Gus had overlooked one important detail. "Whatever you did to those poor fae"— I gestured to the bodies littering the ground between us and the cabin—"won't work on me. I'm human."

He smirked and took a step closer, and Harvey and I took a step back. Harvey had been right; this was just like dancing. Really deadly dancing.

"The spell pulls the subject's soul and magic out, fusing them together. The physical body is no longer needed. The fact that you aren't fae will matter not."

"Blasphemy," Harvey spat, shocking me with his vehemence. "Spells are for witches, to be used by magicless creatures in a magicless realm." Whoa, apparently my friendly merdain fae didn't care for some of Earth's supernatural residents. "The fae don't use them, and certainly not in the midst of Fairie's magic."

I liked to think I was pretty open-minded, and since I'd never actually met a witch, I didn't want to write off an entire race based on rumor or supposition—but the fact that they had a spell to create wraiths, and the recipe called for eating the hearts of real people, made me mentally add them to my naughty list.

"To combine two different types of magic with such contradictory origins will only result in both becoming polluted." The condemnation in Harvey's voice strangled his words, making them barely intelligible.

Until now, I hadn't realized how lucky I was that the vampire and ankou magic inside me could harmoniously exist together. They even got along with the two keys, and a wave of gratitude washed through my veins. Life would be so much harder if all the magics in my body didn't know how to play nicely together.

Another piece of the twisted macabre puzzle tumbled into place. This was why Gus's magic felt tainted and wrong. He'd used two different types of magic that were polar opposites, and now everything his magic touched, including himself, felt oily and disgusting.

A memory of a conversation with Lief came back to me, slamming into my head like a tsunami. *Their magic was so tainted, so* wrong.

At the time, he'd been talking about the females from Earth that Gus and Safeena had kidnapped. They'd been magically altered in the pursuit of turning them into breeding mares to make fae babies. Nobody had been able to figure out exactly what had been done to them, but Lief had described it as an abomination. Now I wondered if it was a similar spell that had changed the poor females.

"This is just one more step in the fae's evolutionary journey." The condescension in Gus's voice was thick enough to choke a horse. I wondered if he'd asked all those he'd already slaughtered if they wanted to be the stepping stones in his scheme to transform the fae race. Probably not.

A lightbulb went off in my brain as I realized this was how he was planning to control Lief. Since the wraiths weren't technically dead, it would be safe to turn me into one of them without any risk to my supposed true mate. And once I was a mindless minion under Gus's control, Lief would do whatever he was told.

I wanted to push Gus down a flight of stairs for the sheer stupidity of his tedious, poorly thought-out pitiful scheme. For Pete's sake, I could come up with at least a dozen better plots on the spot, and I wasn't even a suspense writer. There were about a hundred glaring flaws with the whole concept of holding the dark prince's supposed true love hostage as a semi-corporeal figure made out of magic and soul, then assuming Lief would kindly stand aside so Gus could do as he pleased with the Dark Court. I'm just saying, the dark prince is no pushover.

Before I could call the wannabe out on his pathetic plan, he bent and scooped up the length of abandoned chain from the ground and tossed it across the space between us. "Wrap it around your wrists," he ordered.

"No."

Gus's forehead bunched, and I would have laughed

at his sudden befuddlement if I were a less mature woman. Okay, that's a lie—I'm immature and totally laughed.

His sudden glower chased away any humor I'd been temporarily enjoying, as he stalked toward me. My mind froze up and the muscles in my legs tensed to back away from the man looming above me, but Harvey's cold body held me in place.

Talk about being caught between a rock and a hard place. More like, caught between a ghost and a murderous fae.

Harvey's hand slid from my shoulder to my hip, his fingers firm against my softness. I felt rather than saw his knees bend as he sank down a few inches, and I mimicked the movement.

"Let me guide the sword," he advised.

I nodded, wholeheartedly agreeing since I had no business swinging a sword on my own.

When Gus was only a few feet away, Harvey brought my sword up and across in one swift slashing motion, alerting the gray knight to the fact that my weird golfer stance wasn't just for show. Sensing that I might have a hidden advantage, he tried to raise the crossbow that had been pointed at the dirt, but only managed to lift it a few inches before my blade found its mark. A thin line of red appeared on the fabric of Gus's sleeve.

He inhaled and wrinkles dug into the skin on his forehead, followed by a bead of sweat.

The slight stroke of blood quickly bloomed into a stain that soaked his forearm and dripped on the ground. He opened his mouth but only got as far as, "Wha—" before the lower half of his arm fell off.

Holy hell! His freakin' arm fell off.

My body went all tingly and numb from the shock

of seeing one of Gus's extremities lying in the dirt like a discarded length of sausage tucked into a blood-stained glove. The dark scent of old rusty pennies shoved its way up my nose, making my stomach flip over.

I'm not sure how long I would have lingered there gaping at the bleeding man in front of me, but Harvey directed me forward, like he was a gymnast ventriloquist, and I was his dummy. My body moved with his, fluid and graceful, as he thrust the sword at Gus's chest.

A cloud of dirt filled the air as Gus stumbled backward and fell on his ass. His golden skin was leached of all color, making him sickly white in the dark setting. Air sawed in and out of his open mouth like he was about to hyperventilate.

Guilt filled my mouth, tasting bitter and desperate. There was no other way this could end. If I allowed Gus to live, he'd never stop in his pursuit for power. Just as I'd killed Safeena to keep the people I loved safe, I would kill the man in front of me, too.

I leaned into the motion when Harvey guided my sword backward in an arc. The steady rhythm of his breathing helped calm some of my regret. I didn't want to kill Gus, but I would.

Looking into Gus's nearly black eyes, I projected everything I was feeling at him. All the indecision, remorse, terror, conviction, and belief that I was doing the right thing. I aimed them at him like an emotional missile, hoping it was strong enough to get past his thick skull and sink into the gray matter beneath.

When the heavy blade reached the pinnacle of its path, Harvey hesitated, probably to give me time to adjust my center of gravity. The sudden harsh intake of his breath was the only warning I got before his arms tightened and he spun us around. His crazy-fast fae reflexes made the world blur, and the sword fell from my hands.

Twang! The sudden sound bounced off the trunks of the dead trees, and echoed back down, multiplying as it assaulted my ears. Blinding pain bit into my back, and someone groaned, but I couldn't tell if it came from Harvey or me. My stomach heaved, and I had to breathe in slowly to keep from throwing up.

"Theo…" Harvey's reedy voice trailed off, and his body, hunched protectively around me, disappeared.

Chapter Twenty-Four

Without Harvey's arms to hold me up, I stumbled forward a few steps but somehow stayed standing. I slowly turned, surprised to see that Gus was still sitting on his butt in the dirt. His eyes were glazed, his skin sallow, but there was a hint of a smirk twisting his full lips that made me want to back up even further. And keep going, until I reached another continent. But it was the sight of his crossbow that truly filled me with terror. Still lying haphazardly across his lap, it was no longer loaded.

No, please, no.

Remaining ignorant would have been my preference, but the pain screaming through my back had already taken that option from me. I look back over my shoulder, hissing as my body protested the movement.

No, no, no, please, no.

A thin iron arrow protruded from the right side of my lower back. The bastard had somehow managed to pull the trigger from his defenseless position, and now the sharp pointy tip was lodged somewhere inside me, while about twelve inches of the flat vaned end stuck out behind me. Exactly where Harvey had been standing. While there was no sign of his blood on the shaft, I had no doubt that it had gone through him before coming to rest in my back.

Furious that my ghost had been injured and not wanting Gus to see my pain, I mustered up the strongest glare I was capable of and aimed it at his face like a dagger.

He chuckled, but the sound was strained.

Sweat beaded on my forehead as I stared down at the asshole that was determined to ruin every single good thing in this beautiful realm. My sword lay in the dirt where I'd dropped it, and I couldn't see any more of the iron bolts nearby for Gus to use. It seemed that we were at an impasse.

"Looks like a kidney shot," he commented, feigning nonchalance through his gritted teeth.

Damn it. Not such a stalemate after all. He was immortal, and a severed arm probably wouldn't kill him. His bleeding already looked like it was slowing down. I on the other hand, was human. With my kidney torn apart by the arrow, all Gus had to do was wait and sooner or later I'd succumb to my injuries.

Still, there was one last thing I could do for Fairie and all its inhabitants before I died.

Moving slower than a sloth with arthritis, I reached for my fallen sword.

When I bent forward, new daggers of pain sliced into my back, adding to the agony. My hand was shaking so hard that I had trouble getting a grip on the leather-wrapped handle. Curses fell from my mouth faster than the blood dripping from Gus's stump of an arm.

"What are you doing?" Some of the familiar bluster was back in Gus's voice, reminding me that I needed to hurry.

Since I'd already lost the element of surprise, I saw no reason hide the sword anymore.

"I have Lief's sword." The words wheezed out as my vision began to blur around the edges. If I hadn't felt like I was about to fall on my face, I would have revealed the impressive sword with a dramatic flourish and some witty words.

His dark eyebrows rose comically, as he took in the dirty weapon hanging from my fingertips.

I took a single stumbling step toward him, almost tripping over the too-big boots.

Gus scooted backward, doing an awkward crab walk with his feet and one good hand.

"Stop her!" he cried.

For a moment I was filled with confusion. Then, four black shadows melted out of the surrounding forest, dispelling my mystification.

They surrounded me, blocking out everything until all I could see was misty darkness as their cold fingers dug into my arms and shoulders. "No!" The scream ripped out of me, born of pain and despair. I had to finish this. I *had* to. Gus would continue with his obsession until there was nothing left of Fairie and the fae that lived here. A sob worked its way past my lips, sounding pitiful after the ear-splitting shriek I'd just let loose.

I was afraid to move and injure myself further, but I wasn't going to stand here while the wraiths leaked their filthy dark magic all over me either. Rather than launch a physical assault on my tormentors, I lashed out with my magic. It uncoiled eagerly, running down my arms and slamming into the shadows with enough force that I cringed from the power that ricocheted back at me. I tugged at the oily black magic I could feel animating them, and it flowed into me like curdled cream. My stomach lurched, and I gagged at the foul taste suddenly coating my tongue.

Two of the shadowy figures, the ones closest to me that were holding my arms, winked out of sight. Were they gone for good? Or would they recharge like Vanessa and Harvey, and come back in a few hours?

My body listed to the side. I was close to passing out and reluctantly stopped pulling magic from the two remaining wraiths. I'd been in the dead lands for too long without access to the ambient magic of Fairie, so the sudden boost, even thought it was foul tasting, was better than nothing.

My boots scraped across the ground as the two remaining wraiths continued pushing me away from Gus's prone position.

"*Stop!*" I shrieked, sounding like I imagined a frustrated banshee would.

I tensed, prepared to fight my way past my captors, when I suddenly caught on to the fact that their fingers of death were no longer clamped onto me. Stunned, I looked down and found their hands were just resting on me, but not preventing me from moving. I took an experimental step forward, and they moved with me.

What in the ever-loving hell?

"Kill her!" Gus bellowed, and I could practically hear the ugly vein in his head popping out.

The wraiths didn't move. Not a single inch. My brain struggled to figure out what was going on. Somewhere in the background, Gus continued to issue directives that his minions ignored. It looked like they weren't his minions anymore. Whatever heart-eating ceremony he'd performed to create a link with them had been undone by me draining some of their magic.

"Let me go," I whispered, and nearly fell over when they backed away to the edge of the small clearing.

"*No!*" Gus shuffled backward a few more inches, his eyes bouncing between me and the wraiths in horror. "What have you *done*?"

With no idea how to answer that and not enough energy to waste on a shrug, I chose to ignore his accusing

256

look.

"You broke my bond with them!" Gus continued to fling out a list of my supposed wrongdoings, but if he was hoping for an apology, he was going to be sorely disappointed. His boots scrabbled noisily in the dirt as he used his good arm to push off the ground in an ungainly attempt to stand.

"Hold him," I told the wraiths, trying to mime the commanding tone their creator had used with them. When the shadowy entities palmed Gus's shoulders to hold him in place, his angry verbal tirade dried up with a squawk.

My back burned with vengeance, but I forced my shaking legs to carry me closer to the man sitting in a puddle of his own blood. I was barely able to get my foot high enough to step over his amputated arm; the dirt surrounding it was saturated with blood and the disgusting muddy mixture stuck to my borrowed boot.

The tip of Lief's sword dragged through the muck behind me, leaving a narrow channel.

"You don't have to do this."

Gus's appeal rolled off me like water off a duck's back. He was wrong. I had to do this. I didn't want to, but I had to.

Now that the wraiths were sort of under my command, I could have ordered them to kill him. There was a certain poetic justice there that appealed to my writer's brain. But taking a life was a huge deal, and it wouldn't be right to make someone—or some*thing*— else shoulder the burden for me.

With a grunt of pain, I hefted the sword onto my shoulder. Then, before I could chicken out, I swung it with the last bit of strength I had left.

My knees hit the ground at the same time as Gus's

head.

"Home…" I murmured to the wraiths as the pain took over and I passed out.

****

A familiar rumble worked its way into my consciousness, filling me with a weird sense of déjà vu. I knew that sound better than I knew my own voice. It inspired feelings of loyalty, belonging, and comfort.

Dog? I thought, since my voice wasn't working. I wanted to reach for him, but my arms weren't working either.

The rumble morphed into a growl, making the air around me vibrate.

After an eternity of fighting to pry my eyelids open, I was rewarded with a crack of watery light that stabbed at my peepers like a knife. I groaned and forced myself to look around.

I was still in the dead lands. The black ceiling above me and gnarled twisted branches of the dead trees were a dead giveaway. No pun intended.

The two wraiths held me in their cold grip. My arms were draped across their shoulders, while my feet dangled half a foot above the ground.

Ahead of us, Dog blocked the narrow path. I did a double take when I saw he'd ditched his wolf form for two legs. And as if that wasn't shocking enough, he was *fully clothed.* I'm not even joking when I say he was wearing pants, a long-sleeved shirt, and boots. Everything was completely black, like he'd raided Lief's closet before venturing into the dead lands.

"Dog?" I croaked. Oh good, my voice was working again. And how the hell was I still alive?

Worry and anger battled for supremacy on Dog's face, as his amber eyes bounced back and forth between the shadows and me. His growl, which had momentarily quieted, picked back up. It took a few seconds to realize he didn't like the wraiths being near me.

"It's okay," I told him. "We're sort of friends now."

His lip curled back off his teeth, giving the shadowy figures a scathing look. I couldn't really blame him, since I wasn't particularly fond of them either. The slimy feel of their magic was unavoidable since they were right up in my personal space. Of course, without them, I'd still be lying in a puddle of my own drool next to Gus's decapitated body—so I was willing to admit they were no longer a threat.

"Do you think you could carry me?" The humiliation I should have felt at asking someone to haul my heavy butt home never came. Sometime in the last few days my extra weight ceased to bother me. Well, I mean it still bothered me, but not in the obsessive way it used to. I was guessing it had something to do with the way Farranen viewed every one of my curves as a wondrous gift, rather than a curse.

Dog gave me an insulted look. His eyes seemed to say, *Don't be an idiot. I could carry you home with a dump truck strapped to my back at the same time.*

Cheeky shifter.

Warily eyeing the wraiths, he silently stepped closer.

"Careful, there's an arrow in my back," I cautioned. His answering rumble of disapproval trembled through me, and I tried not to cringe.

Crouching low, he fit his shoulder against my stomach. With his hands around the backs of my thighs, he stood up, balancing me across the broad expanse of his shoulder in a fireman's carry. I bit my lip against a whimper. The sharp stabbing pain from my back had morphed into a blazing ache that encompassed over half my body. Every cell and nerve ending were firing information into my brain at warp speed, overwhelming my capacity to produce any semblance of rational thought.

In his haste to get me out of the dead lands, Dog took off running. With my body jostling against his, I lost the ability to keep my misery to myself and great screaming sobs tore out of me.

****

Leaving the dead lands was like having a circus explode in front of my face.

As soon as Dog stepped out of the dark, silent world that we'd been trapped in, an onslaught of sensations hit me. The assault on my senses was nearly as painful as the arrow currently digging into my internal organs.

Blinded by the bright blue sky that loomed overhead, I shut my watering eyes. The light breeze playing through the bare branches of the trees scoured against my ears after the absence of sound in the dead lands. Even the smell of the freshly fallen leaves and thick patches of grass was overpowering. Once I'd gotten far enough away from the bodies, there really hadn't been any of the stereotypical aromas that should be associated with a forest full of dead things.

The ambient magic of Fairie nearly crushed me with its intensity. Before, it had always felt like tiny little threads of power reaching for me, no bigger than pieces of a spider's web. Now, it was like huge ropes of energy lashing at me, trying to fill all the places inside me that were depleted.

The low murmur of voices ceased at Dog's and my sudden appearance. My sensitive ears heard the collective inhale of multiple sets of lungs, and I cringed when someone called out, "He found her!"

I cracked my eyes open, but from my position on Dog's shoulder, all I could see was a small area of green grass, and the black fabric of his shirt (which still amazed me).

A dozen voices picked up, issuing orders and remarks of astonishment, as they closed in on where we stood. The press of bodies converged around us, and suddenly I was able to pick out the one single voice I'd been hoping to hear.

"*Theo.*" The achingly familiar scent of spicy pine trees washed over me a second before my guardian fell to his knees in my line of sight.

"Hey," I whispered, trying to sound composed even though knives of pain were slashing up and down my back and insides. Dog's shoulder wasn't exactly my preferred method of transportation.

An unnamed emotion shone in Farranen's eyes, making them greener than any eyes had a right to be. With a gentle hand, he carefully brushed away some of my hair that had been pulled free of its braid, before caressing my cheek. A wave of his magic, deep and soothing, slid into me, immersing itself so completely that I couldn't tell where it began or ended. It didn't do anything to relieve the pain coursing through me, but it was enough to distract me from it.

I imagined this was how using drugs would feel. It's no wonder that Fairie didn't need big pharmaceutical companies if magic could produce this kind of a high.

Beneath his cloak, the fine white fabric of his shirt was ripped and stained with blood. Through the hole, I could see that his injury had already healed, adding another scar to the already complicated tale his body told. Obviously, his search for the Army of Light hadn't been a walk in the park, but he'd overcome whatever dangers and obstacles that he'd faced.

Two big feet that would have looked at home on an elephant wearing a burnt orange dress appeared next to my guardian, who was still watching me like he couldn't believe I was here.

"We should get her to the medical tent," a steady voice murmured, perfectly nailing the firm-yet-compassionate-nurse-talking-to-a-traumatized-family-member tone.

"Hey, Eddy." The greeting wheezed out of me. It was hard to draw a full breath with Dog's hard shoulder shoved against my midsection.

"Yes, of course." Farranen's hand dropped, and I instantly mourned the loss of his touch.

Dog started moving, and I lost sight of my guardian. I caught a few glances of polished black boots, gone from my line of vision before I could identify the owners. Without the comfort of Farranen's magic coursing through me, the pain in my body hurtled to the front of my awareness. I kept my breathing slow and even to keep from throwing up. I doubted Dog would appreciate me ralphing all over his first shirt.

The world around me dimmed considerably, and I took it to mean that we'd entered the tent Eddy had directed us to. The sounds of hushed chatter dimmed, signaling someone had closed the tent flaps.

Under Eddy's direction, Farranen and Dog somehow managed to lay me on my stomach on a bed that had been prepared for my arrival. The mattress was firm, and the sheets were ridiculously soft. I felt bad about bleeding all over the pretty white cotton and even worse about all the profanities I'd thrown at the trio trying to help me get settled.

Tears leaked from my eyes faster than I could wipe them away. When they dripped from the end of my nose and chin onto the bedding, turning it brown, I realized my face must be covered in dirt from the dead lands. This wasn't exactly the reunion with Farranen that I had planned.

An intense discussion in hushed tones was taking place above me, but I couldn't focus on what Farranen and Eddy were saying. I wanted to sleep, but the flaming knife of pain in my back wouldn't let me. Turning my head, I found Dog resting his chin on the bed next to me. His sad yellow eyes acknowledged my agony, and when I let out a tiny whimper, he reciprocated with his own.

I'm not sure how long I lay there staring into Dog's understanding eyes, but when his gaze moved to something above me, I turned my head again to see what had caught his attention.

Farranen lowered his face to the mattress, presumably so I wouldn't have to crane my neck to see him. When he took my hand in his, I latched onto it like a dying woman would reach for her lover. Which I sort of was.

"Eddesta thinks the arrow has hit some of your internal organs." He was close enough that I could feel his hot moist breath on my cheek. "We need to remove it."

"It's iron," I reminded him, just in case he'd overlooked the fact that he and Eddy couldn't handle it. None of the fae could.

"Dog has volunteered to do it." His jaw clenched, telling me just how frustrated he was by the fae's intolerance for iron.

A small whine of agreement came from behind me, confirming that my shifter was on board with ridding my body of the arrow.

"Eddesta will put you into a magically induced coma so you won't feel anything." His free hand reached out to stroke my cheek.

"Okay," I said, once it became apparent he was waiting for my consent. Which was understandable since I rarely agreed to do things the easy way. But if Eddy could put me to sleep so I wouldn't feel the pain anymore, then I was all for it. Yes, please—where do I sign?

Farranen's gaze darted to the space above me, and he gave someone a quick nod before he looked back at me.

"Wait!" People could live without both kidneys, so even if one of mine was completely unusable, I should still be fine. But on the off-chance that I did end up dying from this, then there was something I needed to do first.

I focused on the weird blend of magic inside myself. Currently the vampire and ankou magic were weak and restless, probably due to the dismal combination of distress and fear churning through my veins. The ugly magic I'd stolen from the wraiths was still there, but it was thankfully fading. The nugget that represented Lief's key was curled up exactly where I'd left it, as if it had never been MIA in the dead lands. I poked at it with my own magic, and when it roused, I directed it to my empty hand.

Meeting Farranen's apprehensive gaze, I uncurled my fist to reveal the key to the Dark Court. His eyebrows slanted down in warning.

"Theodora, *no*." Ah, there was that new bossy ruler tone that I'd missed.

"Just in case," I pleaded. If I died holding onto Lief's key, I didn't want anyone to have to cut it out of my dead body.

"He trusted it into your care, and you will honor your promise to safeguard it." Fierce lines bracketed his eyes, matching his fierce words. His hand tightened around mine for emphasis.

"Please?" I let all the pain and uncertainty I was feeling leak into my expression, which wasn't very hard since I have a terrible poker face. A few more tears ran down my cheek, adding to the ugly brown stain on the bedding. Vanessa would have been proud that I was finally learning to use my feminine wiles to manipulate a man.

I knew the exact moment that his resolution cracked. "Very well." His lips twisted into a doubtful smile that I wanted to kiss, and he gently lifted the small black key from my palm. The purple jewel in it glittered in the low ambient light. After draping it over his head, it quickly disappeared beneath his shirt, presumably next to its twin.

Chapter Twenty-Five

Have I mentioned how much I hate being an anomaly?

Once again, I found myself on the receiving end of a here's-why-Theo's-not-normal discussion.

"*How* long?" I demanded, while yanking on a pair of black pants.

"Two days." The kindness in Farranen's voice only ratcheted up my own anxiety.

After two days in a magically induced coma, all my injuries had healed. Two freakin' days. That wasn't even *close* to normal.

And not only had I healed, I felt positively rejuvenated. So good in fact, that when my guardian had joined me in the shower to help wash all the blood and filth from the dead lands from my body, I'd taken advantage of his naked state and talked him into some mutually satisfying hanky-panky. Twice.

Now, half-dressed in a sports bra and yoga pants, I twisted in front of the full-length mirror so I could see the place on my lower back the arrow had pierced. The scar wasn't very big, about the size of a quarter. The puckered mark was a shade paler than the rest of my skin and only noticeable because it was the only blemish on my entire body. Still, there was only one other person that saw me naked on a regular basis, and he wasn't bothered by the small round flaw.

How was it even possible to heal such a huge injury

in *two days?*

Turning my gaze away from my reflection, I crossed to the dresser and pulled out the first shirt I saw. It was a deep purple with a graphic of an old-fashioned arrow piercing a thick book. The fletching on the end of the shaft looked like it was still quivering from the impact. I snorted, no longer quite so enamored with Fairie's sense of humor.

"Eddesta and the dark prince await us downstairs." He strapped his sword into place on his back and met my eyes across the bed, silently reminding me that I'd grudgingly agreed to see the healer once I was dressed.

And now I was dressed.

Damn it. I didn't really care why I'd healed so fast. Maybe it was Fairie's way of rewarding me for purging her of Gus's vile influence. When I said as much, my guardian had given me an indulgent smile and told me, "It doesn't work that way." Which only served to piss me off. I mean, this was a *magical realm*, so wasn't anything possible?

Farranen kept my hand in his as we made the quick journey down to Eddy's healing room. I loved the way he kept finding ways to touch me. Living like a hermit for so long had left me starved for physical intimacy—I just hadn't realized it until now. Although, right now he was probably keeping his fingers laced through mine in anticipation of me making a run for it.

As soon as we walked through the door, my mood instantly improved.

Lief and Eddy were standing in the center of the room, with Karista and her flock of pixies nearby. Dog watched the group of smiling fae from the back of the room. His ears perked up when he saw me, and his tail swished back and forth across the thick rug he was lounging on.

Eddy turned and squealed, "Theo!" before opening her arms and launching herself at me. I let out a squeak as I was suddenly engulfed in her big rubbery limbs. With my face smashed up against her generous bosom, I lost the ability to breathe until she finally decided to release me.

I stumbled back a few steps, and Farranen wrapped his arm around my waist protectively.

Since I had no idea what to say to someone that had just tackle-hugged me, I went with, "Hey, Eddy."

She dropped into a low curtsy in front of me, shocking me even further. What the hell was going on? When she stood, one of the pointy ears on her head twisted around to face the pixies, while the other stayed trained on Farranen and me.

"I have most joyous news, my lady!" A tear slipped from her eye, slowly traveling down through the short white fur on her face, leaving a wet track in its wake.

"What news?" Farranen, ever the level-headed one, got right to the heart of the matter.

Eddy's orange eyes widened and slid to the man next to me, like she hadn't realized he was there. "My lord." She followed up the greeting with another elegant curtsy.

Lief, probably growing tired of being ignored, ambled over to us. There was a stiffness in his gait that told me he wasn't completely recovered. I was just glad to see him out of bed and moving around. And wearing a shirt. I'd seen enough of his ripped chest to last me a lifetime. The leather-wrapped handle of his sword looked much cleaner than the last time I'd seen it. I wondered if Dog had gone back for it, since I'd left it next to Gus's body in the dead lands.

Thankfully, Lief wasn't inclined to beat around the bush like Eddy was.

"Karista is with child." The small smirk on his face morphed into a genuine smile full of pride and elation.

Next to me, Farranen inhaled and made a small sound like he'd been kicked.

That's not possible, I thought, even as Lief continued to stare at me with his pale blue eyes twinkling in delight. Of course, I also never thought the formidable dark prince could twinkle—but here I was, obviously wrong about that, too.

"Karista's *pregnant?*" I asked, just to be sure I wasn't misunderstanding Lief's words.

"Yes! I confirmed it myself." Eddy clasped her big hands to her chest, practically vibrating with joy, and I found myself smiling in return. The vibes in the room were contagious.

The flock of excited pixies parted like water as Karista stepped forward, looking stronger than the last time I'd seen her. One tiny hand rested on the slight swell of her belly. When she dropped into a simple curtsy, the other pixies followed suite.

Rising, her pink eyes met mine, full of emotion.

"Congratulations," I murmured softly, genuinely happy for the little female. She nodded, her slight smile understanding.

While it wasn't exactly common knowledge, there were a number of fae who knew I was infertile. Now I wondered if Karista was one of them. My heart squeezed painfully in my chest, but the smile never left my face. This was amazing news—not just for Karista, but for the entire race. There was no way I could begrudge her this wondrous miracle just because I was broken and unable to carry a child.

I knelt so I could see her better.

"The magic grows." Her eyes narrowed in her pale face, and she nodded thoughtfully. "It will thrive." I wasn't sure if she was talking about the metaphorical magic of having a life growing inside her, or the more literal magic that Fairie was made of. Either way, I hoped she was right.

"We will stay until the babe comes," she announced, lifting her pert little nose into the air.

"That's great!" Just when I didn't think my smile could get any bigger—it did. The more fae that moved into the Shadow Palace, the better. Even without the threat of Gus hovering over us, I was happy to know that Karista would be safe within the castle walls for the remainder of her pregnancy.

"Come." Her wings fluttered as she gestured to the group of pixies that had been silently watching our exchange. Every single one of them gave me a respectful nod as they followed their leader out the door.

I stood, feeling more confused than ever.

"The first new blood in over half a millennium, to be born into my court." Unchecked glee radiated from Lief's words, and I glanced over expecting to see him rubbing his hands together enthusiastically.

"How did she manage to get pregnant?" Not that I was trying to rain on their parade or anything, I just wanted to know how it was possible.

"Well, my dear," Lief began in a patronizing tone, "when a male and a female have interc—"

"I know the mechanics of it!" Geez, everyone wanted to be a comedian when it was at my expense. "I *meant,* none of you could make babies for the last five hundred years! What changed?"

"Just as Karista said; the magic grows and will

continue to thrive now that the courts both have strong competent rulers." There was no egotism in Farranen's tone, it was just a statement of fact.

I hadn't really believed that everything Lief and Farranen were doing to help the realm would truly result in a cure for the fae's infertility. The thought left me a little breathless. What was next? Would the dead lands finally recede? Would Eddy be able to fix those suffering from psychogenic atrophy? That would go a long way to keep Fairie's population from declining further. Was there a possibility for more fae babies in Fairie's future?

My stomach dropped as another thought shoved its way into my head.

If all the women in Fairie were suddenly fertile, would Farranen still want to be with me?

It was no secret that he wanted kids.

The familiar buzz of fae magic tore me from my disheartening thoughts, just before a sharp rap at the door announced we had a new visitor. Farranen stepped in front of me as a tall male stepped into the room. I did a double take when I saw the pale gray shirt with gold buttons that marked him as a soldier in the Army of Light.

I tensed—although I wasn't sure if it was in preparation of fight or flight—my reaction instinctive rather than logical since he wouldn't have knocked if he'd been here to attack us. It was going to take a while before my brain was completely on board with the fact that anyone associated with the Army of Light wasn't trying to kill me anymore.

"My lord." The blond fae addressed Farranen with a bow, then repeated the process to Lief, and my mouth fell open in shock. "There's been a security breach," he informed them in a reserved voice.

And just like that, the two rulers of Fairie dropped their casual stances, while identical expressions of fierce determination slid into place. Lief motioned toward the door, and the guard preceded him out. Dog slunk past in their wake. Which was also something I was going to have to learn to live with.

During our shower-time sharing, Farranen had informed me that Dog had pledged himself into the dark prince's service as a tracker of the realm. I got the impression that the position had been offered to him because he'd been the one to figure out Gus had been hiding in the dead lands. Since he wasn't fae, he was the only one who was able to venture into them to find me.

I was pretty sure Lief had invented the honorary position just for Dog, because I'd never heard of it before—but I was over the moon happy to hear that my timid shifter was coming out of his shell. Knowing that he was doing something productive, something that would ultimately help satisfy his protective urges, filled me with so much pride and joy that I thought my chest might actually break open and leak the sappy emotions all over the shower floor.

Instead of following the males out into the hallway, Farranen turned toward me and fisted his hands in my loose hair while simultaneously claiming my lips in a kiss so scorching that I'd almost swear it lit my panties on fire. My entire body was ready to spontaneously combust by the time he released me.

"I'll return," he promised, his eyes dark with passion.

I could only nod, as I didn't trust myself to speak coherently.

****

After all the magical tests that Eddy preformed, I

272

didn't think a simple blood test would be the one to determine why my body had healed so quickly from the arrow.

I sat on the edge of the bed, trying to make sense of the word that the healer kept throwing at me as a diagnosis.

"Immortal?" I asked for the sixth time. Or maybe it was seventh. My head was still spinning, and I'm pretty sure I'd lost track of how many times I'd already repeated myself.

"Immortal," Eddy confirmed with a smile, taking a seat in the high-backed chair next to me.

"But I'm human," I protested.

"Yes. And immortal." She reached over and covered my hands with one of her own.

An immortal human? That was just…preposterous. Not to mention impossible. And crazy. Yet, how else could I explain my rapid healing? I shook my head in confusion. Or maybe it was denial.

"*How?*" I looked up into Eddy's kind eyes, hoping she could explain this in a way that my poor human brain—*immortal* human brain—could understand.

"The best I can guess is, when you formed a permanent bond with Fairie, the magic in your blood triggered a metamorphosis of sorts." Her gaze was shrewd as she considered me, making me feel like a bug under a microscope. "Once the bond was formed, your magic would have grown considerably, but you would have become dependant on our realm to sustain it."

Fuck. She'd hit that nail on the head. Ever since I'd returned home after being kidnapped by Celesta, I'd been living in a haze. And the only thing that was able to drag me out of the fog was my visits to Fairie. Even Farranen and Lief had noticed.

I nodded hesitantly, unwilling to verbally confirm Eddy's theory.

But now that I was aware of my supposed immortality, other pieces were falling into place.

After accidentally killing Safeena, I'd gone home and fallen into a coma—and only woken up once I was back in the magical realm. My broken wrist, along with every scar on my body, had miraculously healed while I slept, but nobody could tell me why.

Actually, there were a few times that I'd been hurt and didn't retain any of the lingering discomfort that would normally be associated with such an injury. When the hawthorn tree exploded next to me, I'd basically walked away with a few minor bumps and bruises. When the wraiths had gotten in a tug of war with my body, I'd literally felt like my joints were being dislocated, yet in the excitement that followed, I'd forgotten about my pain. Draining the oily magic from the wraiths into myself left me feeling like death warmed over, yet hours later I was fine. Even walking barefoot to the dead lands should have left me limping, but my feet had only registered as a nuisance. At the time, I'd chalked it up to adrenaline, but now…Now I wasn't so sure.

And the way my vision had improved. Initially, I'd brushed off the fact that Vanessa hadn't been able to see anything inside the dead lands, while I had, since at the time, I'd been a little busy with trying to stay alive. But now that I thought about it, it weirdly made sense. And when Farranen and I had descended into the Phantom Cliffs, I'd struggled to see—but that far underground I shouldn't have been able to see *anything*.

"Holy. Shit." I was immortal. How the hell had I missed *that*?

Eddy chuckled, making her large breasts jiggle as

she held out a cloth-wrapped bundle toward me. "Here, you'll need these."

I accepted the small bag and peered inside. It appeared to be a pile of thick white cloths. Maybe bandages? Was this her way of saying that I should patch myself up the next time I was shot with an iron arrow? My eyebrows rose inquisitively.

"Theo, I'm guessing your permanent bond with Fairie happened about a month ago?" She leaned forward, clearly anticipating the nod that I gave her. "All the damage done to your body was erased when your immortality set in." Her eyes took on an intensity that made me think I was missing something. After a few moments, she threw her hands up in exasperation and exclaimed, "Your womb, Theo! Your womb has been restored!"

My head snapped back like the words had hands and had slapped me. My womb was gone. An emergency hysterectomy had made sure of that. And a uterus couldn't just grow back... Could it?

A memory surfaced, of me undressing to get in the shower a few days ago and finding a small smear of blood on the crotch of my underpants. At the time I'd assumed it was because I was covered in Lief's blood. But that wouldn't explain how it had gotten *inside* my panties. And all the stomach cramps I'd had in the last few days that I'd written off as hunger or stress suddenly made sense. My terribly bitchy attitude could be explained too.

"No," I whispered because I didn't want to think it could be true. I'd long ago given up on ever having my own children, and to fan the flame of hope now, only to have it smothered again, would crush me.

"Yes," Eddy said firmly, breaking through my inner

fears. "Even now your cycle starts anew." She pointed at the bag I held clutched to my chest. "It's been hundreds of years since the fae have had a need for those. Go and put them to good use."

I glanced in the bag with sudden understanding. They were the fae equivalent of feminine hygiene products. I almost laughed at how stupid I'd been to not figure that out sooner.

Standing, I thanked Eddy in a breathless voice.

Before I left, I turned back and saw a small bloodstain on the white bedding where I'd been sitting. With my face flaming in embarrassment, and Eddy's laughter ringing in my ears, I made a hasty exit.

Chapter Twenty-Six

Once I was back in Farranen's room, I quickly changed into clean pants and made use of the items Eddy had given me.

When I'd gotten my period for the first time at the age of fifteen, it had been all kinds of disconcerting. And now that I was thirty-two, it was no less awkward.

My hands were shaking so badly I dropped the bag of little white cloths, spilling them all over the bathroom floor. I knelt down to clean them up, the tile warm beneath my knees, but all I could do was stare at the mess I'd made. At what they represented. Could I really be a mother someday? I'd spent a decade thinking it wasn't possible. Now I had the option to choose.

I didn't actually know what I wanted.

I sighed and gathered up all the little cloths, stuffing them in one of the empty drawers under the sink. If I really was immortal—my mind was still too freshly blown to even go there right now—then I'd have plenty of time to figure out what to do with my new uterus.

An anxious buzz of fae magic prickled through the air, and I followed it out into the hallway, glad for the distraction. The restless vibe permeated the normally serene Shadow Palace, adding a layer of mystery to every shadow I passed. The feeling increased as I made my way downstairs, until it led me to a group of fae congregating in the foyer.

The lump of unease in my chest abated as soon as I

spied Farranen and Lief conferring with several of the Army of Light. During the more verbal parts of our shower this morning, Farranen had given me the lowdown on his journey to find the missing soldiers, so I wasn't surprised to see they were here at the Shadow Palace.

A month ago, after word had spread that Gus was the queen's true mate—thus elevating him to kingly status—he'd taken command of the Army of Light. Which to me seemed kind of redundant, since his position as the queen's gray knight meant he already outranked all the other soldiers. But apparently that wasn't good enough for him. Anyway, since the queen was dead and nobody was brave enough to contradict Gus's claims, he used the soldiers to slaughter anyone on his naughty list. But not all the males were cool with mindlessly obeying their ruthless new boss and challenged his authority. The majority that sided with Gus were happy to lock the minority in the queen's dungeons. And, no, not the ones where Farranen had been held, and I'd died trying to rescue him. There was a secondary location (probably for overcrowding situations) that was located between the Ragnier and Fallow Woods. Was it a coincidence that the weeden fae resided there and were some of the first casualties? Doubtful.

So, the long story short was that Farranen rescued twenty-five of the missing fae.

I probably could have just said that to begin with, but I'm a writer and telling stories makes me happy.

And as for the rest of the soldiers? Fodder in Gus's insane attempt to "evolve" the fae. From what the rescued soldiers had been able to glean through eavesdropping, the willing soldiers underwent a ceremony before being taken to the dead lands. Most likely it was another witchy spell that somehow allowed them to enter the toxic region.

Impossibly green eyes looked up, taking note of my arrival, and caused my breath to catch in my chest. With a few last words, my guardian disengaged himself from the conversation he was a part of and strode over to where I was standing. The impassive expression on his face cracked, and I caught a glimpse of delight before he leaned down to kiss me.

It was a soft beautiful thing that filled me with excitement and longing, but never went beyond a PG rating.

"You shouldn't be here," he murmured, the warmth in his eyes contradicting his words.

"What's going on?" I asked, taking a step back and letting my hands fall away from his chest. As much as I wanted to keep touching him, PDAs weren't a part of my comfort zone and there were at least a dozen males now watching us with rapt attention.

"It appears that Augustus left behind a mess for us to clean up." Lief joined us, no longer moving as stiffly as he had this morning, with the T'Holly brothers following in his wake.

After hearing that the eccentric siblings had been knocked out, presumably by the wraiths, giving Gus the opportunity to sneak in and kidnap me, Farranen and Lief had been ready to exile the brothers to the dungeons for a decade or two. The pleading I'd done on their behalf had apparently worked since they were still here.

"What mess?" I doubted it was something as simple as a pile of empty beer cans and fast-food wrappers.

"Two wraiths have been spotted outside the castle." Lief's eyebrows slanted down, like he was trying to do complex algebra equations in his head. "They linger by the drawbridge, but retreat when our soldiers get close enough to engage."

Oh, man. I wanted to smack myself for forgetting about the wraiths. In all honesty, I'd thought they'd stay in the dead lands. "Sorry, this is my fault," I told the confused men. During our shower debriefing, I hadn't mentioned anything to Farranen about the two shadowy entities.

"How is this your fault?" Lief asked, sounding genuinely perplexed.

"I sort of stole them from Gus, and then forgot about them." In my defense, I'd had an arrow lodged in my kidney, distracting me. "I'll try to get rid of them."

Nobody stopped me as I marched across the foyer and out onto the lowered drawbridge. And sure enough, two inky black shadows hovered on the other side of the moat, like they were unsure of their welcome. I couldn't really blame them with the way the soldiers were treating them like a threat.

I wrapped my arms around myself, wishing I'd brought a coat. The temperature outside had dropped even further, hovering just above the freezing mark.

They must have followed me back to the Shadow Palace.

"It's okay," I called. "You can come over here."

"Theodora…" Farranen cautioned from behind me. A quick glance over my shoulder confirmed that Lief had followed me outside too.

I turned back to the wraiths, which were in the process of crossing the bridge, but didn't miss the sound of two swords being freed from their sheaths. I wasn't sure what good the blades would be, since the shadows were only corporeal when they wanted to be. Still, if the boys needed to hold onto their security blankets, who was I to judge?

Gus's former minions came to a halt about four feet in front of me, and I smiled. Yes, they'd kidnapped me. But they'd also helped drag my butt out of the dead lands, so a little forgiveness on my part was no hardship.

"Thank you for helping me earlier." I wasn't sure if they understood me or not, but I continued anyway. "I know Gus was your master, but he's dead now, so you're free to go do your own thing."

Still no reaction.

I made a little shooing motion with my hand. "You're free. You can go now."

Did they want something from me? What could I possibly do for them—

Oh, crap.

I knew what I could do for them: the same thing I'd done to their brethren. I'd drained them, essentially ending their existence. Oh God, I really didn't want to pull all that dark oily magic into myself. Still, if this was the only way they could find peace…Then I owed it to them to respect their wishes.

"Do you want me to…drain you?"

A cold blast of wind blew past, making me shiver, but the wraiths didn't move. Jeez, this was more one-sided than any conversation with Dog had ever been.

"If they truly are the physical manifestation of the magic and soul that once belonged to a fae, then they are still constituents of the court they originally hailed from." Speculation and resolve deepened my guardian's voice, and I wanted to throw my arms around him for seeing what I hadn't. "But make no mistake, members of the Light Court are under *my* rule, and I won't tolerate disobedience."

If the wraiths were bothered by Farranen's dire warning, they didn't show it.

"So, are you going to stay?" I asked curiously. Having them around might be cool. As long as their good behavior lasted, their presence shouldn't be a problem.

The wraith on the left floated closer and extended its hand.

I hesitated a moment, remembering the piercing chill of the cold lifeless fingers when they gripped my arm, like a vice made of ice. But the wraiths were no longer under Gus's wicked influence, so I needed to give them the benefit of the doubt.

Holding out my own hand, just as I'd seen Gus do, the wraith settled its insubstantial palm over mine, and an image was thrust into my brain. In it, the two wraiths were patrolling the perimeter of the Shadow Palace, their ghostly forms drifting past the stone walls as they meticulously searched for any sign of trouble.

I blinked. "You want to be soldiers?" Well, I guess technically they still were part of the Army of Light, so it made sense. Maybe they were hoping for some post-mortem redemption from siding with Gus.

Beside me Farranen nodded, and I was relieved he had no objection to adding the wraiths to the ranks of his depleted army.

The inky black shadow withdrew its hand, and both wraiths bent over, bowing toward the man they were willing to acknowledge as their new leader. I let out a startled giggle and watched as they unfolded themselves before floating toward the waiting castle.

"Living with you two is going to take some getting used to," Lief commented, tracking the wraiths with his gaze—but I'm pretty sure the words were for Farranen and I. Because, really, how much trouble could two little wraiths be?

"I think I'll call them Shade and Raven." After all, I had to call them *something*.

Lief muttered something sarcastic and unflattering about my penchant for adopting stray ghosts and turned to go inside.

"He's right, you know." Farranen wrapped an arm around my shivering body and pulled me into the warmth of his, tucking his cloak around us both. "First Dog and I, then Vanessa and Harvey, now the wraiths—you just can't turn away from those in need."

I shrugged. It's true that I used to value my privacy and solitude above everything else, but now I knew there was a very fine line between seclusion and desolation. Hiding from the world didn't equal safety. And it's not like I'd had much of a choice. Who in their right mind would have turned away a starved homeless shifter like Dog? Those big sad amber eyes could melt the hardest of hearts.

But as for adopting Farranen, he was wrong there.

"I didn't adopt you," I protested, wrapping my arms even tighter around his waist as a gust of wind swirled his cloak around my legs.

"Of course you did. I didn't even know how lost I was until you found and saved me."

I tilted my head back to see his face, shocked that he thought he was the one who had been saved. "No, *you* saved *me*. First from Lebolus, then when Gus attacked us."

"True, but you saved me in all the ways that count." Pure affection shimmered in his eyes, reminding me that the fae couldn't lie. "I told you how long I'd waited to find you, Theodora."

Yes, he had. Lifetimes, he'd said. At the time, I'd

written it off as post-coital romantic drivel.

"It was well worth the wait, for the chance to experience this with you." His magic caressed its way through my body, chasing away some of the chill from being outside. When he leaned down, bringing with him the scent of pine trees and cinnamon, I didn't try to stifle my low moan of need that escaped as his lips claimed mine.

"Oh my *God*, you two! Get a room already!" Vanessa's shriek of dismay, which was probably fake, rang through the cool air around me.

"Ghosts," I informed my guardian with an exasperated grin before turning to find two ghosts waiting with identical knowing smiles plastered on their faces. For once, I didn't feel any remorse at getting caught red-handed making out. If anyone had a problem with me kissing the man next to me, then they could shut their damn eyes.

"Theo." Harvey acknowledged me with a small bow. Which was weird, but I was so happy to see that he was all right that I didn't bother to question it.

"Harvey! I was worried the arrow had—" Um, killed him? No, that wasn't technically possible. Injured him? Probably not possible either. I decided to go with "—ah, done some irreparable damage. But you look great!"

His metallic blue skin shimmered with health, the kind that I'd learned meant he was fully recharged. "Yes, I am fully recovered. The injury was quite minor."

"That's the biggest crock of shit I've ever heard!" Vanessa laughed. "You were whining like a baby—"

"I'm glad you're both feeling better," I cut in, not wanting to hear my ghosts squabbling like siblings. "Vanessa, thank you for your help. Weighing me down was a genius idea."

"Whatever." She flipped her hair over her shoulder but couldn't hide the small flash of pride that lit up her hazel eyes. I really should acknowledge her bravery and quick-thinking more often. "It's not like you even needed me. They were already having a hard time dragging your big butt around."

Annnnd, it looked like all my plans to dish out the praise were a bit premature. I turned to the merdain fae, Vanessa's dig at my size already forgotten.

"Harvey, thank you for everything." As far as I was concerned, he'd gone above and beyond the call of duty to help me survive, and I wanted him to know I hadn't taken any of it for granted. He'd put himself between me and the arrow, neither of us knowing at the time that I was immortal. That was something I'd never be able to repay.

His indigo eyes sparkled. "You are very welcome, Theo."

"Harvalin, it would appear that I am in your debt as well." Farranen addressed the space where Harvey was standing, using his benevolent-ruler voice. Which was damn sexy to my ears. "If there's any favor or boon that is in my power to grant you, please advise my lady and I will make it happen."

Looking a little shocked, yet mighty pleased, Harvey sketched a bow toward my guardian. "Yes, thank you—" His eyes jerked to me, and I realized he didn't know what to call Farranen, now that he was a king.

"Harvey says thanks," I murmured against Farranen's shirt as I burrowed a little farther into the warmth of his cloak. "And he wants to know what your official title is so that he may worship you properly."

My indignant ghost sputtered something in denial while Vanessa chuckled in the background.

After a moment's deliberation, Farranen suggested, "The Light Prince?"

"That's not very original." Lief already had the monopoly on being the realm's prince. And since the two of them would be living together in the Shadow Palace, having two princes could get confusing. The light prince and the dark prince. Yeah, that sounded like the name of a bad fantasy movie from the eighties.

"Traditionally, the only other title associated with a male in my position would be king," he mused, not sounding terribly enamored with the honorific.

"You don't like 'king'?" It seemed like a good fit for the regal man I was currently trying to steal body heat from.

"Many will associate 'the light king' with Gus's outrageous play for power." A muscle in his jaw clenched, and I couldn't blame him for not wanting the second-hand moniker.

"Does it have to have 'light' in it?" I'd never heard anyone call Safeena "the light queen." Everyone had just referred to her as the queen.

"Not necessarily," he hedged, probably leery of whatever road my imaginative brain was leading me down. Which was justified since I was already combing through the possibilities.

I mentally compiled a list of his best attributes, knowing it would only continue to grow the more I got to know him.

Hmm…The strong king? No, that was a bit too tyrannical, and the realm had enough of that style of leadership with Safeena. Maybe the cold king, on account of the way he donned a cold impassive mask for the rest of the world? No, that sounded like the name of a tofu wrap at a new-age hipster restaurant. The brave king would have fit, but the name sounded flat when I tested it on my lips.

I glanced behind me to see if Harvey or Vanessa had any input, but they were gone. Probably for the best, since I'm sure Vanessa would have had a few inappropriate suggestions.

I contemplated the resourceful king, the wise king, the courteous king, and the steadfast king, but they all weren't quite right. The so-smoking-hot-he-sets-my-loins-on-fire king sounded good to me, but I doubted the rest of Fairie would appreciate my candor.

"Theodora?" Farranen's fingertips, surprisingly warm, traced a path down across my jaw as he tipped my head back.

"Farr…" His name slid from me on an exhale, and I recognized the rightness of the unfinished word.

My rigid guardian, with his well-defined sense of right and wrong, had recognized the disorder within his own court and, despite his strict adherence to following the rules, had been willing to shift allegiances for the good of the entire realm—which highlighted his greatest trait of all: his impartial, unprejudiced ability to be fair.

"The fair king," I breathed, and the magic from his key, safely tucked back inside my body, gave a little thrum of approval.

His full lips pulled into a smile that was warm enough to chase away the chill from being outside.

Chapter Twenty-Seven

After instructing the T'Holly brothers to spread the word of his new designation, Farranen had glamoured me a warm green cloak before taking me by the hand and leading me back out into the cool morning air.

"Where are we going?" I asked, scanning the clouds that were slowly drifting across the dreary sky. The wind had a certain bite to it that made me think it was going to snow soon. While my cloak and boots would keep me warm even if the temperature dropped, I hoped we weren't going far. I still hadn't told Farranen about my new status, and the longer I waited, the more anxious I grew.

I eyed the small pack on his back suspiciously. It could easily hold enough provisions for a day or two. Hopefully we wouldn't be gone long enough to need them.

"It's a surprise." The look he gave me filled my tummy with butterflies.

We turned off the main road after a few minutes, and I followed him through the trees, lost in my own thoughts of how I was going to inform him of my immortality.

Hey, honey, don't worry, I'm still human—but now I'm immortal, too, might do the trick. But then again, it wasn't so much the dialogue that I was worried about, but his reaction.

When he'd told me, *For as long as you'll have me,*

I will be yours, I'd felt the vow woven into the fabric of the words. But at the time he'd assumed that I'd only had a handful of decades left. Now that my lifespan had no expiry date, would he change his mind? Forever was a really, really long time—it was literally, well…*forever.*

It only took about fifteen minutes to reach our destination, which wasn't nearly long enough to reach any sort of definitive conclusion about how to bring up the subject of my expanded life expectancy. Then again, we could have walked for another year, and I probably still wouldn't have known what to say.

"We're less than half a mile from the Shadow Palace." Farranen stopped near the top of a small rise, standing just as tall and regal as the trees surrounding us. "Close enough that the dark prince will still be able to draw power from his key, but far enough away to have a small amount of privacy when we desire it."

"Okay…" Where was he going with this? Yes, a little alone time with the fair king would be nice, but why here?

Farranen took my hand and tugged me the last few steps to the top of the incline, tilting his head toward what was waiting beyond the small hill.

"My cabin!" I shrieked, once I'd caught sight of the recognizable brown structure.

Uncaring that I was likely to trip and fall, I ran down the leaf-covered slope, not stopping until I was standing next to the back stairs of my cabin. My fingers trailed across the worn railing that was as familiar as my own shadow. With joy beating through my veins, I ascended the creaky steps to the back porch. It was the same back porch that I'd fallen off when I'd smashed a supernatural law enforcement agent in the head with a hammer for trying to take me into custody.

"How?" I demanded, turning to face the man that was watching me from the bottom of the staircase.

"While you were recovering from your arrow wound, I sent one of the remival fae to retrieve it. The Shadow Palace is your home now, but I thought you might need a place where you could get away from the stresses of court life occasionally." He continued to regard me with a hint of vulnerability peeking out from behind the cool façade that he'd schooled his features into. Like he wasn't sure how I'd react to having my property relocated without my permission.

I smiled. "Thank you." The meager words couldn't convey the extent of the gratitude I felt at having this meaningful part of my life back. Until this very moment, I'd been regarding my stay in Fairie as temporary, knowing that the life I'd been living on Earth was waiting for me to return. But now that I had my cabin, it was like the last piece of the puzzle had fallen into place.

Well—actually this was the second last piece of the puzzle.

I took a deep breath and held out my hand in silent invitation.

Without even knowing what I was asking for, Farranen swiftly climbed the five short steps between us and put his hand in mine.

The next words out of my mouth were long overdue. "I would like to take you inside—" I risked a look at my guardian through my lashes. "—and make love to you."

His eyes went wide.

I almost laughed at his comical expression, but I didn't want him to think this was a joke. Because I was dead serious. Saying the words out loud made me blush, but I knew it would get easier with time. And I planned to say them *a lot* in the future.

His lips parted, hopefully in eager acceptance of my proposition, but I cut him off before I lost my nerve. There was something else I needed to tell him that was even more important than sex.

"I love you," I told my shocked guardian. "I love you, and I'm sorry it took me so long to admit it." And it wasn't just him that I'd been keeping it from; in hindsight, I hadn't been willing to acknowledge it to myself either. The prospect of giving him this kind of power over me was less terrifying than it used to be. I was still scared, but much less so than I previously was.

His satisfied smile let me know he wasn't going to hold it against me. With a knowing look, he tugged on my hand so I was forced to take a step forward, right into his personal space. Being surrounded by his warmth and spicy scent made my knees weak. "I'd like to tell you that the words are unnecessary, since your sentiments are already obvious through your actions, but I'll admit that hearing the words brings me great joy."

Some of that aforementioned joy was shining out of his eyes right now, bright enough to set certain parts of me on fire. Set the whole world on fire, actually.

I licked my lips nervously. Would he still look at me with such joy when I told him that he wouldn't be rid of me anytime soon? The empowerment that I'd been enjoying from finally being able to discuss our sex life out loud dried up. I still had to tell him about my newly discovered immortality, but I couldn't for the life of me figure out the right combination of words.

"What?" The slightest wrinkle marred his smooth forehead, as his eyes traced across my face. Dang, his superior fae eyesight missed nothing. "What's worrying you?"

"I..." Damn it, I was screwing this up.

I made a fist with my free hand that he quickly engulfed in his before bringing them both to his chest.

Farranen continued to regard me, the vivid green of his eyes popping against the paleness of his hair as the breeze teased it around his shoulders.

"Harvey bowed to me. That's so weird, right?" Oh God, I was rambling. A reasonable little voice in the back of my head was screaming at me to shut up, but I ignored it. "He's never done that before, so why would he start now?"

"Because he recognizes you as my equal." His tone was puzzled, like maybe the peculiar topic was a metaphor he hadn't grasped yet.

It wasn't. I really had been wondering about all the bowing that seemed to be happening lately—not just by Harvey, but Karista, Eddy, and the T'Holly brothers as well—and I was totally delaying the inevitable discussion regarding my loss of mortality.

"As do all the fae."

"What does that mean?" I asked, hoping he would have a long-winded answer for me.

"Now that I have publicly claimed you as my chosen, you will be afforded the same respect and deference that I am."

I blinked. Well, that didn't sound so bad.

Mirth smoothed the concern from his face, and he let out a masculine chuckle that wrapped itself around me. "Did you not notice the concessions the realm has made to please you?"

"Concessions?"

He gestured vaguely, encompassing the space around us. "The flannel sheets, always tucked in tight enough to strangle the mattress, the textured tiles in the bathroom to keep you from slipping, the wardrobe full of comfortable clothing rather than evening gowns. In all my years, I've never seen such an abundance of cake so readily available."

My mouth fell open, and I gaped at him. "All those things are for me?"

"All those and more. The realm seeks to satisfy you. In all likeliness, the amalgamation of the castles was brought about by your desire to see the two courts united."

Uh, what? Until now, I'd believed my thoughts about Fairie's social structure were private. How the hell had Farranen, not to mention the entire realm, known what I was thinking?

There was no humor in the low chuckle that rumbled in his thoat. "You may not have voiced your opinion on the matter, but anytime the realm's political disarray was discussed, the outrage on your face spoke louder than any words could have."

I wanted to believe that my harsh criticism of Fairie hadn't been so obvious, but it was hard to argue with his logic. All the new little details that I'd thought were perfect, *were* perfect, because they existed with me in mind. The idea of it was…shocking.

"Well, that's…nice." It was strange to think Fairie knew me so well.

He arched a brow. "*Nice?*"

"Awfully nice," I amended.

His tiny little forehead wrinkles returned. "Is Harvey's unusual behavior what really worries you?"

The concern in his voice was obvious, but it was the compassion that finally broke through the wall my words had been hiding behind.

"Eddy figured out how I healed so fast." I took a deep breath, and then slowly let it out. "I'm immortal." I bit my lip again and risked a glance at the man that had earned my love. *Better to get everything out in the open now,* I thought. "And my uterus grew back."

His head snapped back, and his hands tightened on mine painfully, reminding me that he wasn't human. "*What* did you say?"

"I, ah…I'm immortal and I have a uterus?" The words sounded surprisingly small in the open air of the forest, since their value was greater than anything that had ever crossed my lips before.

His hands, strong enough to take a life when needed, gentled where they held mine, surrounding them with his protection and love.

"Truly?" he asked, his eyes regarding me with so many emotions that I couldn't even name them all. Shock, hope, anticipation, joy, disbelief, and maybe even a touch of fear. They shimmered there, laid out for me to examine at my leisure, because he'd long ago stopped wearing the cold façade around me that he donned for the rest of the world. And since he deserved no less than my own honesty in return, I gave it to him without hesitation.

"Truly."

His gaze traveled lower to my stomach, like he could see through the fabric I was wearing, past my skin and bones, all the way down to the newly formed organ in question. "Are you…" His eyes returned to mine, bearing a vulnerability and desire that wasn't there a second ago. "…with child?"

"No." I shook my head, a sharp pang of disappointment striking me behind my breastbone.

I wasn't sure if it was a reaction to the disappointment reflected in his eyes, or if the unwelcome emotion had originated from some subconscious part of myself that I hadn't yet had time to examine. I would need more than an hour to do some serious self-reflection before I could develop an official stance on whether I wanted to become a mother or not.

And after seeing the fragile yearning written on Farranen's face, I knew the decision wouldn't be up to me alone. Something as momentous as creating a brand-new life would affect us both. Although, it was obvious what his vote would be. Judging by his expectant expression, he was already picking out baby names.

"But theoretically, someday I could be." I purposely left the timeline vague in a way that would have made any fae proud. I still hadn't wrapped my head around the whole immortality concept, but if we truly had forever to be together, then there was no reason to rush headfirst into family life. I was perfectly content with just the two of us.

And Dog.

And Harvey and Vanessa.

Okay, Shade and Raven were growing on me too.

And I had my fingers crossed that I hadn't seen the last of Sepian or Svencer.

Even Lief was among those that I considered mine. While most of my feelings for Dog and the ghosts were of a maternal nature, the dark prince was closer to a flirtatious half-cousin that didn't recognize the typical boundaries that family should.

Maybe Farranen had had a point earlier when he said I adopt those in need—only I hadn't realized until now how much I needed them in return. For all intents and purposes, these magical beings had become my family.

A single snowflake landed on his shoulder, and I reached up to brush it away. My head tilted back, my eyes widening as hundreds of tiny flurries slowly drifted down toward us. It looked like Fairie was almost done correcting the natural order of seasons that had been thrown off for so long. At this rate, it would only be another day or two until both realms were blanketed in a thick white cover of snow.

"Theodora?" Strong hands framed my face, and I blinked.

I met his eyes with a small grin, embarrassed that I'd become lost in my thoughts. "Sorry."

"We don't have to decide right now."

"I know," I murmured. And I did know. He was leaving the metaphorical ball in my court, giving me the time and space to figure out what I wanted. Which made the decision so much easier.

I already loved and trusted this man more than I thought possible, but the idea of sharing something so intimate and wonderful with him should have scared me. It didn't. It actually filled me with the same kind of joy that was radiating from his hopeful eyes. The kind that made me want to rush in headfirst, consequences be damned.

He leaned down until our foreheads were touching and only a breath of air spanned the distance between his lips and mine. "With or without a child, Theodora, I am still yours."

I was helpless to deny this man anything—

especially since the thought of adding to our unconventional little family filled me with something warm and fuzzy that had nothing to do with my magic, rather than the apprehension I was expecting.

Still, since such a monumental decision shouldn't be made hastily, I mentally pushed all thoughts of hypothetical babies to the back of my mind and focused on what was right in front of me.

It didn't look like my new immortality was going to be a problem, since he hadn't batted an eye when I'd dropped the news in his lap like a hot potato. I closed the remaining distance between us by rising onto my tippy toes and kissed him with a heat and enthusiasm that he gladly returned. When he pulled away to trail his lips across my jaw, I didn't try to hide the satisfied sigh that worked its way out of my chest. God, was there anything about this man that wasn't pure carnal sin?

"I believe I'd like to take you up on your offer for lovemaking." His voice was a sensual caress, only rivaled by the lips that were now working their way along my neck.

"Oh, God, yes—*crap!*" I pulled back, halting the progress his mouth was making toward my cleavage. A deeper blush crept up my already flushed face. "Damn it! I've got my—ah…*monthly.*" Gah, I'd finally matured enough to say "lovemaking," but I was incapable of telling him I'd gotten my period. It's like I was fifteen years old, all over again.

His understanding smile only made my embarrassment that much more intense.

"You had no complaints when I pleasured you this morning. *Twice.*"

My eyebrows rose as I recalled our mutual

enjoyment of each other in the shower. An eager smile bloomed on my face, as I caught on to his reasoning.

A masculine chuckle rolled out of his throat and followed us as I tugged him through the backdoor to my cabin.

If he was willing to forego my bed with the perfectly tucked sheets, in lieu of my ancient cast iron tub and crappy water heater, then so was I.

As if he could read my mind, he murmured, "Don't worry, I'll keep you warm."

A word about the author...

Born and raised on the beautiful Canadian prairies, Everlyn prefers to spend her time outdoors with her family kayaking, skating, fishing, and hunting. She loves reading and writing about vampires, witches, fae, and zombies that get to find their own version of happily ever after.